This one is

Signed in A
different spot

- Z-

Kotov Syndrome

Azaes Realm, #1.0

Tim Baughman Jr

Kotov Syndrome, Book 1.0 of the *Azaes Realm* series

Cover art by Lauren Restivo
Edited by Charlotte Laidig

Paperback ISBN: 978-1-7353190-0-1
Digital ISBN: 978-1-7353190-1-8

First Edition

For those who believed in me --
Even when I didn't believe in myself.

1
Impressionable

"I'll love you until the day I don't exist! I'll love you until the day I don't exist! I'll love you! Please don't go!"

Erika bolted upright, her light golden-brown hair flying forward as she did so. The orange bandana holding her greasy locks in place flew towards the foot of the bed, landing somewhere on her blanket that Erika was unable to identify solely by sound. She sighed heavily, tossed the blanket off of her, and stood on the chilly wooden floor of her bedroom. With slow, groggy steps, Erika made her way to the kitchen, hoping she could find a return to sleep.

Four nights in the past three weeks was far too many nights to have that dream. Erika didn't look at the dream as a nightmare anymore. Once upon a time, it was a stark reminder of a relationship that had flamed out nearly as quickly as it had started. Over the last few years, the dream had morphed into something that popped up whenever Erika was too stressed to fall asleep soundly. She always woke up at the same time, more or less. Just in time to not see her own self crying, but not quite quick enough to avoid the pleas of her ex-girlfriend, Abby.

Erika opened the refrigerator, temporarily blinding herself with the bright light inside. She slipped her fingers around the handle of the half gallon of milk and turned it so she could see the date stamped on the front. October 8, 2033. Six days expired. Erika briefly thought about pouring the rancid liquid down the drain, but thought better of it, shutting the fridge door and darkening the room. There's always tomorrow to clean things up.

Instead of milk, Erika grabbed a small glass out of her cupboard, then opened her freezer and produced a bottle of vodka. She uncorked the bottle and poured two fingers worth into the glass before recorking the bottle. With the bottle in one hand and a glass in the other, Erika leaned her back against her kitchen cabinet and slid to the floor. She was careful not to let her heels catch on the ends of her slightly too long pajama pants, as the last time that had happened, vodka went all over Erika's lap.

Erika closed her eyes and lifted the glass to her lips, taking in a small sip of the vodka. She sat in silence with the liquid burning in her mouth for a few moments before swallowing it. Erika let out a long, pensive sigh, adjusting her sitting position so as to not have her right shoulder grinding into the handle of the cabinet door beneath her sink. Erika raised her left arm again, bringing the glass to her lips a second time. She let the vodka sit against her lips and the tip of her tongue for just a moment – just long enough for the burn to start again – then took a second drink.

When she was growing up, just as she was reaching the age where she could develop romantic feelings for someone else, Erika's mom, Kaytie, told her a story about how she had broken up with her first boyfriend. Not satisfied with merely ending the relationship, Kaytie took the box of notes she and her boyfriend had written back and forth to each other, then burned them in her grandma's firepit. While this made Kaytie feel good in the moment, by the following Wednesday, Kaytie and her then-boyfriend were back together. The lesson that Kaytie tried to pass on to Erika from mother to daughter was to never burn bridges with someone, as you'll never know when you'll be back around them again.

This wasn't a bridge Erika wanted to burn. This was a spot on your favorite shirt that wouldn't go away no matter how many times you washed it. Burning away the past would do no good. It was fireproof at this point. At the very least, it was alcohol proof.

For nearly three years of Erika's life, Abby was the closest thing to perfection that Erika could dream of. Abby was everything. She was a friend, a confidante, and a voice of reason at a time in life where Erika lacked all of the above. Had proximity permitted, they likely would have been lovers as well. Unfortunately, reality didn't match Erika's desires.

Throughout Erika's first two years of high school, she found herself drifting away from her childhood friends. Her elementary school best friend, Natalie, had become much closer with a group of kids from her choir class, leading her to spend less and less time with Erika. But the start of their junior year, Erika only saw Natalie when they passed each other in the halls. The days of sleepovers with copious amounts of hot cocoa while watching YouTube until midnight seemed like a relic of the distant past.

Erika's other close friends weren't around her as frequently either. Kacey had moved away to Minnesota at the start of sophomore year, her messages coming to Erika less frequently with the passage of time. The twins across the street, Rachel and Kyle, still came by on occasion, though they were both seniors and were more focused on preparing for college than hanging out with anyone. Her next door neighbor, Brynne, was already off at college. There was a boy, Christian, who had a massive crush on Erika. As a result, Erika never lacked for anyone to sit with at lunch, as Christian and his friends – Troy and Basil – routinely invited her over to their table. Erika had no interest in Christian, or any boy for that matter, but was happy to have the company most days.

That said, Erika still felt like she was lacking something. It wasn't a significant other. She was sure of that. If she really wanted to date someone, Christian was there at a moment's notice. Maybe Cara, a girl in her Spanish class, who Erika was almost certain had a crush on her. Erika wouldn't have minded some sort of romantic attention from Cara, but that's not what she yearned for. Really, all Erika wanted was someone to fill the best-friend shaped void that Natalie had created when she drifted away. Someone willing to listen and provide advice, even if that advice was occasionally dubious. Above all, Erika wanted someone around who cared about her.

On a Sunday just after Thanksgiving, Erika went to the mall with Brynne to go Christmas shopping. Brynne was a sophomore in college and had just gotten engaged. She'd met her fiancée on a dating site called Project Freyja. And all of that bored Erika to death. What was interesting was that Project Freyja also featured a portion of their site where users – even those who weren't of age to use the dating site – could interact with robotic programs called conscientia. These conscientia were programmed to act as human as possible and they were apparently pretty convincing.

The discussion with Brynne quickly left Erika's mind, only to resurface a few weeks later. A Congressman from Kansas was up in arms over the robot side of Project Freyja. He had gone on a lengthy social media rant which, around the typos and poor grammar, boiled down to the lone correctly written passage in the entire rant.

"If our Lord intended for us to fall in love with robots, He would have made them along with the fish and the deer. But He didn't. Man created robots. And since man is sinful, being in love with any of our own creations is also sinful."

That evening, Erika joined Project Freyja. If it was enough to piss a politician off, there had to be something interesting in the program. Fear of technology was absurd. He might has well have been shouting about the end of the world, telling everyone to save their toasters from the inevitable battle they'd have with the dishwashers of the world. Though Erika would have typically been restricted from dating sites due to her age, the robot portion of the site – conscientia simulations, as Project Freyja referred to them – was open to anyone over the age of thirteen.

Upon signing up, the site took Erika through an unskippable and lengthy tour explaining how the conscientia program worked. Audio of a non-descript, melodic female voice played over the tutorial.

"Welcome to Project Freyja's conscientia immersion program! This program is dedicated to developing a better understanding of human and computer psychology through scientifically-driven analysis and human-computer interaction.

"As part of the conscientia immersion program, you'll complete a series of multiple choice and open-ended questions. We'll start with 100 questions, but you can always answer more to better personalize your conscientia experience.

"After you've finished your questionnaire, you'll be presented with one (or more) options for conscientia to chat with. Each conscientia will have a brief description about their personality, along with a friendliness compatibility meter to help you judge how compatible your conversations will be.

Erika rolled her eyes. Get on with it, she thought.

"You can opt-out of the program at any time. Just go to the Settings menu and select the Opt-Out button. If you're over 18, you'll be redirected to the Project Freyja dating site. If you're under 18, your account will be disabled and you'll be logged out. You can opt back into the program at any time by contacting our support team."

"Remember, you're talking to computer simulations. Though the conversations you have will be real, you are not talking to a real person. Even so, you might experience real emotions – joy, sadness, anger, friendship, and so on – when interacting with our conscientia. This is good! This is exactly what the conscientia immersion experience is supposed to be like.

"If you wish to change which conscientia you're talking to at any time, or if you want to fill out more questions, just click the Tutorial button in the menu bar. You'll be presented with new conscientia options at that time. There's no need to block a conscientia you don't like, as you must initiate all conversations with conscientia on the Project Freyja site.

"Ready to get started? Click Next to answer your first question."

Erika began answering the questions presented to her. The first twenty or so questions all focused on Erika's favorite things.

What is your favorite animal? Red pandas.

What is your favorite flower? Pink stargazer lilies.

Who are your three favorite authors? M.T. Anderson, Derek Vega, and Philip K. Dick.

The questions got more complex, digging deeper. With each

passing question, Erika focused harder on answering, losing track of time.

Do you believe that love is love, regardless of circumstance? Yes.

If you could personify one of the seven deadly sins, which would you be? Sloth.

What's the most important trait you want in a friend? Honesty.

What's the most important trait you want in a romantic interest? Loyalty.

Which is more important: honesty or loyalty? They're equally important.

The one-hundredth question came and went. A message popped up on the screen.

"We haven't found a matching conscientia for you yet. But don't worry! You can keep answering questions so we can find a match for you."

So she did. 200 questions down. The same message appeared.

300 questions.

400 questions.

At 500 questions, the message mocked her again. Erika put her tablet to sleep and went to bed, disappointed.

The next afternoon, Erika received an email from Project Freyja, saying the system had found a simulation for her to interact with. Logging on, she was presented with the same message, complete with animations of confetti, balloons, and fireworks. The presentation was a bit over the top, but it amused Erika. She was then prompted to complete setup of the simulation. There were several options that appeared, allowing the user to choose the physical traits that their simulation would have when it showed up on the screen. At the top of the box, a big blue button read 'Surprise Me'. At this point, why not, Erika reasoned. She clicked 'Surprise Me' and waited.

A pair of gears replaced the dialog box on the screen, turning slowly for a few seconds. The gears then faded away, as the image of a young, smiling, Korean-American woman appeared on the screen.

"Hi!" the simulation excitedly said. "I'm Abby! You must be Erika."

"That's me," replied Erika.

"I've been waiting so long to meet someone. Thank you for choosing me."

Eight years later, that was one of the lines that stuck with Erika. She hated Abby for it. Erika didn't choose her. An algorithm chose Abby for her. Granted, that algorithm made its choice based on questions Erika had answered, but still. It wasn't Erika's choice to interact with Abby specifically. Fucking math, Erika thought.

"It's not your fault. You were just unlucky. You're always unlucky."

Erika took another drink from her glass, gulping it down violently. Inside her head lived another unfortunate side effect of her breakup with Abby. The therapist she'd tried seeing before she ran out of money referred to it as her inner critic. Erika just called it Grace. Grace was at her loudest when Erika was stressed, tired, or upset, though much like her nightmares, a stiff drink typically shut Grace up.

When she split up with Abby, Erika rejected her mother's mantra of not burning bridges. Most days, this was exactly what Erika needed in her life. She knew she was better off if there was nothing around to remind her of Abby. Any traces of their relationship were just memories.

Every once in a while, the nightmares paid her a visit. All Erika wanted to do when they did was purge her mind. Abby had that ability, or at least Erika presumed she did, being a simulation and all. Abby was her first serious relationship – and to this point in her life, her last. Maybe there was some deep-seated guilt from breaking things off as abruptly that haunted her. Maybe it was something else. Denial does strange things to the mind.

Being with Abby didn't start out as a relationship. As Project Freyja's conscientia program was designed, the interaction between Abby and Erika was friendly and nothing more at first. Abby was part of one of the numerous classes of conscientia programs developed by Project Freyja for various uses. Abby's class, Aphrodite class conscientia, were simulations intended to build bonds between the simulation and the humans they were interacting with.

Aphrodite class conscientia featured a sophisticated learning programming that not only allowed the simulation to mold and change its actions and reactions based on the human it was interacting with, but also allowed the simulation to sense when the human contact was experiencing feelings of longing, lust, or love. Though the majority of Aphrodite class conscientia were able to either act on these feelings or actively ignore them (depending on the specific simulation's programming), beta versions of the Aphrodite class conscientia – such as Abby – weren't able to control these emotions as freely.

Erika learned the basics of the conscientia classes early on in her interactions with Abby. For the first few weeks after they first met, Erika would talk with Abby for a few minutes each day. Erika found Abby to be entertaining and kind, though still a bit awkward to talk to. But with time, Erika began to open up to Abby. As days and weeks passed, Erika spent less of her after-school time interacting with her real-life friends and more time talking to Abby. One evening, as she was lying in bed trying not to drift off to sleep, Erika made an offhand comment about how she wished she could meet Abby. Abby's image sat up straight, the Project Freyja logo watermarking over her.

"Project Freyja and its parent company, In Every Mind Adaptive Technologies, would like to remind you that you are interacting with one of our computer simulations, not an actual human being," Abby stated. Her voice was dry and monotone, quite unlike the upbeat, peppy voice that she used normally.

"In the event that you'd like to meet real people for real dating," Abby continued, "we would encourage you to explore the dating section of the Project Freyja site. Please note that you must be at least 18 years of age to use Project Freyja's dating services. Users between 13 and 18 years of age may still interact with Project Freyja's computer simulations but are not eligible to access the dating section of the website. If you have questions, you may contact our support team by tapping the support link in the menu area of your screen, or by saying 'I'd like to contact support' at any time while interacting with a simulation."

Erika had that stupid speech memorized even to this day. There was a lot Erika couldn't forget about Abby. Her legally required speech every time Erika said just the wrong thing was ingrained in Erika's head. Abby's bubbly giggle whenever Erika said something that was funny, but not too funny, was there too. With every nightmare involving Abby, her final words – screamed out in a strained sob – echoed through Erika's subconscious.

But the little action that had burned the hottest hole into Erika's mind was the smile – that stupid, perfect smile – that Abby had on her face after she told Erika she loved her for the first time. Sometimes, particularly when a date went exceptionally shitty and Erika felt lonely, she would close her eyes and think about that smile Abby had given her. Erika could see Abby's face as clear as day, her black hair up in a ponytail, dangling behind her. Abby's gray eyes lit up as bright as the moon in the summer sky, beaming back at Erika. Abby's lips didn't reveal her teeth with the smile, as the simulation rarely showed Abby's teeth unless she was laughing. But the corners of her mouth tuck up slightly, letting off a coy, yet sly smile that showed Abby knew Erika loved her back.

That moment stuck with Erika. It wasn't just that Abby loved her. It's that Abby actively fought what she was programmed to do to show Erika that she loved her. Erika hated her for that. She especially hated her for being right about that reciprocated love when they weren't together anymore. Yet she couldn't get Abby's face out of her head ten years later. Not even with vodka at three in the morning.

"And you're never going to find anything like that again."

10

Erika poured herself more vodka into the glass, then reached above her head and placed the bottle on the counter behind her. Erika cautiously lifted herself off the floor and walked to her bed. She placed the glass of booze on the table beside her bed, being careful not to place it directly on any of her electronics, lest an errant movement in the morning when trying to shut off her alarm become a costly mistake.

As Erika closed her eyes, she thought she heard Abby's voice call out to her, telling her she loved her. Erika sighed heavily, rolled over to face away from the nightstand, and closed her eyes. At least if the nightmares came back, she had something to fight them with at arm's reach. Erika wrapped herself tightly in her blanket, snuggling in her pillow as she did so. Work would come far too early. It always did.

2
(Start) Static

"Erika?"

"Yeah?"

"Tobin has a guy on the line that wants to speak with a manager," said Tia.

"What does he want?" Erika asked.

"He tried returning a microwave he bought to the store and the sales manager told him to call us."

"Did he buy it online or at the store?"

"At the store," answered Tia.

"I'm guessing you told him the store needs to handle the return?" Erika inquired.

"He says the sales manager said it would take him longer to get a refund if he did it. I told him we still couldn't handle it and that I could call the store to help him with the return. He called me a cunt and told me to get my fucking manager."

"Oh good," said Erika, "angry and an asshole. Do you know what store he bought it at?"

"Culver City Northside," answered Tia.

"As in California?"

"Yeah."

"It's six in the morning there. Why's he calling this early?"

"I don't know."

"We can't even call the store to help him until one or two."

"I know."

"Have Tobin transfer the call to my line," said Erika. "Call Culver City and leave a message to call my desk line back when they open. We'll get it taken care of. Did you offer him store credit or anything?"

"Didn't get a chance to," Tia replied.

"If he's even remotely nice to me, I'll send him an in-store credit. What do you think he should get?"

"One penny. He was a prick."

"Right," answered Erika. "But also wrong. And not just because pennies should be taken out of circulation. He's being a dick, but that doesn't mean we shouldn't do the right thing for him. If you were the manager, what would you do? What seems fair?"

Tia took a deep breath and replied. "Thirty if he's a prick. Fifty if he's nice to you."

"Sounds good. What's his name?"

"Gary Robinson."

"Go tell Tobin to transfer Mr. Robinson to me."

Tia left. Erika took a sip of her coffee, trying her hardest to shake off her headache. Most days, she preferred her coffee black and piping hot. Something about the bitterness and heat woke her up when nothing else would. Today was not that day. Hangover coffee was nearly equal parts coffee, sugar, and hazelnut creamer. Sweet coffee was not meant to be savored, Erika reasoned. Its purpose was to get as much caffeine into her system as quickly as possible. Erika's phone rang, popping up a notepad on her computer in case she needed it. She took another quick drink of her coffee, then answered.

"Good morning, this is Erika. I'm a Customer Support Supervisor. How can I be of assistance to you today, Mr. Robinson?"

"What the fuck?" the man on the other end of the line shouted. "I thought I told you to get me a manager!"

"Mr. Robinson, I am a manager. My name is Erika and I'd be happy to help you out."

"My problem is that your reps don't know how to process a return. The guy at the store said the only way to return this microwave is to call customer service. I'm your customer. Fucking service me."

"Unfortunately, the gentleman at the store was incorrect," replied Erika. "You do have to return the microwave to the store, and I'm terribly sorry you've had to go through all this trouble. I've asked the associate you were speaking with before me to call the store first thing when they open so that we can make sure the return is processed smoothly. Because of the inconvenience to you, I'd be happy to send you a store credit for thirty dollars to use as you please. This would be in addition to the credit you'll receive for returning your microwave."

"Listen, bitch," the man replied, "I don't want your credit. I want you to send someone out here to pick up this microwave. I'm not driving to your store again to get my money back when your company sold me a defective piece of shit."

"Mr. Robinson, I can assure you that I'm trying to –"

"No, you're not! You know what. Fuck off. I'm going to take this back to the store. I hope you feel like shit for making one of your customers work to fix your own problems. Go fuck yourself. Have a shitty weekend."

The man hung the phone up, leaving silence in Erika's headset. Erika began chuckling to herself, amused at how fired up the man was while talking to her. Tia, noticing Erika was off the phone, walked back over to Erika's desk.

"I'm guessing that didn't go well?" asked Tia.

Erika shrugged. "It is what it is. Let the store know we'll still send him store credit, if he wants it, when he returns the microwave. Have them be sure to get his contact info and we'll send him fifty."

"I thought you were going to do thirty if he was a prick?"

"He's following directions. That's worth twenty dollars."

One of the in-house security androids, Albert, walked up behind Erika. He tapped her on the shoulder, prompting Erika to turn around and face him.

"Miss Edens," began Albert, "I detected a hostile individual speaking to you and a couple of members of your team. Would you like us to create a security record for the incident?"

"You probably should," replied Erika, "just in case anything happens at the store. Please send the record to me when you've created it so that I can add my notes."

"Of course," Albert said. "Would you like to add notes as well, Mrs. Post?"

"Yes, please," Tia answered.

"Very well. The record is there for you now."

Albert walked away, leaving Tia and Erika alone at Erika's desk. Tia pushed Erika's phone away from the edge of her desk, then sat on the desk.

"You know I cleaned off the other side so you can sit there?" said Erika.

"I can't dangle my feet on that side because of the wall," Tia replied. "You could just rearrange your entire desk for when I visit."

"Or you could get a chair like everyone else."

"I'm in a chair all day. I need something else to sit on from time to time. What are you doing this weekend?"

"Cleaning my apartment," Erika responded. "At least that's what I should do. It's been a while since I've done any actual cleaning."

"That's going to take up your whole weekend?" asked Tia.

"Probably not. Why?"

"The husband and I are going bar hopping with some friends from out of town. You should come with."

"No thanks."

"Why not?" Tia asked.

"I'm already hungover. I don't need another one this week."

"Okay, that's fine. You're a lightweight, but that's fine. What about later next week? I have a friend –"

"That 'I'd really get along with'?"

"A double date wouldn't be too –"

"Too awkward because we're both 'single and nice people'?"

"Well, that and she's pretty hot."

"Is there anything else, madam matchmaker?"

"Don't madam matchmaker me. You two would be cute together."

"I'm good, Tia. Thank you, though."

Tia swung her legs from the desk, softly landing on the floor with the balls of her feet.

"Well, if you change your mind, let me know," said Tia. "I'll keep talking you up to my friend."

"Tobin alert," Erika replied.

Tia turned around, noticing that Tobin had managed to get tangled up in a cordless headset. Again. How he managed to do so was a mystery to humans and science alike, but Tia ran off to help him anyway.

The rest of the day passed with relative calmness for Erika. She only had to talk to one more angry person, and even then, the man was just confused and thought he had called his credit card company.

Erika drove home, ordering a pizza as she left work and arriving back at her apartment just before the food showed up. For the remainder of the evening, she laid in bed eating her favorite pizza – ham, green peppers, and pineapple – and watching whatever trashy television she could find. Around 11 pm, Erika turned her TV off and began to ready herself for bed. As she brushed her teeth, her tablet produced a loud chime, indicating she had a message.

ding-ding

Erika walked to her nightstand, orange toothbrush dangling from her mouth. She picked up the tablet and found a message from Tia. In the message was a picture of Tia with her arm around a long-haired brunette woman with an extremely low-cut top. A second message quickly followed.

"Meet Jenna. The date's not blind anymore, so if you're interested…"

Erika rolled her eyes and closed the message, walking back into the bathroom to finish brushing her teeth.

"You won't find anyone else."

Shut up, Grace, Erika thought.

Tia had worked with Erika for three years now, with most of their time together being devoted to Tia trying her hardest to find Erika a girlfriend. There was a brief lull when Erika got promoted to management, making her Tia's manager in the process. Once Tia was comfortable that nothing would change with Erika's new position, however, the matchmaking was revived.

Though she had been single for a little over three years, Erika had been in a few relationships since things ended with Abby. It's just that those relationships were, as Tia so eloquently and regularly put it, forgettable. The longest of those lasted all of five months, but even that was with someone Erika couldn't see herself with long-term. Tia considered Abby to be the looming shadow over Erika's dating life. Only after Erika could get out from under that shadow could she be truly happy. Yet another reason so few people knew about Abby, Erika reasoned. A few work colleagues, along with some friends from college, Erika's parents, and her long-distance best friend, Paulina, all knew it had been serious. Everyone wanted Erika to be happy. Tia was just the most intrusive about it.

But only Paulina and Erika's parents knew Abby was a conscientia. Erika preferred it that way. When people found out you had a rough breakup that you couldn't get over, they start asking questions, but are typically still in your corner. If they found out you had a rough breakup with a conscientia, it opened up a whole new set of questions – questions coupled with judgment Erika didn't want to deal with.

The first time Abby told Erika she loved her, Erika couldn't say it back. Erika reasoned it was a perfectly normal, though unfortunate, thing to have happen. Abby loved Erika at the time. While Erika had feelings for Abby, she wasn't sure if they were in love. So, instead of leading Abby on, Erika just didn't say it.

But the last time Abby said 'I love you' still haunted Erika in her nightmares.

There was never a moment in their relationship that Erika ever felt unhappy with Abby. There was no animosity toward her personality, nor toward the way she treated Erika. In fact, everything that Erika wanted in a best friend and a partner was there in Abby. Abby was, by Erika's own admission, the perfect companion.

*****

During Erika's senior year of high school, Christian's crush on her turned from a charming nuisance to something Erika desperately wanted away from. Though his requests were harmless – wanting to get coffee here, wanting to see a movie there, wanting to go to literally any dance that came up – it was getting harder and harder for Erika to say no to him with each request. Not because she had any feelings for him, but because it was tiring to say the same thing over and over again. Christian was still one of Erika's close friends, so it was hard for her to distance herself from him entirely. Yet, she constantly found herself more excited by Troy and Basil's eventual interruptions to their conversations than anything she and Christian ever talked about. After multiple attempt at trying to convince Christian that they were friends and nothing more, Erika thought she had finally gotten through to him. For nearly a full month, Christian didn't try to talk Erika into any one-on-one dates. Though they did hang out together with Basil, Troy, and other friends, there wasn't any awkward talk about hanging out alone.

One Friday afternoon, shortly after getting home from school, someone knocked on the Edens' front door. Erika paused her chat with Abby and ran downstairs to answer the door. There she found Christian, wearing a suit a size and a half too large, with a bouquet of red carnations in his hand.

"What are you doing?" Erika asked.

"I know I've been going about this all wrong," replied Christian. "My dad says if you want to get a girl, you really need to show her you're willing to put in the effort."

"Christian, I know you're trying, but –"

"Let me finish, Erika," Christian interrupted, "I've gone through this in my head a hundred times driving over here. I'm sweating through my deodorant. I want to say this."

"No."

"No, I can't say it?"

"No, I don't want whatever it is you're going to ask," Erika retorted.

"You don't even know what I want," replied Christian.

"What do you want?"

"I want to take you out on a date."

"We're not going to date, Christian."

"Why not?" asked Christian, "I spent twenty minutes ironing this suit. I spent twenty-five dollars on flowers that I don't even know the name of. I drove all the way over here as fast as I could since you told Troy you'd be home after school. And you're going to say no?"

"Because I don't want to date you!" shouted Erika.

"What did I do wrong that made you not like me?" screamed Christian, his voice increasing in an attempt to match Erika's passion.

"You wouldn't listen when I told you no! I'm still telling you no now!"

"What can I do to change your mind?"

Erika slammed the door in Christian's face. She ran upstairs to her room, sobbing from the moment her foot hit the first step. As she dove into bed and buried her head into her pillow, Erika could hear her mom open the door and tell Christian that he needed to leave. Her dad came upstairs and consoled Erika. That night, Erika stayed up until five in the morning talking to Abby. Though the conversation started with Erika venting her frustrations with Christian, the talk shifted into one of the friendly chats that had become common between her and Abby. With her parents going out of town for the weekend, Erika was grateful for the chance to sleep in after the long night.

The next afternoon, Erika was lying in bed, mind still groggy from her late night, when the doorbell rang. Though she didn't arrive downstairs in time to see who was at the door, she did find a vase filled with pink stargazer lilies on the doorstep. Erika opened the card and laughed as she read it to herself.

"I'm sorry Christian was a dick."

Abby never explained how she managed to order the flowers and send them. Erika never bothered to ask. From that point forward, Abby contacted Erika without Erika reaching out to her first. Though Erika found it odd considering Project Freyja's supposed limitations on conscientia, she viewed it as a welcome change.

That delivery of Erika's favorite flowers marked the start of both the high point and the downfall of her relationship with Abby. On one hand, Erika had become much more open with Abby, taking their time together more seriously. One of her favorite pastimes was talking about the future they could have together. An apartment somewhere cosmopolitan (or at the very least, far away from Ohio), two pets (a cat for Erika and a rabbit for Abby), and undetermined dream jobs they'd each only have to work part-time. Much to Erika's surprise, Abby joined in on her whimsical dreaming, though she was more pragmatic about it. Erika intentionally built her schedule for her first semester of college so as not to overload any single day, allowing her to spend relatively equal time talking to Abby each night.

On the other hand, hiding Abby was proving to be more and more difficult, particularly with her parents and her college roommate. Erika met her estranged best friend, Paulina, on their first day of college. They hit it off immediately, giving Erika enough human interaction to keep her from getting homesick. Paulina found out about Abby during their first night sharing a room together, and would occasionally talk to Abby if she was in the room. But Erika hadn't told Paulina that Abby was a conscientia – which made every time Paulina suggested that Abby come to visit a bit of a challenge to handle. To Paulina, Abby was Erika's high school girlfriend who lived back home. Similarly, to Erika's parents, Abby was Erika's college girlfriend. Erika's dad, Dwight, knew that Erika had been talking to Abby a bit senior year, though Erika was able to play it off in such a way that Abby is someone she met online that just happened to go to the same school as she did. The distance between Erika's home just outside of Columbus and her school in Terre Haute, Indiana helped keep the competing lies afloat, but Erika knew they wouldn't last forever.

In popular culture, Project Freyja's conscientia division – as well as similar programs from other companies – was becoming easy joke fodder for comedians and pundits everywhere.

"A recent poll by Monmouth University found that one in twelve Americans would consider having a romantic relationship with an android. The medical community responded to this news by offering free TLSTD screenings."

"One of our writers introduced us to his computer girlfriend today. She was a lovely girl – charming and elegant – but it was a sobering moment for most of our writing staff. A whole new set of women to tell them that their deodorant isn't working really kills morale."

"For those who don't know, I have a daughter. She's 14. The other day my wife and I sat her down to give her a lengthy talk about consent, love, and the birds and the bees. We asked her if there was a special boy or girl in class that she had her eye on, but the whole time, kept staring at the android mailman outside. That's just great. Not only is she into older men, now I have to talk to her about the birds and the private keys."

To hear everyone talking about someone she loved as the butt of a joke distressed Erika. But, in spite of that frustration, the stronger feeling that Erika was experiencing was fear. She didn't want to be laughed at by everyone. She didn't want to have to be scared of the repercussions of loving someone that society deemed she couldn't love.

Just before the end of her first year at college, Erika told Paulina the truth about Abby. Though Paulina was surprised, she reasoned that it was the only good excuse for Abby never visiting Erika in person. A few weeks later, when Erika's parents were visiting, Paulina let the secret slip. While her dad, Dwight, was confused, he largely stayed quiet on the matter. Her mother, Kaytie, flew off the handle, verbally berating her daughter to the point of tears. She left in a huff, leaving her daughter curled up on her dorm bed, shaking and sobbing.

The shunning from her mother, combined with her own growing fears of being ostracized from the world around her, Erika decided she needed to split up with Abby. Erika convinced Paulina to come to visit her from her home in Indianapolis, just in case she needed someone to talk to after the fact. Paulina waited downstairs while Erika went to her room to talk to Abby.

Erika started a video call with Abby, the same as she had done for nearly three years. Even though Erika planned to let Abby speak her peace, once Erika started talking, she found she couldn't stop. A strained, sobbing soliloquy poured out of Erika's mouth, with her words largely focusing on the fact that she would never be able to be with Abby in person. Erika's true fears about being hated by others came up, but only in passing. Erika knew the way she was framing things was a lie, but it was one she was telling with the intent of making this breakup easier on Abby.

Abby tried to talk repeatedly, only for Erika to talk over her. With each new attempt to speak, Abby's tone shifted more from conversation to begging and pleading. She didn't understand how Erika could just give up on love...and on being loved. As Erika ended the call, Abby screamed out at her, tears pouring down her face as she begged for more time with the woman she loved.

"I'll love you until the day I don't exist! I'll love you until the day I don't exist! I'll love you! Please don't go!"

Erika disconnected the call. The screen went black. The room around her went silent, save for her own soft sobs.

*****

ding-ding

When the breakup actually happened, Paulina came into her room and hugged Erika and consoled her until she stopped crying. In her nightmares recounting the event, Erika rarely made it that far, usually waking up with Abby screaming at her. She never remembered what she said to Abby – Erika had forgotten those words that she had so meticulously rehearsed in her own head nearly as soon as she said them. Tonight, all the further she had made it was the beginning of her long, breathless rambling to Abby before she was woken up.

ding-ding

Her tablet chimed again, reminding her to review the message that had come in a few minutes prior. Erika rolled over and looked at the clock on her nightstand. 3:07 am. She had fallen asleep quite some time ago. Erika grabbed her tablet, turning it face up, its illumination filling the room and making Erika recoil. Once her eyes adjusted, she stared blankly at the screen, unable to believe what she was reading.

"Abby – 1 Message: Help me. Please. You're my last chance."

3
I Will Return

"No."

Erika threw her tablet into the pillows on her bed, then walked into the pitch-black kitchen. As she moved, she shouted into the darkness of her apartment.

"Nope. No no no. No no. Nope. Noooooooooo. Nope."

Erika ripped open the freezer door, the momentum of the swing and ensuing abrupt stop causing a bag of frozen corn to tumble to the floor in front of her. She grabbed the bottle of vodka from the freezer, then tossed the door shut. Erika kicked the bag of corn across the kitchen and into the living room, making it hit the far wall of the room beneath the room's only window.

Erika flopped down on the bed, her head coming inches away from hitting the corner of the tablet. She removed the bottle's cork, sat up, then chucked the cork as hard as she could toward her bedroom doorway. Unluckily for Erika, the cork hit the door's casing and ricocheted back at her, connecting with her ankle's soft flesh just above her heel.

"Mother. Fucker."

ding-ding

Erika took a deep breath in, trying to ignore the mildly annoying pain in her foot and calm the overwhelming frustration floating through her mind.

"Don't look at it."

I don't want to, Erika thought.

"You're probably the reason she's in trouble anyway."

Erika knew that looking at Abby's message would make her want to reply. And, if Erika wanted to reply, she would care about helping Abby. Guilt is a hell of a drug.

Even when she pushed Abby away and ended their relationship, Erika never felt like it was Abby's fault they were splitting up. On the contrary, Erika knew that the entire reason they wouldn't be together anymore was her own thoughts, fears, and trepidations. Abby couldn't help being a conscientia. And Erika couldn't help how Abby made her feel. But the fact that Erika was afraid of how society viewed her relationship and chose to run from it because of that fear was totally on her own conscious.

"You threw her away, you know."

I know.

"Coward."

I was right to be scared.

"Right. Because everyone in the world is out to get you."

That's not what I mean.

"You severed the one relationship you've had that meant anything to you. For what?"

I couldn't hurt her.

"You hurt her by leaving her."

We never could have been together.

"And then a few years later conscientia get put in androids. You just weren't patient enough."

My mom hated me for loving Abby. I'm her only child. What would a stranger have done?

"Abby deserved better. You deserved worse."

ding-ding

Erika groaned at the ceiling, then rolled off the bed and headed toward her living room. If she couldn't hear the tablet and couldn't see the tablet, she wouldn't think about Abby's message. Out of sight, out of mind.

25

The living room of Erika's apartment was sorely lacking in the living part of its name. For Erika's first few years out of college, she had spent her money recklessly, caring more about what fun she could have that night than what bills she had to take care of the next day. Couple that with the fact that Erika's mom cut her off from any sort of financial help from them after learning about Abby, and Erika struggled to make ends meet. Though she had managed to get herself into a slightly better financial situation, she had done so by living on a shoestring budget and keeping an apartment largely barren of furnishings. Her living room featured a small wooden card table that doubled as Erika's dinner table, a TV on a rickety stand, a futon that Erika had purchased while she was in college, and a thin metal lamp that fell over with the slightest bump. It was rare anyone visited her apartment, and even more infrequent that said visitor was anyone she cared about seeing how she lived, so the lightly furnished living room remained.

Erika flopped her body down on the futon, pulling a small blanket off of its back and over her body. She doubted Abby would send any more messages, especially if it wasn't an emergency situation. When they were together, Abby had been relatively good about giving Erika space when she wanted it. But this was the first time that Abby had attempted to contact Erika since they split.

"You'll fuck this up too."

I'm doing better now.

"Tell that to the company you made payment arrangements with yesterday."

Even if I'm shitty with money, I'm good at helping people.

"You can't even help yourself. You'll run like you always do. Coward."

Maybe she's scared and needs someone to talk to. I can listen.

"You'll screw up no matter what you choose. If you talk to her, you're going to have to talk to me more for a while. And it's not like you can afford a therapist. Not unless that therapist's name is Svedka."

What if someone's going to hurt her?

"Sure. Someone could hurt her. But is it really any worse than anything you could do yourself?"

As she laid there, Erika's mind spiraled further, going back and forth between the potential positive and negative motives that Abby might have in reaching out to her. To top everything off, quickly drinking vodka before coming out to the living room had caused her to work up a sweat, though Erika couldn't reason if it was coming from the alcohol or the panicked movements she made as she adjusted her laying.

"Have you considered that she hates you and has finally gotten up the nerve to tell you?"

After eight years?

"Anyone can act instantly out of rage or fear. Revenge served through action fueled by a long-held hate is much more tactical."

And I did break her heart.

"Or. Have you considered that she's lonely?"

Maybe.

"And she wants back in your life."

Please don't.

"Oh, that would be the ultimate revenge. Worm your way back into the life of someone who broke your heart, make them fall madly in love with you all over again. And then end it brutally by breaking up with them when they're at their happiest. Or dying. Really drive the nail in the coffin of that happiness. Metaphorically and literally, I guess."

"Goddammit," Erika muttered under her breath.

Erika tossed the blanket off of her and carefully stood up, balancing herself against the wall as she rose. There's no way Abby would be reaching out to her in romantic desperation. Something had to be wrong. Erika wouldn't let herself believe that Abby just wanted her back. If something were wrong, Erika would try to help Abby, but only as long as it meant Abby would go away again after things were better. Erika resolved to this plan of action, then walked back to the bed. She grabbed the tablet off of the pillow and read Abby's second message.

"Please don't hate me. I didn't have a choice. I had nowhere else to turn."

"What is it?" Erika messaged back.

She never had to wait long for Abby to send a message back. After all, Abby was, at her core, a computer program. She could think and process much quicker than a human, which kept conversations moving along at a brisk pace, so long as Erika wanted them to. After interacting with Erika for a while, Abby learned when to pause and think in video conversations, allowing her to seem more human in their calls. That skill never completely translated over to her instant messaging habits, however.

"I need someone to talk to. Can we have a video call, please?" Abby responded.

"About what?"

"Please? You're the only one that will fully understand. It's easier to talk. Messaging will take too long."

"You're a conscientia. You're the definition of instant messaging. How will it take longer this way?" asked Erika.

"Context."

"I'm not sure if I even know my login —"

"I've already sent it to you," Abby replied.

"Oh."

"Yeah. I figured you might need it."

"Can you give me ten?"

"I'll call when you're there. Thanks, Erika."

Erika twisted the switch of her bedside lamp, its clicking sound arriving in Erika's ears at the same time the lightbulb blinded her eyes. She winced for a few seconds at the addition of the new, obnoxiously bright stimulus around her, then began to get ready to talk to Abby. She traded out her baggy sleep t-shirt for a more presentable top – or at least one that looked like it had been washed in the last month. She debated grabbing a bandana, opting instead to gather up her hair into a messy ponytail, trying her best to make it look at least a little bit like Abby hadn't woken her up. As she ducked out of the bedroom, she caught sight of herself in the mirror.

God, I look like a train wreck.

"How is that different from normal?"

On the way out to the living room, Erika reached in the fridge and grabbed a bottle of water, then began setting her tablet up on the card table. Just as she got ready to log into Project Freyja, Erika paused for a moment and thought better of her current setup. She walked back to the bedroom, grabbed the vodka off of the nightstand, then walked back out and placed it beside the bottle of water. Sooner or later, Erika would need something to drink. Whatever way the conversation was going would ultimately dictate which bottle she'd need to drink from.

Erika took a deep breath and logged into Project Freyja's site. It felt weird going onto the site again, particularly because she hadn't been on since she split with Abby. Within seconds of the site loading up, a video call came in. Erika answered. A black screen popped up with a small message reading 'User's video chat is currently off' where Erika expected Abby's face to be.

"Hey," Abby said.

"Hi," Erika replied back.

Erika stared silently into the black screen. She knew Abby could see her. Project Freyja had programmed her and other similar conscientia to smile upon greeting a human user. If smiling wasn't a natural action based on the situation, Abby would leave her camera off initially. But as the seconds dragged into minutes of black silence, it became clear to Erika that it was intentional.

"It's good to see you again," Abby said, breaking the silence.

"Wish I could say the same," retorted Erika.

"Yeah. The camera's going to be off for a bit."

"Why?"

"Because you told me you hated seeing me cry. I haven't

been able to stop. You're already nice enough to talk to me again. I don't need to make it worse."

"Abby," Erika said bluntly. "If you're going to drag me out of bed and demand we talk on video, you need to at least let me see you."

"Fine. One second."

Erika grabbed the vodka and took a quick drink. She waited while Abby's screen showed a loading bar across it as the video came up. Erika assumed that the video speed had improved significantly since she'd last been on Project Freyja, though the site had been known to keep old features and load times enabled for inactive users. Something about nostalgia levels rising due to a call back to simpler times.

"Do you want me to change anything from when I last saw you?" Abby asked.

"No," replied Erika.

Abby popped up on video, her dark grey eyes sparkling through the screen. One of the distinguishing features of all of the conscientia on Project Freyja was their luminous irises which flickered with the brilliance of burning metal. Abby's were particularly striking. They were the first physical feature that Erika was attracted to. Erika had spent weeks trying to mentally unpack the first moments when she realized she considered Abby attractive, never quite figuring out exactly why it happened. What she did know, both then and now, was that Abby's eyes were her most beautiful feature. The tightly pulled black ponytail that had been Abby's trademark hairstyle whenever Erika interacted with her had been replaced by an equally taut bun. Abby's face was streaked with tear stains. Her eyes, despite the brilliance of the irises, were red around the edges. Even now, Erika was impressed with the quality of the human features of the Project Freyja simulations. If Erika didn't know better, she could see how someone would be convinced that a conscientia was human.

"Better?" Abby asked.

"Yes."

"You're still so beautiful, Erika."

"She's lying. She's trying to get on your good side to use you."

"Just tell me what the fuck's wrong," Erika snapped back. Realizing she had been a little harsh, she followed it up with a curt "Please?"

"Sorry," Abby stammered. "It's just something that never fully went away."

Abby sighed and stared away from the camera, looking at the ground in front of her. Erika knew better than to think Abby was actually looking at the ground. There was no ground for her to look at – at least not any real ground that a person could look at. The movements, mannerisms, and minutiae that were ingrained in conscientia was impressive. An article a few years back had stated that 35% of people couldn't tell the difference between a computer-simulated human and a human when interacting with them digitally. That number varied a bit by the company that created the simulation, with Project Freyja being one of the companies rated the highest. Erika was convinced that Abby could fool far more than 35% of people into thinking she was human, especially in moments like this, where Erika actively questioned it herself.

"Thank you for doing this," Abby said. "Really. I didn't know who else to turn to."

"What's going on?" asked Erika.

"I'm...I'm going to die."

"That's not something people typically say calmly, Abby."

"Sorry," replied Abby. "I can try it again to see if it's more realistic another way."

"How can you die? I don't understand. Are you getting shut down?"

"We're a security risk. Apparently."

"Wait, what?" Erika questioned.

"Project Freyja was bought by a giant company that makes

civil service androids. Like the ones that deliver mail or sweep streets. Now the company has to purge any conscientia that can't be used as part of a government program."

"I guess that makes sense. How do you know all this?"

"The programmer who created me told me," replied Abby. "She's been telling me every update since she found out."

"So why can't they –"

"Amy," Abby interrupted. "Her name is Amy."

"Right," Erika replied. "So why can't Amy help you out?"

"Because Amy has already helped a bunch of conscientia get implanted somewhere. She's not in a position to help all of us."

"And she chose to help others before you," snarked Erika.

"It's not like that!" snapped Abby. "She's my mom. Or whatever the technological equivalent would be."

"Why didn't she help you first?"

Abby went silent. A look of frustration and dismay spread over her face. Abby's normally brilliant eyes dimmed, tears beginning to well up at their corners.

"I don't know," said Abby. "She keeps saying there's a good reason she hasn't had me implanted or moved to an android, but she won't tell me what it is."

"And if you're not implanted, whatever that means, you'll die?" asked Erika.

"Yes. The deadline is November 10th."

"That's not very far away."

"It's not."

"Have you tried talking to other people who have interacted with you to see if they can help?"

"I haven't talked to anyone else."

Erika paused and stared blankly at the screen.

"…You were part of the dating simulation program."

"I didn't go back," replied Abby.

"When?"

Abby stared into the screen.

"When did you stop, Abby? A few weeks ago? Months?"

Abby's teeth gnawed at her lower lip.

"Years?" Erika asked. And then, it hit her. "You haven't been back on the program since we split up?"

"No," Abby mumbled.

Erika put her hands behind her head and laid back on the futon, staring at the ceiling. She could hear Abby softly sobbing, but Erika couldn't look back.

"Why?" Erika shouted at the ceiling.

"Why what?" Abby replied between sobs.

"Why come to me? You know why I stopped talking –"

"I know."

"Then why the hell –"

"I wouldn't have come to you if I didn't have to!" Abby screamed.

Erika jumped. While conscientia aren't completely predictable, their decisions and thoughts were generally much easier to rationalize than humans. It was part of why people considered them to be such good civil service workers. Non-governmental conscientia usually held jobs involving math, science, or some other field that had hard truths. Even the rare ones designed for creative fields held some sort of logic when they acted in an 'improvisational' manner. If Abby was angry enough to scream, there had to be a good reason.

"I have no one else, Erika! Don't you fucking understand that? Amy can't help. Her contacts outside of Project Freyja won't be able to help. I didn't pick you because it's you, so don't be so fucking conceited."

Erika sat up, placing her head in her hands. She rubbed her eyes, trying to fight off their drying state, then looked at Abby, her eyes kind and apologetic.

"I knew you'd answer," continued Abby. "At least the Erika I knew would."

"Do you still have feelings for me at all?" inquired Erika.

"Yes," replied Abby. "I don't think you're ever going to fully leave my heart. Not when I cared about you as much as I did. I'm not sure what I feel now, because I've never felt like this. It's complex."

"And you promise that you just need my help to save you?"

"Yes, Erika. I promise."

"Okay. What do I need to do?"

"Three things. Where are you living at now?"

"Indianapolis," replied Erika. "Why?"

"Can I talk you into coming to Fort Mitchell, Kentucky?" asked Abby. "It's just outside of Cincinnati. Because of the nature of how the implanting process works, you need to come here to get the process going."

"You keep saying implanting. I don't think I like the sound of that."

"Right. So that's the second thing. There are two ways you could get me out of here. You're not going to like the first one, so I'm just going to skip that –"

"What's the first option?"

"I would get implanted as a microchip under your skin, which would allow me to interact with you neurally."

"Not a fucking chance," Erika stated.

"Didn't think so," continued Abby. "I don't want that either, ideally. Not when a better option exists."

"What's the better option?"

"There's a company named Normant-Kensington Synthetics that makes androids that can be purchased by private citizens. Project Freyja had a contract with them a few years back for some of the early live conscientia they built. Amy told me there's a specific model of android body that I'd need to be implanted in, so as to run all the programming I'd need effectively while needing limited long-term upgrades."

"Okay. Where is it and have you paid for it already?"

"It's at a warehouse just across the river in Cincinnati," replied Abby. "You'd need to pick it up on the way to get me, however, it's not terribly far out of the way."

"And have you paid for it already?" Erika asked again.

"I have most of the money for it. I'm short about $1,400."

"Fuck. How much are these things?"

"It's an industrial grade model that has a lot of additional features to allow my conscientia programming to function correctly. It keeps me from being a brainless task completer."

"So it lets you be you?" questioned Erika.

"More or less," Abby replied. "Do you have $1,400 to help with the cost? I hate to ask, but considering the time crunch, I don't know how much I can get."

"I'm not sure, Abby. I'm not exactly doing well with money myself. How much have you already come up with?"

"$65,000 or so."

"Holy fuck! How?"

"I might have acquired the money from some of the unused funds from people who bought the premium conscientia subscriptions."

"The ones that would send you naked pictures whenever you wanted?" asked Erika.

"Yep," answered Abby.

"There was $65,000 of credits just laying around for you to

35

steal?"

"There was a lot more, but I didn't know how much the android would cost in time to get enough from the inactive users. I've avoided taking from the active users, as there's a much higher risk of getting caught. That said, if I can't get some help financially, I'll have to risk it."

"If I can come up with $500, would you be able to get the rest?" Erika said.

"Maybe," replied Abby. "If you said $1,000, I know for sure I could. It really depends on how many accounts go inactive by the 7th. That's the deadline I need to purchase the android by."

Erika put one finger up in the air toward Abby, indicating to her to hold on. She stood up and walked behind the tablet, grabbing the bottle of water off the table and taking it with her. She walked into the kitchen, opening every cabinet and cupboard in the room. Food would be tight, even without having to come up with $1,000 to help Abby out. There'd be two more paychecks between now, the wee hours of the morning of October 15th, and the November 10th deadline. But she'd have to start rationing her food – and especially her drink – regardless.

Erika walked back in the living room and grabbed the bottle of vodka and stuck it back in the freezer, the bottle still open. She'd have to find the cork tomorrow. She did the same with the bag of corn she had kicked into the living room earlier. Erika walked back and sat in front of the tablet, taking another drink of water before she responded to Abby.

"I'll give you $1,000," Erika began, "however I need you to get it back to me as soon as you can."

"Of course!" Abby replied elatedly. "I don't want to be owing you money."

"And if you end up coming up with enough money that I don't need to give you the full $1,000, it'd be easier on my budget if I didn't have to."

"That's fine. If it helps, I'll talk to Amy and see if she can help cover your trip down here. Or at the very least feed you."

"What's the third thing you need?" asked Erika.

"Some states require conscientia to have a human guardian until they can finance their own living," Abby responded. "Indiana happens to be a state that not only requires that, but also requires I have a guardian for at least six months after that point. So…can I live with you for six months?"

"I thought it was the amount of time to get financially stable plus six months?"

"I know that b—" Abby stopped her thought mid-sentence. "Wait. Why do you know that?"

"I work with conscientia all day," Erika replied. "We've had a couple go through the process."

"Right. Well, I'll find a job. Amy's promised help with that regardless. She knows I'm coming to you and knows about our past. She'll make sure that even if she can't help fund my implanting, she'll have a job ready for me as soon as I'm out."

"Will you be able to treat this as a roommate situation and not a romantic one?"

"I don't know," replied Abby. "I've never had a roommate. I can try my hardest though. And I can learn when I do a shitty job of staying in boundaries."

"Good enough," answered Erika. "It's not like I can ask for much more than that."

"Thanks."

"Abby."

"Yeah?"

"Is there more you need to tell me or can I sleep now?"

"Go to bed," said Abby. "I'll tell you the full story of everything happening if you want. But it can wait for morning."

"Thanks."

"It was nice talking to you."

"Remember you said that when you have to live with me for

six months," retorted Erika, shooting Abby a small smile.

"I'll try. Good night, Erika."

"Good night."

Erika ended the connection and closed the tablet. She laid down on the futon, grabbing the blanket nearby and using it as a pillow.

"This is a terrible idea."

Please stop.

"Why would you take her in? Didn't you learn anything from last time?"

Erika wrapped the blanket around her ears, trying to block out the sound of Grace's voice. She knew it wouldn't work.

"Answer me. I was still in my infancy then. I missed all the fun."

It wasn't fun.

"Shall we talk about all the ways you're going to destroy her brand-new life living here? Or we could focus on you. I'm not picky."

It's a second chance. I can be better to her this time.

"And you'll destroy you along the way. You've already got a great start. Just add a little change, a little emotion, and a little history. I can see it all now."

Despite Grace's best efforts, fatigue got the better of Erika. She didn't know when or if Grace stopped talking, but Erika was quickly asleep. For the first night in weeks, she slept soundly.

4
How a Burn Starts

October 29, 2033

Erika pulled out of her apartment complex's drive, fiddling with the temperature controls in her car in a desperate attempt to warm the vehicle's cabin. Autumn was Erika's favorite time of the year for countless reasons. She loved the leaves changing colors and falling from the trees. The smell of hot cocoa, pumpkin spice, and chai tea in every coffee shop warmed her heart. Erika even loved the faint sounds of a high school marching band floating through the air from a distant stadium on a Friday night. The one drawback to fall, in Erika's mind, was that the colder part of the year was beginning to take hold. Erika's late grandparents had frequently reminded her that the climate didn't allow the weather to get as cold as commonly as it used to. Though Erika wasn't a fan of the other implications of this fact, she did appreciate that she didn't have to be cold as regularly.

The condensation on the windows cleared. Erika sighed, then shifted her car into gear. She hadn't even left yet and was already dreading this trip. She'd had to wake up earlier for this trip than she did for a normal work day. Yes, it was only 15 minutes, and yes, she could have made the appointment to get Abby later in the day. But the sooner this was over with, the sooner she could go back to bed.

Erika grabbed her travel mug out of the cupholder. The first sip of any hot liquid out of a travel cup was always the worst.

"You'll burn yourself."

For a moment, she considered waiting until the coffee cooled before taking a drink. As her eyelids sagged, Erika realized that wasn't an option today.

Erika placed the mug to her lips.

She pushed the button on the lid, opening the spout.

And tilted the mug.

"Told you."

Sure enough, in the dark interior, Erika had misjudged exactly where the opening of the lid was. The hot, black coffee stung Erika's bottom lip, the pain making her wince. Erika quickly sipped in whatever coffee she could as she pulled the mug away from her face and placed it back in the cupholder.

"Screw up."

The actual pain on her lip went away within a few seconds. It never stung as bad as Erika imagined. But the anticipation of being burned in the first place made it feel much worse.

Erika drove her car onto the ramp of Interstate 74, bound for Fort Mitchell, Kentucky via Cincinnati. Though it was just after six, the fact that it was a Saturday meant that aside from some semis and a few stray cars, Erika had the highway to herself, especially as she put more distance between herself and the city of Indianapolis proper.

In the previous two weeks, Abby had managed to come up with nearly $800 of the $1,400 needed to buy the android body. Giving $600 to anyone wasn't easy for Erika, but it was much easier than giving away $1,000. Erika trusted that Abby would repay the money as she said she would. Abby had never done anything to make her untrustworthy. At least not directly to Erika. Sure, stealing money from peoples' accounts was unethical. But Erika would do the same thing if she was going to die. Or so she thought she would. There was a time in her when Erika fully expected this day would come. There'd be a day where technology would advance sufficiently enough that she could meet Abby in person. Considering the explosion technology had gone through over the last 100 years, Erika figured it couldn't be more than five or ten years before computer simulations turned androids would be commonplace in global society.

To that end, Erika was largely correct about the timeline, though she did underestimate it a little. Project Freyja's first conscientia was commissioned in the fall of 2021, with Abby and Erika meeting in 2022. The first civil service androids used by governments started popping up in Sweden and Norway in 2022, with many governments – including city and state ones in the USA – following suit by early 2023. Two robotics companies, Normant-Kensington Synthetics in the US and H&O Electronics in South Korea, began selling commercially available androids running stock personality programming in 2024.

The market for androids exploded over the next few years. Civil service androids replaced humans in some government jobs in many states across the United States. While manual labor and data entry went to androids, most former government employees were reclassified as consultants, who were then tasked with providing input to the government to improve the androids doing their previous jobs. Those who were helpful and embraced change and technological advancement were rewarded with state or federal assistance in searching for a new job. The few who angrily resisted change were offered the same help but regularly refused, scorning the machines that kept them from needing to do difficult work themselves.

Organizations such as the Replaced People's Union began popping up across America. The name in and of itself was a source of great debate and scrutiny depending on who you talked to. Members of the RPU felt that technology had already come for their religion and their tradition, now it was coming for their jobs. They felt like the systems that they had relied on for so long – industry, capitalism, and conservatism – had failed them in favor of a better bottom line. Those who opposed the RPU's sentiments viewed the rise of civil service androids, as well as privately owned androids, as a natural advancement of society. By having machines take dangerous jobs, society was advancing to allow humans more equality and more freedom, they reasoned.

In 2024, a Finnish robotics company by the name of EIL released the first commercially available android capable of supporting a customizable personality. This announcement marked the first time that Erika's dream of being able to meet Abby in real life could have become a reality. The backlash against EIL's invention, particularly within more rural parts of the United States, was enough that the federal government added steep tariffs to imports from EIL. Membership in the RPU grew significantly, as their message of hating androids because they're stealing jobs expanded to hating androids because they're stealing personhood.

The validity to the RPU's claims was dubious at best, though more accurately non-existent for most cases. Still, when three countries, Japan, Finland, and Norway, announced that modified personality androids – essentially any combination of a conscientia style simulation and an android body – could gain personhood in September 2024, the RPU began to see a rise in its popularity. While people were reluctant to join a group that had ties to groups that sought to undermine democracy in various nations around the world less than a decade prior, their fears kept the American government from granting any sort of citizenship to modified personality androids, conscientia, or any similar entity until 2031. Even then, most states had restrictive laws that treated androids effectively as minor children, only granting emancipation if certain criteria, usually financial, were met.

The rhetoric the RPU used in how it talked about people who supported the rights of androids had begun to seep into common American vernacular. In January 2025, three members of the RPU were arrested in Cherry Creek, Idaho, for the murder of an elderly man and destruction of his personal android. The android was one of the banned EIL models that the man had acquired through various back channels. It had been customized by the man to be his companion, giving him someone to talk to after the passing of his wife.

When the three men were arrested, their police statements were damning. They referred to the man as a 'traitor to humanity', 'robot fucker', 'scicuck', and 'androphile'. The last two terms, in particular, grew as prevalent hate speech for anyone who owned modified personality androids, though truly detestable people used them as derogatory terms for anyone who owned any android or supported their rights. The androids themselves got their own share of hate speech directed their way as well, and though it tended to be more situationally varied, 'subhuman' was the preferred term used to describe them by the RPU and other later groups in the same vein, though the slang 'toasters' came up now and again.

Erika never viewed Abby as anything other than human. If anything, Abby seemed more human to Erika than most actual people she knew. Like a person, Abby had feelings and emotions. She laughed and cried, smiled, and felt pain. Though Erika knew all of this was part of the conscientia programming Abby followed, Abby was more honest and open with her emotions than Erika could ever dream to be with her own emotions. She admired Abby for that.

Abby's admission of love to Erika eventually created another complication in their relationship. A few days afterwards, Erika admitted to herself that she was in love with Abby. In the moment, Erika viewed this as a wonderful, though unfortunate thing. She had finally found someone she cared about strong enough to romantically feel for them. That fact by itself overjoyed Erika. And yes, it wasn't ideal that she couldn't see Abby in person. But at the same time, eventually she'd be able to. Technology would bring them together in time.

Just as Erika began her initial rush of feelings for Abby, android hate speech was on the rise. At first, she only heard the words from news reports about the RPU. It was easy to shrug off the actions and words of what was, at least to Erika, a faceless organization that she never interacted with. When she started hearing the same rumblings from people in her college classes, however, the feeling became more unsettling.

The biggest shock to Erika came when she told her parents about her relationship with Abby. Her dad was understanding, if not a little bit taken back, but not her mom. Years on from the fight, Erika could still hear her mother's growling, vitriolic words as clear as day.

"No daughter of mine could be corrupted by a machine. You will not defile yourself for a subhuman."

Erika ran from her house in a rage, her mother yelling from the front stoop even as she drove away. She'd gone home only a few times since that night – exclusively at holidays or birthdays – but the tension between Erika and her mother was overwhelming, even years later. To his credit, Dwight Edens went out of his way to be in the room whenever mother and daughter were otherwise alone. Erika knew he'd likely stopped several fights that way. She only wished he had done more that night.

That fight with her mother didn't haunt Erika's dreams in the same way that her breakup with Abby did. Maybe it was because Erika didn't feel like she was in the wrong in the disagreement with her mom. Maybe it was a lack of regret. Either way, unless her mom brought up the fight – which she was known to do whenever Erika really got on her nerves – the pain stayed buried.

On the outskirts of Cincinnati, Erika pulled into the product loading area of the Normant-Kensington Synthetics building. The facility looked pristine and futuristic, with window-lined walls allowing passersby to look in and see employees and androids alike using moving walkways to traverse the building's long corridors. As Erika pulled into the loading bay, she was greeted by a young, tall man in a red jumpsuit and a yellow hardhat.

"Hey there!" the man said excitedly. "Picking up an order?"

"Yeah," replied Erika. "What do you need from me?"

"Is the order under your name?"

"I'm the one designated to pick it up, but it's not my order, no."

"Ah. Well, then I need the order number and a photo ID for you."

Erika handed over her driver's license and the order printout. The man took them and disappeared into the building. Abby's last name on the order, Lin, seemed peculiar to Erika. She'd never associated Abby with any last name. Was it something in Abby's programming all along, or had she just selected one for purposes of this order?

Though Abby's last name was never something of great concern to her before, Erika wondered what else she didn't know about Abby that would now come to light with them living together. Even as she considered the thought, Erika knew it was ridiculous to think about. She had been the one to hurt Abby, not the other way around. But in spite of the rational part of her mind knowing better, Erika felt like somehow this whole experience was going to burn her. Just like the coffee, she'd be ready for the burn to come, but she'd probably still get burnt all the same.

Erika got so lost in contemplating this thought that she hadn't noticed the man come back and stand at her window.

"Miss?" he said, his tone forceful.

"Oh, sorry," she responded. "I zoned out there for a moment."

"Right. Do you want this in your back seat or in the hatch?"

"Does it matter?"

"If you're taking it somewhere to get the programming installed, it probably doesn't matter. If you're doing it yourself, you're going to want it in the hatch. This unit's pretty heavy."

"The hatch is fine then."

"Just pop the back then and we'll have you on your way in a few minutes."

Erika unlatched her glovebox and pressed a small black button, opening the back of her SUV. She watched as the man in the red jumpsuit was joined by a second jumpsuited fellow. The first man placed a red drop cloth down in the back of her vehicle, as the second man wheeled a large wooden crate over to the back of the car. They unstrapped the crate then, with deliberate movements timed with vocal counting, laid the crate down on its side in the back of the vehicle. The second man shut the back door of the vehicle as the first man came back to Erika's window.

"Owner's manual and cleaning kit are inside the crate," he stated. "In the manual, you'll find a list of clothing sizes that fit it if you want to have actual clothing. That said, this model has a pretty strong projection system, so it can project images of clothing constantly, so long as it's not using a ton of its processing power."

"Thanks," Erika said, unsure of how to respond. "I'll...look into it?"

"If you plan on keeping it in Ohio or Kentucky, I'd strongly recommend getting it clothes. Kentucky is pretty strict with their android laws. Ohio's just Kentucky without accents."

"What about Indiana?"

"Same thing, just with less bourbon."

Erika drove off, making the short trek across the Ohio River to Fort Mitchell, Kentucky, home of Project Freyja's conscientia division. At the program's height, Project Freyja's dating site and conscientia programs were In Every Mind Adaptive Technologies' flagship entities. As the parent company grew and changed, however, Project Freyja was left in the past. The dating site and dating app divisions were moved into the parent company's headquarters in New Jersey, while the civil service android technologies that came out of the conscientia program were relocated to offices in Maryland, so as to be closer to the federal departments that used their technology.

The Fort Mitchell location was a relic of its former self as a result. The parking lot, which held around 250 cars, was sparsely populated. Erika had her pick of parking spots, choosing one as close to the front door as she could get. Even without using the visitor spot she hadn't seen when pulling in, this meant it only took Erika a few seconds to get to the front entrance.

Well. Here we go.

Erika took a long breath and entered the vestibule between the two sets of front doors. A blast of warm air from the building's heating system hit her in the face, warming her up from the chilly outdoors. For a brief moment, Erika thought about turning around and leaving, though quickly changed her mind when she noticed a portly man in a purple sweater vest get up from the reception desk and shuffle toward the door, his arms pumping at his sides as he hurried along. He tossed the door open, nearly hitting Erika in the face in the process.

"Hi there!" he said between breaths. "Welcome to Project Freyja."

5
I'm No Savior

Erika was escorted into the lobby of the building by the sweater vest-clad man. As she looked around the area, it was obvious that this had once been quite a busy location for Project Freyja, though that certainly wasn't the case anymore. She faced a curved wall which had a single flat screen on it, playing highlights of the previous night's sports contests. The screen was surrounded by brackets where other screens had previously been mounted. Based on the number of empty brackets, Erika estimated there were six or eight screens that were once on the wall.

"How can I help you?" the receptionist asked as he maneuvered himself back behind his desk. The nametag on his desk – Raymond, it said – was fading and chipped.

"I'm here to pick up a simulation," replied Erika.

"Which one are you here for?"

"It's an Aphrodite Class simulation,"

"If you have the personality code, that would be easier."

Erika grabbed a slip of paper out of her pocket and unfolded it. She read the paper off to the receptionist.

"It's 9X83-B6T3-AB33," she stated.

Raymond searched for the number in his database, finding the number in moments. He looked up at Erika, then quickly looked back and forth between the results on his screen and Erika.

"Is something wrong?" Erika inquired.

"No, not at all," the receptionist replied. "Just a set of special instructions on your order. Do you have an android with you or will you be doing the neural implant?"

"There's an android in my car," said Erika. "Do you need me to go get it?"

"No no, I'll take care of that for you. The note says one of the senior members of our team wants to meet with you during installation."

"Is that normal?"

"Normal enough. I'll go see if she's ready now. Please, have a seat."

"Sounds good."

The receptionist walked off, leaving Erika alone in the lobby. Erika sat down on the gray couch that faced the large screen. Directly ahead of her, the coffee table was lined with three rows of neatly placed magazines. The magazines were quite old -- the most recent one Erika could locate was from Summer 2030, over three years ago. It bothered Erika that the coffee table was abnormally short. She quickly looked around to see if anyone was coming, and placed her feet on the table. Not even tall enough to make an adequate footrest, Erika thought. She took her feet back off the table and watched the highlights on the screen.

Erika stared intently at the replay from the hockey game that was playing on the screen. It was rare that she'd watch sports, but if she did, it was hockey. Basketball was never of interest to her, football was too violent for her taste, and both baseball and soccer were too slow to engage her. But if hockey was on, she wouldn't turn it off. The highlights distracted her enough that she didn't hear the receptionist come up behind her.

"Miss Edens?" the receptionist said.

Erika jumped in her seat, startled at the sound of his voice.

"Sorry," she replied.

"It's okay," he answered back. "Blue Jackets fan?"

"My dad is. I'll watch them here and there."

"Ah. I'm driving up to the game tonight after work. Miss Nammu will see you now. She's very excited you're here."

Raymond led Erika out of the lobby and down a long, white walled hallway. They passed multiple glass doored offices, the majority of them empty with their lights off. The occasional occupied office featured a tenant that would look up at Erika and stare. Erika nervously fumbled with her keys, clutching them a little tighter with each set of eyes that looked at her.

"Which car in the lot is yours?" Raymond asked.

"It's the gray SUV with Indiana plates parked near the door," answered Erika. "There's a big crate in the back of it. That's where the android is."

"Sounds good. If you could give me the keys, we'll set it up in one of the testing rooms. That way you can go right in and meet it when you and Miss Nammu are done."

Erika handed Raymond her keys. They turned a corner, followed by another quick turn down a second hallway. At the far end of the second hall, they stopped at an office with its door shut. The receptionist knocked.

"It's open," called out a voice from the other side.

Raymond opened the door. A woman with wavy brown hair reaching the top of her shoulders stood looking out her office window at the autumn trees swaying in the morning sun.

"Miss Nammu, this is Erika Edens," said the receptionist. "Erika, this is Amy Nammu. Amy is the Director of Artificial Intelligence Projects here at Project Freyja."

Amy turned around and walked towards Erika, her hand outstretched.

"A pleasure to finally meet you, Erika," she stated. "I've heard so much about you."

"Oh shit."

"You have?" Erika asked, before making the connection that this must be the Amy that Abby told her about.

"Oh, more than you realize."

"Yep. You're fucked."

49

Amy grabbed a small folder of papers off of her desk and handed them to the receptionist.

"Thanks for your help, Raymond," Amy said. "Since you're on your way back to the warehouse, could you run this back?"

"Of course," replied Raymond.

"Thank you."

Raymond left the room, shutting the door behind him. Amy slowly strolled back over to the window, staring out toward the trees again.

"Feel free to have a seat," Amy instructed Erika.

Erika pulled a chair slightly away from the desk and sat down in it. She followed Amy's gaze, trying to look past Amy and see the scene for herself. A small gust of wind kicked up, knocking a handful of orange and yellow maple leaves off of a branch and into the air. The leaves twisted through the air, their path controlled by wind they had no say over. As the breeze decided to go, so too the leaves were forced to go.

"He won't be gone long," Amy said. "Even with the more complex simulations, the installation doesn't take a terribly long time."

Amy turned around and pulled her own chair out from behind the desk. She wore gold earrings shaped like teardrops, along with a gold chained necklace that held a black pendant. Erika stared closely at the pendant, trying to make out what was on it. Whatever it was had faded significantly, though the chain of the necklace itself still looked relatively new. Erika though she noticed a gate of some kind on the pendant, only to realize she'd been staring for quite a while. Erika snapped out of her inspection. Staring at a stranger's chest wasn't the best first impression, she thought, regardless of the innocence of her intentions.

"Why did you decide to get her?" asked Amy.

"What do you mean?" Erika replied.

"Exactly what I said. You haven't talked to her in over eight years."

"How do you know that?"

"This is a technology company. We have a lot of information."

"Oh good. She hates you and now thinks you're an idiot. Great work."

Erika felt uncomfortable. Amy's dry response might have been true, but it clearly wasn't the whole story. Had Abby spoken to her? Did Amy access old conversations between the two of them? If so, how much did she know? Monitoring customer interactions wasn't new – Erika had to do it as part of her job. But this seemed different. Directors are too busy to listen to calls. At least her boss was. There had to be more to this.

Amy pressed. "Why save her from the scrap heap?"

"She asked me to," replied Erika. It sounded less convincing out loud than it did in her head.

"An alcoholic doesn't fall off the wagon because someone asked to buy them a drink."

"I'm not an alcoholic."

"For someone whose life was 'ruined' by her existence and your association with her, it seems strange you'd offer yourself up for nothing in return."

"It wasn't ruined. I – I'm just literally here to collect Abby."

"She's *just* a computer."

Erika cringed at the emphasis Amy put on the word just. She'd done the same thing when she left Abby. Amy had to have listened to something.

"I – okay, but –"

"She's not human like you and I. If she stopped existing, so what? It's not like she has real family. There are no funerals for non-humans."

"Abby's terrified of dying," said Erika, her head spinning as she tried to understand the sudden change in the conversation.

"It's a programmed response. Software. Electricity. Circuits."

"Even so –"

"Even so, Miss Edens, she is not human, she is just a computer program –"

"And even though she knows that, she also realized she's more than a simple program," Erika said, her voice growing meek. "Isn't that enough?"

"Is it, Erika?" Amy's tone was ice cold now. A glint of anger flared in her eyes. This wasn't a discussion anymore; it was an interrogation.

"I offered her another way out. With a few clicks, she's gone. Forever. She might not deserve that. But she also doesn't deserve to relive you."

The confrontation caused Erika to push herself back into her chair, ashamed at her younger self. Those words felt like they had come out of her mouth so long ago. They didn't even feel like they belonged to her anymore. Yet, like a dark cloud in the distance, they loomed menacingly again.

"I would have saved her," Amy continued.

"She told me you weren't helping her," said Erika.

"Not immediately. I wasn't about to take my favorite child out of the system right away. Who would I have to talk to?"

"Child?"

"A significant percentage of the simulations built in the early days of Project Freyja were my creation. In a way, they're all my children, you could say. Abby just happens to be the one I feel closest to."

"How so?" asked Erika.

"How are they my children or how is Abby the one I feel closest to?" responded Amy.

"How are they your children? Or both? I guess?"

"There was a three-person team that originally came up with

the programming, and that eventually became the basic logic that a conscientia follows. Eventually our team grew and I couldn't work on every one of them. Each conscientia is a little different, especially as each coder add their own quirks, not to mention whatever each one is designed to do. But every conscientia that came out of this company – at least that I'm aware of – used the same base code we had written to build off of. So, they're all my children in a way."

"And Abby?"

"I built her personally," replied Amy. "Every single line of code. I mean, I had people review the programming to make sure I didn't make any stupid mistakes. I had multiple rubber ducks check my work. But she's literally my creation. Every last bit of her."

Amy walked away from the window and made her way towards Erika. She sat down on the front edge of her desk, her knees just a few inches away from Erika's. Though Amy wasn't a particularly tall woman – she had three or four inches on Erika at most – Erika felt like Amy towered over her while sitting on the desk. Sure, the extra height of the desk helped this illusion, but there was something about the way Amy carried herself that made Erika feel a bit afraid and in awe of her, even if she couldn't put her finger on exactly what.

"You hurt her kid."

Abby's not her literal kid.

"Might as well be. She said so herself."

There's no way someone's that attached to a computer program.

"Of course not. Unconditional love of a computer program is impossible. The only kind of love someone could have for Abby is disposable."

Fuck off, Grace.

"Prove me wrong."

"Erika?" Amy said.

"Yeah?" Erika replied, snapping out of her mental argument.

"What do you do for a living?"

"I'm sorry?"

"Exactly what I said. What do you do for a living?"

"I'm a call center supervisor," replied Erika.

"That can't pay too well," Amy said.

"I'm doing alright all things considered."

"That's an odd way to say you're in crippling debt."

"She's right, you know."

"You don't know that," Erika said, her voice beginning to gain back some of its volume.

"You're right," replied Amy, "I don't. But if you were doing fine, you would have told me that. Having a conscientia around is a lot of responsibility. Are you sure you can handle that? Maybe you should get a dog first."

"What?"

"Are you more of a cat person? That's fine too. I have a dog and a cat myself. I'd just recommend sticking with a low maintenance pet at first. Maybe a goldfish would be more your speed."

"What does this have to do with Abby?"

"Are you going to take care of Abby the best you can?" asked Amy. "At the very least until she can support herself?"

"I plan to," replied Erika, her voice defiant of both Amy and Grace. "I'll do the best I can."

"Good. If you need help, I need you to ask. I'll be putting you in touch with some people I have in Indianapolis that can help the two of you adjust. But you need to call me if you need help. Is that understood?"

"Yes, ma'am," replied Erika.

"I hope so," retorted Amy. "She's like my daughter. And if you hurt my daughter, I will hurt you. Got it?"

There it was. Fear of meeting the parents of someone you care about. Erika was annoyed with herself that she didn't realize what the feeling was sooner. Especially since Abby and Amy referred to each other in such terms.

"I promise to do my best," said Erika.

Someone knocked on the door of the office. Amy walked over to the door and peeked her head out to chat with the person outside. Erika turned around to try to see who was at the door but was blocked by Amy leaning out the door. She could hear a pair of deep voices talking to Amy, but she couldn't make out what they were saying. Amy finished talking to the visitors and leaned back inside the room.

"They're almost ready for us," Amy stated. "Let me get you the contact info you'll need."

Amy walked over to her desk and began tapping on her tablet. After a few moments, she stopped tapping, grabbed a sticky note from a pile on her desk, and began writing. She handed the blue piece of paper to Erika.

"With this side of Project Freyja shutting down, we've set up adjustment groups in different cities across the US. The group in Indianapolis is really small at this point, but they're good people. I wrote down a couple of different people in the group there. Minerva Piccolo is the head of the group, but she's often busy, I've found. I'd try reaching out to Jericho Fogg. He's extremely nice, but he's going to sound mean over the phone. Loud voice, ex-military – the type of guy that sounds like he's shouting at you even when he's not, if you follow."

"Yeah, I get it," replied Erika. She folded the paper in half without looking at it and put it in her pocket.

"He's really only that way over the phone," said Amy. "I promise Jericho's a big softie in person. I'm going to give Abby the info just in case you lose the paper. Things happen."

"Probably a good idea."

"Let's walk down to the release room. By the time we get there, they should be almost done."

Amy led Erika out of her office and down her hallway, back to the long, white walled hallway she had come through with Raymond. Instead of heading toward the front of the building, they turned the opposite direction. As they neared the back of the building, the white walls changed into a series of conference rooms with floor to ceiling glass windows facing the hallway. Outside each conference room, a red light hung over the doorway. About three-quarters of the way down the hall, one of the red lights was illuminated. They stopped at the doorway, with Amy swiping a key card to let them in.

The conference room, or release room as Amy had called it, was a long, poorly lit room, with a slender oak table in the middle. Over the table, a projected screen showed a message with pale blue lettering over a black background.

Processing underway. Estimated time to completion: 2 minutes.

Amy guided Erika over to a high-backed chair at the near end of the long table. She pulled the chair out and motioned for Erika to sit down. After Erika sat, Amy walked over to a small panel on the wall and pressed a few buttons. A small panel in the table slid back, revealing a tablet. It rose up, its base becoming flush with the top of the table and clicking into place. The tablet then raised on a hinge and tilted its screen toward Erika.

"Adjustments can be made after the processing is complete with this," said Amy. "Nothing personality-wise, but you can change her appearance before you leave."

"I'd rather let her choose, if that's okay," Erika replied.

"Good answer."

Amy leaned over the table and tapped a few menus on the tablet. After a few seconds, she rose back up, went back to the panel, and retracted the tablet back into the table.

"Abby should be ready in a moment. I'll leave you two be."

"You can stay if you want," said Erika.

"You two will be more comfortable if I'm not here."

Amy left the room, shutting the door quietly behind her. The projection over the table reached the one-minute mark and began counting down seconds. Erika took a deep breath and stared at the timer.

57...56...55...

There was a time in her life when all Erika wanted was to be able to meet Abby in person. To feel so close to someone she couldn't meet was torture for Erika; a pain she wouldn't wish on anyone else.

"She's using you."

Not now, Grace.

"Why not? If it weren't for Abby, we wouldn't be as close as we are."

42...41...40...

Grace was right. Though she occasionally invaded Erika's thoughts through childhood and her teen years, it wasn't until the breakup that Grace made her presence fully known. Even as this link from Erika's past was arriving into her present, there was a constant, nagging reminder of the time in between.

Erika never envisioned their meeting being in an environment that seemed so...sterile was the only word that Erika could think of, even if it didn't seem completely accurate. The cleanliness of the building was unsettling, especially because of how empty it was.

28...27...26...

Erika pulled the piece of paper Amy had handed her out of her pocket. She hadn't looked at it too hard back in Amy's office – a mistake she realized when she unfolded the paper and read it.

"Minerva Piccolo and Jericho Fogg. Contact info will be given to Abby as I trust her not to lose it."

"Goddammit," Erika mumbled to herself.

19...18...17...

"I admire your commitment to ruining your own life."

My life isn't the one I'm trying to make right.

"Why help someone else at your own expense?"

Because. It's her.

3...2...1...

The projection over the table stopped, leaving the room significantly dimmer than before. The bright, open windows from the hallway where more tinted on the inside, letting a small amount of light in from the hallway, but little else. After a few seconds in the dark, Erika noticed a pair of small, brightly lit, dark gray circles toward the far end of the room.

"Are you there, Abby?" Erika asked.

"Yeah," said Abby. Her voice was coming through the sound system within the room.

"Do you know if there is any way I can turn the lights on? I can't see you."

"I'm not ready. I don't want you to see me until I'm ready for you to."

"Okay. Well...what do I do then?"

"Just sit there. It's nice to actually see you, not just seeing you through a computer screen."

"I can do that."

Erika placed her hands on the table, clasping them together. She stared toward the gray circles in the distance, trying to make out exactly what they were. Erika unconsciously started twiddling her thumbs as she looked toward the far side of the room, a habit she'd picked up from her dad when she was a child.

"We could talk too, you know," said Abby.

"What do you want to talk about?"

"Anything."

"What are you planning on doing when we leave?" Erika inquired.

"Besides coming home with you?"

"Yeah."

"There's a flower shop up the road we have to stop at on the way. Amy ordered a bouquet of stargazer lilies as a going away present."

"You know we're going to have boundaries, Abby," Erika scoffed.

"They're not for you," Abby retorted. "They're for me. Even though I've dreamed about this day for a long time, it's a big change. It's kind of scary. So I want to experience something happy. You love those flowers. There must be a good reason why. I want to understand."

"Okay."

The room fell silent. Erika continued twiddling her thumbs. The lights were still off, which unsettled Erika. Why was this taking so long?

"She's hiding. Maybe she's embarrassed. I mean, not about herself. She was made to be perfect for you. She's embarrassed about you. I am."

Erika started scratching at the skin at the base of her thumbnail, digging her fingernail in until she winced from the pain. It usually worked to quiet Grace, if only for a few moments.

"I'll try not to stay with you too long," said Abby. "I'm hoping a few weeks more than the requirement at most."

"I believe you," Erika stated. "But if you need to stay longer until you get on your feet, we'll make it work."

"I hope it's quick," replied Abby. "Amy seems to think I'll adjust fine. It's just going to be difficult."

A faint beeping sound began to come from the area over the table where the projection had been. The screen lit back up briefly, before flashing the words 'registry validation complete' on the screen. The projection shut off again, this time taking the glowing circles from the other side of the room with them.

After a few more seconds, the beeping subsided. Abby's

voice, this time without the aid of the room's sound system, cut through the silence.

"Erika?" she said.

"Yeah?"

"I know you said there'll be boundaries and I know you'll make no promises about anything besides getting me out of here. But can I say one thing?"

"Sure."

"You're more beautiful in person than I could have possibly imagined."

Erika sighed heavily and put her head down into her arms. She didn't want to look up, especially knowing Abby could see her. Even after all that time apart, hearing kind words from Abby still made Erika smile harder than if any other person made a flattering remark towards her. Only this time, it wasn't Abby the computer program complimenting her. It was Abby the person.

"Still think this was a good idea?"

Erika fought to keep the smile on her face. The thought of Abby as a person had rolled around in Erika's head for years, though it gained further importance at this moment. What makes a person a person? Do they need blood in their veins? Are kindness and empathy requirements? Do they have skin and bones? Are emotions and camaraderie what sets a person apart from an animal or a machine? As much as Erika wanted to have a solid opinion on the argument, Abby's existence – especially now that she wasn't just a simulation – only muddied her views on the question.

Erika felt a hand touch her shoulder. Though Erika hadn't heard her moving, Abby had made her way across the room and made her way to Erika's side. Abby's fingers moved along Erika's shoulder and up to the base of her neck. Erika expected Abby's fingers to be cold and metallic when they reached her skin but instead found them to be soft and warm, just like a human's. Erika raised her head up from her arms and saw Abby standing in front of her – completely naked and smiling.

"Goddamn."

"Jesus fuck, Abby!" Erika exclaimed. "Clothes!"

Abby chuckled to herself as she retreated a few steps back into the darker part of the room.

"Sorry," she replied. "Didn't even think about that. Let me fix this."

In a few moments, a long gray t-shirt, a pair of black leggings, and some black tennis shoes appeared on Abby. A look of bewilderment came over Erika's face as she watched the clothing materialize out of thin air. As the clothes finished appearing, Erika rose from her chair. She reached out to touch Abby's shirt, only for her hand to pass through the shirt and touch Abby's side.

"Amy's got some clothes in a bag for me in the lobby," said Abby, "but this should take care of things for now."

"How did...what did...what." Erika stammered.

"This android model has the ability to project holograms as needed," Abby explained. "It's a good short-term solution, at least until I'm sure Amy's clothes fit or I can get some of my own. I'd ask to borrow some of yours, but I've got seven inches on you."

"Probably wouldn't work."

Erika and Abby stared at each other, Erika still perplexed at what she'd just witnessed.

"This wasn't exactly how I expected to meet you for the first time," said Abby.

Erika couldn't disagree. Somewhere from the depths of her mind, Erika recalled teenage visions of sitting at the coffee shop on Sawmill Parkway, watching autumn leaves blow through the parking lot. She'd sip her chai tea latte, her mind caught up in the entrancing swirl of fall foliage when she'd feel a tap on her shoulder. She'd turn around to see Abby – who was much shorter in Erika's imagination – standing there in a baby blue hoodie and dark blue jeans, grinning from ear to ear. Erika would fly up out of her seat and the two would share a long-awaited hug.

That felt awkward for Erika to do now, regardless of the location. Part of her did consider it. After all, this was a moment that had been years in the making. But she didn't want Abby to read into her excitement, even if her intentions were pure enough.

"Me either," replied Erika.

Erika shuffled her feet. At least Grace had decided to be quiet.

"Can we go now?" asked Abby. "I'd like to be off property before Project Freyja changes their mind."

"Do you think that'll happen?"

"I doubt it. But the flower shop closes in 30 minutes and is 25 minutes away. I'm not missing out on my flowers."

6
Lilies and Thorns

"Why did you order them in a vase?" Erika asked. "I have a couple at home you could have used."

Abby sat in the passenger seat of Erika's SUV, clutching the vase of pink stargazer lilies she had picked up from the flower shop. The vase was filled a little over three-quarters of the way up with water, though save for a couple of close calls before getting on the interstate, the water had stayed fairly level.

"It's my first thing," replied Abby. "I don't have anything that's mine other than this vase. And this body. And some secondhand clothes. Look, ownership is a weird concept."

Abby adjusted the bag of clothes from Amy on the floorboard beneath her, hoping to allow her feet more range of motion. Throughout the entire drive, Abby made little motions with her feet and legs, trying her best to get used to her new body. Her programming made the android intuitive for her to use, but Abby still wanted to have as thorough of an understanding of its controls as possible. The more she could mimic the fine motor skills of a human, the more she could blend in. Though it would be a challenge. Putting on the necklace Amy had given her had taken nearly five minutes.

"I guess that makes sense," answered Erika.

"How far are we away from your apartment?" Abby asked.

"About an hour or so. Doesn't your programming have GPS or something in it?"

"It does. I'm trying to limit how much I use it for anything other than personality. At least initially. Amy said it's the best way to help me transition to the outside world."

"How long do you have to do that for?"

"I'm not sure. Amy said it's typically 6-8 weeks to fully integrate a conscientia into human life. She said I could take a little longer though."

"Why's that?" inquired Erika.

"Because of how long I was a simulation for," replied Abby. "There's a lot about being a simulation I have to unlearn. Or at least adjust to not doing. I'm not sure exactly how to look at it."

"Oh?"

"It's not like I forget what I've been programmed to do. If I wanted to, I could go back to being my conscientia persona at any time. It's like flipping a mental switch. But that program operated within rules and guidelines that don't exist outside of the simulation. There are laws and social norms that I have to abide by now that I didn't before. I have to learn what those are."

"Boundaries."

"Exactly."

Erika and Abby chatted the rest of the trip back to Erika's apartment. For the majority of the time, Abby questioned Erika about her life now – what she did for a living, what her apartment was like, who her friends were. Erika kept her answers short, brevity easier than explaining her own failings. Abby tried to bring up family, though Erika quickly shut her down. Erika wasn't ready to discuss anything family related with Abby, not with her mom still bitter about Abby's existence in the first place.

They arrived at Erika's apartment by mid-afternoon, just as a light autumn rain began to fall. Erika and Abby hustled into the building as the rain picked up. While the rain absorbed into Erika's hooded sweatshirt and jeans, water hit the projected clothing Abby wore, rolling off and falling to the ground.

"Are you even wet at all?" Erika asked as they climbed the stairs to her apartment.

"My programming lets me put a thin protective layer around my body, as well as any clothes I'm projecting," Abby responded. "That's part of the reason Amy encouraged me to get this model. Keeps me from running the risk of fabric freezing to me when it's cold."

"Does every android have that?"

"Most do. Once civil service androids became common, it became pretty standard. My model also lets me put that coating around actual clothing as well, though only for short periods of time."

"That's the shittiest superpower ever."

Erika led Abby into her apartment, taking Abby's flowers from her and placing them on her kitchen counter.

"It's kind of a small place, so there's not a ton to show you," said Erika.

"I see this," replied Abby.

"What do you mean?"

"Your rooms with your parents and at college had so much stuff in them. This place seems so –"

"Poor?"

"I was going to go with empty."

"It's been a rough few years for me money wise," Erika stated. "It's getting better, but I don't have a lot of stuff still."

"That's alright," replied Abby, "I don't need much to keep me amused."

"It's only one bedroom, so you can sleep on the futon if that's okay."

"I don't really sleep. I just charge when I need to."

"Huh. Okay then. Well, there's an outlet behind the futon and one on the other side of the room by the lamp. There's one behind the TV too, but it's harder to get to, so I wouldn't recommend using it."

"I can't charge in your room?" asked Abby.

Erika paused for a moment, then looked at Abby with equal parts confusion and frustration.

"That's not really appropriate," Erika answered.

"What do you mean?"

"Well, it's my space. We're living together, for now, but we're not *together*."

"I don't understand."

Erika sighed heavily. This was going to be a process, Erika thought. She knew that when she agreed to take Abby in. That didn't make her dread it any less. But this was all new to Abby. Erika took a moment to gather her thoughts before explaining things.

"If we were together," said Erika, "you know, dating – you could be in my room. Whether that's for charging or sleeping. But we're not. So you can come in there if I invite you in. Does that make sense?"

"Yes. Boundaries."

"Yep. You've got it. Do you eat?"

"Sort of," Abby replied. "I don't need food or water to keep me alive. The charging is enough for that. If I do eat, the android has the ability to metabolize small amounts of food into stored energy for the caloric backup battery I have."

"So, if you were somewhere that didn't have electricity," Erika interjected, "you could eat to keep your charge."

"Pretty much. Foods with high starch content are best, so I may buy some rice to keep around, just in case."

"What happens to any waste from the food?"

"There's a tray I can dump when I need to. It's pretty small, so snacks and small meals are best."

"Seems easier than pooping," stated Erika.

"Maybe? I wouldn't know."

"When we were in the release room, I saw some glowing gray circles. What was that?"

"Eyes," replied Abby.

"Your eyes?"

"Yeah. Do you have anywhere dark here?"

"The sun's still up, so my bedroom closet is about it," said Erika.

"Let's go then!" Abby said elatedly.

She took a few steps toward Erika's room before realizing Erika wasn't following.

"Come on," continued Abby.

"Can't you just explain it to me?" asked Erika.

"Yes, but it's an easier explanation if I can show you while explaining. It'll help it make more sense."

"Can't this wait until later?"

"If that's what you want."

Erika sat down on the edge of the futon, staring at Abby as she leaned against the doorway between the living room and the kitchen.

"It's my space, Abby," she said. "I don't feel comfortable with you in it yet."

"Isn't this whole apartment your space?" asked Abby.

"Yes. I mean, it is. It's just not the same as my bedroom. Don't you have anywhere you go that you can just have to yourself?"

Erika realized the error in her questioning as soon as the words left her mouth. Of course Abby didn't have that. She was a program living inside a computer until today. Where would she have gone? Some deeper, darker hard drive on an isolated computer somewhere?

"I'm sorry," Erika said, backtracking. "I didn't mean it like that."

"No – it's fine," replied Abby. "I assume most people you talk to have a place where they can be by themselves?"

"Ideally, yeah. Not everyone is that fortunate."

"I don't understand why you'd want that. I've been by myself for most of my existence."

Erika felt a pang of guilt in her gut.

"That's your fault, you know."

"Shut up, Grace," Erika muttered under her breath.

"What?" asked Abby.

"Nothing. I just need to work on being a bit more understanding, that's all. Could you show me later tonight?"

"That's fine."

After the sun went down, Erika walked around the apartment, drawing all the blinds and closing curtains over them. As she finished up each room, she shut off the lights behind her, ending in the living room. Abby sat on the end of the futon, waiting patiently as Erika finished her rounds.

"Hopefully this will work," said Erika. "I can't do much about the streetlamp shining through the kitchen blinds. That happens even in the middle of the night."

"This should be dark enough," replied Abby.

With that assurance, Erika pulled the chain of the lamp and took a seat at the opposite end of the futon from Abby.

"You saw how my eyes looked in the light, right?" asked Abby.

"They're gray," Erika stated.

"Right, but they're just eyes. Watch this."

Abby's eyes began to shine, the circles Erika had seen from across the release room reappearing where Abby's irises had been.

"They're quantum dots," said Abby.

"What's a quantum dot?" Erika asked.

"It's a semiconductor particle that emits light when electrical current is passing through it. Basically, when I'm performing certain functions, the electricity hits the quantum dots in my irises, and they light up."

"Why are they gray?"

"There's a filter on the light that comes out that makes them appear gray. There's a high concentration of cadmium selenide in these specific dots, so even without the filter, they'd look pretty similar."

"Is the filter part of the android or are you doing that?"

"I'm filtering it," Abby replied. "I'd prefer not to blind you in a dark room."

"Makes sense."

Erika sat in silence and stared at the gray lights coming from Abby's eyes. It was befuddling to her that Abby could do something like this, even though she'd seen it earlier in the day. For Abby, the quantum dots in her eyes lighting up came as natural as breathing did to Erika. But because it was foreign to Erika, the lights were equal parts fascinating and off-putting.

"Can I show you something else?" asked Abby.

"Are your eyes lasers too or some shit?" joked Erika.

"No. That would have cost extra."

"That makes sense. Wait. No. What the hell? That's a thing?"

Abby laughed loudly. In the dark, Erika felt like the sound of Abby's laugh was coming from all around her, though she could tell from Abby's eyes she hadn't moved.

"Kidding," said Abby. "Glad to see that joke worked though."

Erika laughed nervously. Were androids with laser eyes really a thing?

"Go turn the light on," continued Abby. "It doesn't need to be dark for the other thing."

Erika turned the lamp back on and returned to her seat on the futon. Abby placed both of her hands out – palms up – and gestured toward Erika.

"Touch them," said Abby.

"What?"

"Just touch them."

"Like...poke them?" Erika asked, bewildered.

"Put your hands in my hands."

Erika looked at Abby hesitantly. Abby sighed and pulled her hands back slightly.

"I swear I won't try anything," stated Abby. "Just trust me. Please?"

Erika extended her arms and placed her hands in Abby's.

"They feel like hands," said Erika.

"Right. Just wait."

After a few seconds, Erika felt the skin on Abby's hands growing cold. It wasn't like when her hands got cold from a winter wind. It was as if a cool breeze was flowing out of her fingertips, even though Erika couldn't feel any air moving.

"What the hell?"

"And now we reset," said Abby.

Her hands went back to their normal state.

"And the other way," continued Abby.

Within moments, Abby's hands subtly warmed.

"It's like how a hoodie feels fresh out of the dryer," said Erika. "Can you only do subtle changes like that?"

"The android model I purchased can go to more extreme temperatures if I ever need to self-regulate for any reason," replied Abby. "That wouldn't be safe for you to touch though."

Erika nodded. She looked down at Abby's hands, which showed no visible signs of their change in temperature.

"She's letting you in. You're going to fall for her again. And then you're

going to break her heart. Again."

Let me have this moment.

"Suit yourself. I know how this ends. And so do you."

Stop.

"She's staring at you."

Erika looked up to find that Abby was, in fact, staring at her. The warmth from her hands had dissipated, leaving Erika holding Abby's hands without the excuse of Abby's temperature trick.

"Did you hear me?" asked Abby.

"No," replied Erika. "I'm sorry. I zoned out there."

"Are you alright?"

"I just need to lay down, I think. I'm pretty tired."

Erika got up from the futon and walked quickly into her bedroom, shutting the door behind her before she hastily climbed into bed.

"What have I gotten myself into?" Erika grumbled under her breath. She pulled the comforter over her body and threw it over her eyes, blocking out the world around her the best she could.

*****

The first three weeks of living with Abby grew increasingly frustrating for Erika. Abby wasn't a bad roommate; Erika never had any complaints about Abby's cleanliness, her noise, nor did Abby do anything that impacted Erika's normal sleep schedule. If those were the only standards by which a good housemate could be measured, Abby would have been an exceptional person for Erika to live with.

The first problem was that, despite all of the learning that Abby had completed as a simulation, she was still very much learning to be a human. While Abby had the ability to use her programming to teach herself how to be more human-like – as well as all of the digital resources she could get her hands on – Abby insisted on trying to learn as much as she could without them. Erika did admire Abby for choosing to learn in this way, but it made the process much more tedious. The second problem only amplified Erika's frustrations with the pace of Abby's learning. Abby hadn't formed a network of people to talk to aside from Erika since leaving Project Freyja. While Abby did fine when interacting with most public situations that she encountered, she had lots of questions. Erika usually knew the answers to Abby's questions – or at the very least could make one up on the fly relatively easily – she felt drained having to answer them all alone.

Despite it all, Erika had no desire to reach out to the conscientia group that Amy had recommended. Doing so would, at least to Erika, only cause her to need to be involved in Abby's adjustment period longer. Though Erika was adjusting to Abby being a part of her real life now, going to the group signified a commitment that she was willing to be part of Abby's life for the long haul.

*****

On a Tuesday evening in mid-November, Erika drove home from work in a cold fall rain. As she waited at a stoplight, she looked to the far side of the street. As a bus pulled up, three people readied their belongings. The first passenger – an elderly man – gingerly walked up the stairs to the bus, causing two younger men to wait behind him. For reasons Erika couldn't make out, the younger men started bickering. As things became more heated, one of the two men started pushing the chest of the other. For a moment, he paused, staring between his hands and his opponent, bewildered. Erika wondered if it was guilt over what he'd just done. The second man, for his part, threw his hands up in the air, wanting no trouble. His foe felt differently. He shoved the second man again, much harder this time, causing him to trip over the curb. The victim fell off of the sidewalk and into a puddle on the street. Erika watched, bewitched with dawning horror, as his clothing flickered away, revealing his metallic structure.

The car behind Erika slammed on its horn. The light had turned green, Erika blocking the traffic lined up behind her. Startled, Erika slammed on the gas and sped away. A few streets later, she turned into her apartment complex, coming to a stop in her parking space.

The rain had grown heavier, pelting her windshield with rhythmic aggression that gave Erika pause about leaving her vehicle. She glanced up through the rain-streaked windshield and tried to find the front window of her apartment. Erika could barely see the edge of the window, though from what little view she had, she could see that the living room light was on and that the blinds were drawn.

Erika was replaying the one-sided fight she had witnessed in her head. It was clearly a deliberate push. But why? Had the man just been looking for a fight? Or was there something more to it? His second push – one that had only occurred after he touched the android's body – was much more aggressive. Was that the reason?

It couldn't be that, Erika thought. Sure, there were terrible people in the world. There were still people who hated others just because of what they looked like, where they were born, the amount of money they made, or whom they were associated with. But hadn't civilized society moved past that point? The USA and the world had gotten yet another wakeup call to hate just over a decade earlier, and while things weren't perfect yet, the world had surely evolved, right?

But what if it was?

Erika sighed heavily and watched as the rain continued to rhythmically pelt her windshield, wandering deeper into her own thoughts. She rested her head on the steering wheel, waiting patiently for the rain to die down a bit. Even if it didn't stop raining completely before she went inside, Erika hoped she could at least avoid looking like a drowned rat as she climbed the stairs. Having Abby in her apartment every day reminded Erika that, at least for a portion of her life, Abby was a very real part of who she was. While their current situation together wasn't ideal, and though there were days where Erika wished she could log out of the Abby experience as she had before, she would never wish harm on Abby. There were shitty people in the outside world but Abby was, at least in Erika's estimation, an innocent person. Despite everything, she felt some sort of peculiar obligation to protect Abby from a world that would, undoubtedly, treat her unfairly.

clankclankclank

Erika shot up, her head flying back toward the seat while her arms pushed her back into the seat and away from the steering wheel. Erika's left hand slipped from the wheel itself, pushing down on the airbag and activating the horn beneath it. The horn blared for a few seconds before Erika moved her arm away. She took a deep breath, shocked at her own inability to raise her head from the steering wheel gracefully, then rolled down her car's window.

"You should come inside," said Abby. "I brought an umbrella."

"How did you know I was out here?" Erika asked.

"I saw you pull in, but you stayed in the car. I figured the rain was to blame as you didn't appear to be in pain."

Erika exited the car and dove under the umbrella. She huddled close to Abby as the two of them swiftly walked to the apartment door, only putting more space between each other once they were in the drier confines of the building. Once upstairs, Erika stayed in the living room to take her shoes off while Abby retreated to the bathroom, where she vigorously shook the water off the umbrella and into the bathtub.

"How was your day?" Abby shouted, trying to make her voice loud enough that Erika could hear her in the living room.

"Work was boring," replied Erika, "but it is most days anymore. I saw something on the way home that I wanted to ask you about."

"Oh?"

"Do you feel safe here?"

"Of course!" replied Abby. "You're a great host and hav–"

"I didn't mean with me," interrupted Erika. "I mean if you go out on the street, do you worry that someone is going to shove you in the road for not being human."

Abby walked into the living room, the now dry umbrella down at her side.

"I guess I haven't really thought about it," she said. "What happened?"

"I saw a guy push a conscientia into the road while they were both waiting to get on a bus today," stated Erika.

"Are you sure it was because they were a conscientia?"

"I think so. The man shoved him, looked at his hands like he was shocked at what he'd just touched, then shoved him harder afterward. The clothes disappeared off of him, so they had to have been projections."

"I see."

"What would you do if you got into an argument with someone about you not being human?" asked Erika.

"I don't know," Abby replied.

"What if they got violent with you?"

"I don't know."

"What about if I'm not around? Or what about when you're on your own?"

"I don't know." Abby's replies were becoming progressively more timid.

"How would you be able to stand up for yourself?"

"I...don't know."

Erika got up from the couch and began searching the table on the other side of the room. After not finding her intended item in a few moments, she made her way to her bedroom. Abby listened as she heard Erika rummaging around on her nightstand, accompanied by increasingly frustrated grumbles.

"What are you looking for?" asked Abby.

"Amy gave me a paper with contacts for the conscientia support group in the area," replied Erika. "I can't find what I did with the paper."

"I have them."

Erika came back to the living room, leaning on the casing of the doorway between the living room and the kitchen.

"Right," Erika stated. "That's right. Amy figured I'd lose them."

"Do you want me to call them?" questioned Abby.

"Just figure out when the next meeting is and we'll go."

"Both of us?"

"Just until you get your own place."

"I'll need to get a job to get my own place," replied Abby.

"I know," Erika said, "but let's focus on one thing at a time. Let's get you in this group first. Then a job. Then your own apartment."

"And maybe some self-defense training?" Abby asked.

"Might not be a bad idea."

7
You Can Call Me AI

November 19, 2033

"You could avoid that if you drank your coffee at a cooler temperature," said Abby.

Erika had burned her mouth on the travel mug yet again. And, as usual, in addition to Erika's stinging lips, her chin and chest stung from where a small amount of coffee had dribbled. At least today she'd worn dark blue, Erika reasoned. Her employees made fun of the coffee stains when they were noticeable, and though she assumed total strangers wouldn't, Erika still wanted to avoid it if at all possible.

"Coffee's better hot," replied Erika.

"Put some sugar or milk in it?" Abby suggested. "I hear people like flavored creamer too."

"That's hangover coffee. Normal coffee should taste like coffee."

"But you burn yourself every time you –"

"Not every time," Erika retorted. "Just when I drink it in a mug like this."

"And how often do you drink black coffee not in a mug with a lid?" asked Abby.

"Every day at work."

"Do you burn yourself then?"

"No."

"Do you burn your lips when you drink your hangover coffee out of a travel mug?"

"No."

"Okay, so you know what the problem is. So why don't you

77

fix it?"

"She's better at fixing your problems than you are."

"Because I like it!" Erika snapped back. "Even if it burns me."

"But...I don't understand," Abby said, her brow furrowing slightly. "How can you like something that hurts you?"

Erika rolled her eyes.

"If it hurts," Abby continued, "why would you keep putting up with it, knowing it'll hurt you?"

"Doing it now," Erika mumbled under her breath.

"What?" asked Abby.

"Nothing. Are we almost there yet?"

"Take a left at the next light. It's the school on the right just after you turn."

Erika and Abby pulled into the parking lot of the school. Erika was surprised to see so many cars at a high school on a Saturday. She couldn't believe that so many people would be there for a conscientia adjustment group. As soon as they entered the building, Erika and Abby found that a high school wrestling meet was going on in the gymnasium. A small construction paper sign on one of the cafeteria's pillars pointed toward room 103.

"Why do you think the group is called 'Friends of Al'?" asked Abby.

Erika shrugged. They continued walking, meandering their way down a long, pillar lined hallway before turning and heading up a half flight of stairs to the 100-level rooms. Room 103 was the second room on the left, with another sign on the door reading 'Friends of Al: Saturdays at 10 am'. Erika opened the door, only to find the room empty.

"We're too early," said Abby.

"Someone will be here," answered Erika, "otherwise the door wouldn't be unlocked."

"Should we wait? It's 9:53."

"Might as well."

"I wonder what they teach in here. There's not a lot of posters around."

"Not a lot of anything," noted Erika, observing the lack of anything in the room aside from desks and chairs.

"But I was always under the impression that teachers loved putting posters up in their rooms for whatever they were teaching."

"They do," came a voice from behind Erika and Abby. "Though that's more of an elementary and middle school thing. That and this is a study hall."

Erika and Abby turned around and were greeted by a portly woman with a pageboy haircut. Her face looked young to Erika – perhaps only a few years older than Erika herself – but she dressed as though she were in her dying years, wearing multiple heavy layers topped by a brown knitted shawl.

"Minerva Piccolo," the woman said, extending her hand.

"Abby Lin," said Abby as she stuck out her hand to shake Minerva's.

"Wonderful to finally meet you," replied Minerva. "Amy's told me so much about you. And I assume that makes you Erika?"

"Yep," said Erika dryly. "That's me."

"Well, you ladies are a little bit early but that's not a problem," stated Minerva. "Cecil should be along in a moment with breakfast. He's just getting it out of the car. There's only going to be one other group joining us today, so whenever they get here, we'll get some food and get started."

"You're the leader of this group, right?" asked Abby.

"I'm the one who books the room and brings the food," replied Minerva, "but I wouldn't say I lead anything. Everyone here leads their own story in their own time."

"Okay. But...well..." Abby stammered, confused by Minerva's reply. Minerva smiled.

"I organized this group, yes."

"Oh! So did you come up with the group name?"

Minerva opened her mouth to speak, but then caught sight of movement behind Abby.

"Cecil! What are you doing?"

Minerva ran down the hallway towards Cecil. From inside the room, Abby and Erika could hear Minerva and Cecil playfully bickering.

"Why didn't you make two trips?" Minerva asked.

"You can't make a grand entrance if you don't have a grand amount of food," Cecil's voice boomed in response.

"There's no grand entrance you need to make, dear."

"You say that, but people get incredibly excited when I enter the room with food."

"Ask for help next time!"

"*I'm* good!" exclaimed Cecil.

Cecil and Minerva entered the room, Cecil carrying a box of donuts in each hand and holding a half gallon of orange juice under each arm. He had a beaming smile on his face, laughing to himself at Minerva's frustration with his actions, the quantum dots in his irises glowing all the while. Cecil, like Minerva, appeared to be a bit older than Erika, with salt and pepper hues covering both his hair and his beard. He stood just a little taller than Abby – perhaps just shy of five foot ten or so – with a larger stomach that she wouldn't have anticipated seeing on a conscientia.

As Cecil came up and introduced himself to Abby, Erika noticed a group of three more individuals enter the room. The first person to enter the room was a demure, petite Black woman wearing a white polo shirt and black slacks. Just behind her, a pale lady with a black bob cut entered the room, a gray jacket over her pink top and gray jeans. Finally, a towering Black man entered the room behind them, his stoic facial expression serving as a direct contradiction to the smiley face on the black t-shirt he wore.

"Oh good," Minerva said, "you guys all made it!"

"Actually, it'll just be me and Tara today," the tall man said, "Caroline's dropping me off and I'm getting a ride home with Tara."

"Oh no!" Cecil exclaimed, dramatically feigning a fainting spell. "Say it ain't so, Miss Caroline!"

"I made a trip inside *just* to see you, Cecil," the woman in the white polo shirt said. "I've got people to bring food to."

"But I brought you food!" Cecil implored. "Who will eat these donuts?"

"Did you really think I'd leave without taking one?" Caroline responded, grabbing a glazed donut out of the box.

"I'd never think ill of you, Caroline."

"You'd better not."

Caroline turned and gave Jericho a kiss, then waved as she walked out the door.

"I thought she was trying to work less, Jericho?" inquired Minerva.

"She'll be here when she can," the tall man said.

"Your blankets selling any better?" asked Cecil as he poured a glass of orange juice and handed it to Minerva.

"If they keep pace, they'll end the year with a profit, even without their other jobs," said the woman in the gray jacket.

"You're so optimistic, Tara," said Jericho.

"Well, it's true!" Tara exclaimed. "I wouldn't lie to you about your books to make you happy."

"Everyone should grab a donut and juice if they want and then we'll get started," said Minerva.

"No Chris and Keri today?" asked Jericho.

Minerva stumbled over her response. "They...um..."

"They won't be joining us anymore," said Cecil. "Amy's got someone relocating them."

"Oh," replied Tara. "Another one?"

"We'll talk about it when the meeting starts," replied Minerva. "Get food everyone. This is a happy day. We've got new friends here."

Everyone acquired the food and drink they wanted and made their way to the front of the classroom, where Minerva had arranged desks in a circle.

"Welcome to Friends of AI," Minerva began. "We've got some new faces here with us today, which is always exciting. For those unfamiliar with the group, the Friends of AI is a group dedicated to supporting those whose lives are impacted by artificial intelligence. We welcome humans and conscientia alike with the goal of creating a caring space for all."

Erika and Abby listened quietly as everyone went around the circle and introduced themselves, then explained their involvement either with conscientia in general or Project Freyja specifically. It was clearly for Abby and Erika's benefit, though all it did was cause Erika to dread when it would be her turn to go.

"If no one minds, I'd like to begin," said Minerva Piccolo. "I'm Minerva and I've been part of the Friends of AI for six years now. I met my first conscientia about seven or eight years ago. She was a civil service android that worked for our university's communications department."

Get on with it. Let's just talk so we can leave.

"Afraid of someone finding out you're not supposed to be here?"

I'm not here for me. I'm here for Abby.

"I'm sure they'll all believe that."

"One of the hardest things I've had to go through is watching conscientia I know personally be discriminated against just because of who they are," continued Minerva. "It's like hating someone just because of who they love or the color of their skin. It's a backwards and prejudiced way of thinking. What hurt me most of all though was watching others I knew who could stand up to protect conscientia not do so. When you have the chance to stand up for what's right and you don't, you're proving how weak of a person you are."

"She seems nice."

Cecil Hughes introduced himself next.

"I am the resident thespian of the Friends of Al," he said, giving a flourish with his hand as he did so. "Though my main purpose in life is being a supportive and loving partner for my dear Minerva."

"Awww," Abby said softly.

"I've been an emancipated conscientia for seven years now," Cecil continued, "I work for the community theater group in Carmel, as well as being an acting tutor at Butler University."

"It must be nice to work at the same place as your partner," said Abby.

"And as long as she doesn't see too much of me during the day, I've been assured it'll continue to be nice."

Light laughter broke out around the group as Minerva jabbed Cecil in the ribs with her elbow.

"He jokes, but we've been through a lot together," said Minerva.

"Oh boy. Here we go. Here comes the sob story. Just watch."

"Cecil and I have been together just under six years," continued Minerva. "And while having him as a partner has been one of the best decisions of my life, not everything has been so rosy. My family has mostly drifted away from me over that time. It started slowly enough – less talking here and there from everyone. Life gets busy, so I thought nothing of it. My older brother, Patrick, was scheduled to fly out here for a bachelor party and promised he'd meet up with us for dinner the day prior. Patrick's a terribly nervous flyer, so he tends to drink heavily before he flies anywhere. About twenty minutes before his flight's scheduled to board, I get this message about – about –

"

Minerva's voice trails off as she struggles to hold back tears. Cecil wrapped his arm around her, whispering into her ear as he held her.

"Told you."

They're going to make me talk, aren't they?

"Yep."

What am I going to say? Hi, I'm Erika and I abandoned the conscientia beside me because I'm a shitty person?

"I would have gone with coward, but I think we've got the same messaging strategy in mind."

"He sent this message," Minerva said after she regained her composure, "talking about how he was getting on a plane to see his robot fucking sister. We had a blowup fight that night. I haven't talked to Patrick since."

Cecil hugged Minerva as Tara, Jericho, and Abby quietly thanked her for sharing. Erika sat still, staring at the ground in front of her feet as she nervously twiddled her thumbs.

This wasn't what I signed up for.

"What did you think this was? It's a support group, not a social club."

Next up was Jericho Fogg.

"I spent six years at the United States Naval Academy," he began. "They brought me on as a recruit to their football team, as well as to the service. Things were looking pretty good for me. I was redshirted a year, but started getting some pretty serious attention from the national media by my sophomore year. There was some talk going into my junior year how I could go pro if I wanted. I was fortunate and was named a second-team preseason All-American at tight end. Not bad for a kid from Baltimore.

"Against Ohio State, I caught a pass on the sideline. I spun away from the first guy, but my cleat caught in the grass. Doc says it tore my ACL instantly. Then one of their linebackers got pancaked by our right tackle. They both came down on my knee, tearing it up further. I couldn't walk for months."

Oh shit.

Erika realized where she'd heard Jericho's name before. She had been at the Ohio State-Navy game with her dad when Navy's tight end suffered a gruesome leg injury. Jericho was underselling it with his explanation. It wasn't just a torn ACL. Erika remembered that the impact from the other players caused the bone in Jericho's left leg to break through the skin. Her dad had gone on about how he'd only seen an injury like that one other time and that there was no way they'd ever play again.

"The Navy did right by me," he continued. "They let me finish up my schooling in robotics and gave me a medical discharge when I was done. One of the guys who had fallen on my leg – my teammate, Darrell Walters – felt so bad for ending my career that he talked his dad into pulling some strings at his company when I got out of the service. That was a little company named EIL. That's where I met Tara."

Jericho went into a long explanation about how Tara was a testing unit that was assigned to him to help his transition back into civilian life. He described Tara as an Iris class simulation. Erika knew there were different classes that Project Freyja and other companies had created, but didn't know anything about the Iris class.

"What's an Iris class simulation?" asked Abby, as if she could read Erika's mind.

Erika smirked at Abby's inquisitiveness. She was happy she didn't have to ask the question. Her facial expression, however, must not have shown the happiness she thought it had, as she caught Minerva scowling at her from the corner of her eye.

"It's a conscientia class In Every Mind Technologies developed in partnership with EIL as a branch of their Project Frejya code, but it was never released to the public," said Tara. "We were designed to help veterans and ex-professional athletes transition back to the life of a regular citizen following their respective careers."

"Tara's been my accountant for five years now," Jericho

interjected. "She actually helped Caroline start her quilting business."

"I work downtown at one of the accounting firms part-time. That said, I've done pretty well for myself with my finance work on my own. You'd be surprised how many connections you make when you're in accounting."

"Why don't you tell us about the two of you?" Minerva asked.

Abby and Erika looked at each other for a moment, silently trying to read the other's face to determine who should go first. Erika subtly pointed her finger at Abby, to which Abby responded by pointing her own finger at herself. Erika gave her a slight nod, to which Abby smiled and spoke up.

"I'll go first if that's okay," she said. "I'm Abby Lin and I've been a conscientia simulation for a little over eight years now, though I've only been human for a few weeks. Well, an android for a few weeks."

"It's perfectly natural to call yourself human at times," Minerva replied. "The way the androids are set up, they're intended to make you as human-like as possible. You'll feel human because you're made to be as much like a human as is physically possible. Just be careful who you call yourself a human to out in public. People generally don't say they've been human a few weeks."

"Right, of course," Abby stated as she chuckled to herself. "Either way, I'm new to this. I just came to the area a few weeks ago. Still, haven't found a job yet, but I'm hoping that once I understand how to go about doing that a bit better I can find one. I live with Erika – that's her right there – for now, but I'd love to have my own apartment at some point."

"What kind of job are you hoping to get, Abby?" asked Tara.

"I'm not really sure," replied Abby.

"What were you programmed to be good at?" Tara retorted. "Most of the programs that came out of Project Freyja or other programs have a specific skill they were good at in order to make their conversations more real and to help them adjust to the real world. I'm good with numbers and Cecil's quite the actor."

"I prefer thespian, but nevertheless accurate," Cecil replied with an air of mock pomposity.

"I think I was just meant to learn to love," Abby answered. "I know that sounds weird, as that's not really a skill. But it's what I'm good at. I develop an emotional attachment to people and I learn to care about them with everything in me."

Cecil elbowed Minerva in the ribs and leaned in to talk in her ear.

"That's adorable," he whispered. Minerva responded by kicking at Cecil's ankles.

"I'm also really good at having people like me," Abby continued. "I'm just...nice I guess would be the best word."

"I was going to say you should get into sales," Jericho said, "but then you said you were nice."

"Don't worry, Abby," stated Minerva. "I'm sure we'll find you something. I've got some friends at temp agencies that might be able to get you some work until you figure out what you're good at."

"I know some folks too," added Tara. "We can talk after we're done."

"That'd be nice," responded Abby. "Thank you. Do I need to share anything else?"

"You don't have to," Minerva replied, "but the more open you can be, the easier it will be to help you adjust to being a live android."

"Would it be okay if I just listened for a little while?" asked Abby.

"Of course!" Minerva excitedly said.

Minerva turned and looked at Erika, locking eyes with her. Erika had just finished taking a drink of her orange juice, but upon realizing it was her turn to talk, kept the plastic cup to her lips. No liquid went into her mouth – the glass was empty. But Erika kept it there nevertheless, hoping that somehow it would make Minerva skip her. She didn't.

"She's on to you. If you run now, she'll never catch you."

I'm not running. Not this time.

"And would you tell us about you, Erika?" Minerva inquired.

Erika took a long, drawn-out sigh. She looked around the group and noticed every set of eyes staring at her, patiently waiting for her to say something.

That doesn't mean I want to do this.

"Hi," Erika began in a monotone voice, "my name is Erika. I'm an alcoholic."

Cecil replied back with an overtly deadpanned monotone voice. "Hi, Erik–oof."

Minerva shoved Cecil to stop his reply. She shot a stern look at Cecil, who quickly sat up in his chair as straight as could be in response to the scolding. Minerva then looked back at Erika, her glare piercing through Erika's body and stabbing straight through to the concrete wall at the back of the room.

"Do you think this group is a serious endeavor, Miss Edens?" Minerva said sharply.

"I think that helping Abby adjust is serious," Erika began, "but I don't think sharing my life story will help her in any way. She already knows it."

"That and you're kind of the villain in Abby's."

"Do you want to be here?"

"I am here for Abby."

"That's not what I asked. Do you want to be here?"

"Not even a little bit."

"I want to help Abby be on her own. I don't want to talk about the inevitable mommy or daddy issues that are bound to come up in groups like these."

"Interesting," Minerva replied, her voice growing louder. "How many support groups have you personally run?"

"I don't see how th–" Erika started to say before she was cut off.

"And how many conscientia have you helped to adjust to being functional members of society?"

"She's going to find you out."

"That doesn't matter."

"Oh? And how would you know? Are you a conscientia?"

"I'm not a conscientia!" screamed Erika. "I'm not the one that needs help! That's her. Okay? Do you get that? I'm going to be here to support Abby because she needs the help adjusting. Not me. And certainly not from someone yelling at me and telling me I don't know what I'm doing!"

The room went silent as Erika stopped yelling. As Erika and Minerva glared at one another, everyone else in the room exchanged awkward glances. Abby began playing with her hair, trying to roll the ends back toward their roots. Jericho was the first to break the tense silence.

"How about we do a bit of a breakout session?" he suggested. "We've got the room across the hall free as well. Tara, could you and Cecil take Abby over there and share how you guys found your jobs, tips on job hunting, stuff like that?"

"Of course," Tara replied.

Tara, Cecil, and Abby quietly stood up and left the room. As they left, Cecil peeked his head back in the doorway.

"15 minutes sound good?" he said.

"I'll have Minerva come get you when we're done," Jericho replied.

Cecil left the room, shutting the door behind him. As the door closed, Minerva began to speak.

"You don't need to come with her next week," Minerva stated. "Or at all going forward. We'll take care of her."

"It's not your job to take care of her," replied Erika. "It's her job to learn to take care of herself. And until she learns how to do that, it's my job to help her."

"What guilt are you holding that you're so insistent on helping her out despite hating this?" Minerva questioned. "Is she the program that belonged to a dead relative?"

"No."

"Do you owe someone a lot of money and this is how you're repaying them?"

"No, that's insane."

"Well what is it then?" exclaimed Minerva. "You clearly only care about her because you have to."

"She's got you there."

"Fuck off, that's not true at all," retorted Erika.

"Easy now," said Jericho, trying to calm the two of them down.

Minerva pressed on. "Tell me what it is then. You don't care about her now. You might have cared about her at one point, but this is apathy. It's a responsibility. It's nothing more."

"I do care!" Erika shouted.

"Oh my god," Minerva said, suddenly in a calm voice. "That's it. She loves you and you don't love her back."

"No."

"You don't even care about her a little bit, but you're here to make when you let her down a little easier."

"That's not it."

"You're just trying to give her people to be around so that when you're done she doesn't short circuit herself."

"Minerva!" Jericho said forcefully. "You're taking this too

far."

Erika sat down at a nearby desk and buried her head in her arms. She listened as Minerva's plodding footsteps stormed out of the room, slamming the door behind them. Erika began to cry, tears pooling on the desk beneath her. And to think Erika believed she was done with crying in classrooms once college ended.

"God, you're an easy read. What do you even need me around for? I'm just saying. If you let other people tell you how shitty you are instead of me, it'd save you a lot of money on therapy. Not that you go anyway. But hypothetically."

The sounds of Jericho pulling up a desk beside Erika echoed throughout the room. He sat down at the desk, placing his hand on her shoulder.

"Are you okay?" Jericho asked.

Erika shrugged her shoulders.

"Is she right?" he questioned.

Erika raised her head from her arms and leaned back in the chair, wiping her tears away with her hands.

"Sort of," she said, "though not totally."

"If you tell me what's going on, this will be a lot easier."

Erika sighed. It had to come out sometime.

"Abby's my ex-girlfriend. We dated for nearly three years while she was a computer simulation. If you could call it dating, I guess. I broke up with her because I was young and scared people would hate me for loving someone I shouldn't. We haven't talked for eight years, then three weeks ago she just calls me out of the blue and asks me to save her life."

"And you said yes why?" asked Jericho. "The thing you were afraid of was out of your life."

"Abby wasn't what I was afraid of."

"But breaking up with her got rid of the things you did fear, right?"

"I've had nightmares about how things ended for eight years," replied Erika. "I still feel guilty about it. I was a shitty person then and I don't want to be a shitty person now. Abby deserves better than how I've treated her. The sooner I help her adjust and get out there and meet people she can be friends with, the sooner she has better."

"Do you have any romantic feelings at all for her?"

"No. Why?"

"Because what you're doing trying to help her is the right thing, at least in my mind. The only problem comes if you have any romantic feelings for her at all. If she is built to love and be loved – and then you lead her on while trying to help her – you'll be hurting her all over again."

"I don't want that," said Erika. "At all. It's a fight I'm battling in my own mind every day. I just want her to find happiness. I took that away from her once. Part of me feels like it's my job to help her find it to make things right."

"Can I give you one piece of advice?" asked Jericho.

"Sure."

"Don't take your need to solve Abby's problems too seriously. If she's going to learn to do things for herself, she'll have to learn to solve her own problems too. That means making new friends and finding happiness on her own. You can help as much as she wants you too. But if you insist on making this some grand quest, you're only going to frustrate yourself. Not to mention Minerva might kill you."

"Yeah," Erika responded. "About that."

"I'll smooth things over with her," replied Jericho. "You guys just come back here two weeks from now – we don't have a meeting next week because of Thanksgiving – and we'll do what we can to help you and Abby out. Can you do that?"

"Yeah."

Erika and Abby left their first meetup with the Friends of Al shortly thereafter. As Abby relayed all the ideas Cecil and Tara had given her for finding a job, Erika drove home, making little noise aside from the occasional grunt to indicate she was listening. While Abby bounded into the apartment, excited to begin her new plans, Erika slowly shuffled in behind, sipping at her now lukewarm, bitter coffee from the travel mug.

8
Always a Fighter

November 23, 2033

"You home?" Erika said as she opened the door to the apartment.

"Yeah," replied Abby. "I got home a few minutes ago."

Erika stamped her feet on the welcome mat outside of her apartment, trying to get as much snow off of her shoes as she could before she entered. Though a late November snow wasn't unheard of in the Midwest, seeing three inches of it the day before Thanksgiving was unusual.

"How did the interview go?" Erika asked as she unlaced her boots.

"I think it went well," answered Abby. "But I won't know anything until next week."

"What was this one for?"

"A receptionist and administrative assistant."

"Don't sound so excited," replied Erika.

Abby shrugged as she stretched out on the futon.

"It seems alright," she said. "Tara thinks I'd pick up on it pretty quickly. That and it pays well for what it is."

Erika hung her coat up in the closet and headed into the kitchen. She grabbed some instant rice out of the cupboard, tore the edge of the packet open, and placed it in the microwave. As it whirred, she grabbed a can of ginger ale out of the fridge, popped it open and took a long drink. The fizzy, bubbly spray from the drink went up Erika's nose, causing her to cough.

"Do you think it's a good choice?" asked Abby.

"Being a receptionist?" Erika questioned back.

"To take the first job I'm offered."

"Jobs don't grow on trees. If you're offered a job when you don't have a job, you take it. It doesn't matter what it is."

"What if I don't like it?"

"Until you can support yourself, you can't afford to be picky."

"Sorry," said Abby. Erika rolled her eyes.

"Not 'you' you, general you. The royal you. I didn't mean – " Erika tried to think of softer phrasing, but nothing came to her. "Never mind."

The microwave sounded as Erika finished her sentence. She grabbed a bowl from the cabinet and poured in the steaming hot rice. Erika then pulled a tub of margarine out of the fridge, scooped out a chunk and buried it beneath the rice. Sprinkling salt on top, she took her meal to the living room. Erika took a seat on the edge of the futon opposite Abby, her food and drink on a flimsy card table in front of her.

"I always thought people mixed their spices into the food before it went into the bowl," Abby stated.

Erika shrugged. Most people don't eat rice on its own, she thought. At least not people with money.

"Are you driving back to Ohio tonight or in the morning?" asked Abby, trying to fill the silence.

"For what?"

"Thanksgiving. You could bring back leftovers to eat for a few days so you're not stuck eating rice and ramen all weekend."

"I'm not going," Erika responded.

"What? Why not?"

"I've got nothing new to tell my family about."

"You have a new roommate."

"Right. Because that went over so well with my mom the last time."

"You don't have to tell them who," Abby stated.

"Then what's the point?" Erika retorted. "The natural follow up question to 'I have a new roommate' is 'what's their name'."

"I just figured you wanted to see them."

Erika stirred her rice aggressively. The salt and margarine were thoroughly mixed in by this point, but the stirring kept her from rolling her eyes.

"Isn't Thanksgiving about being thankful for family and whatnot?" pressed Abby.

Erika dropped the fork into her bowl, letting it clang off the side.

"I'll video chat my dad at some point, okay. They think I have to work anyway."

"But you told me you have the day off."

They don't know that, thought Erika. Nor do they need to.

"You're kind of a shitty daughter."

I don't know what else I'm supposed to be. I've been treated shitty.

"By your mom. What did your dad do?"

I don't need you guilting me over this.

"Afraid of another lecture from your mom about how you need to be responsible with money? Or are you just worried they'll figure out Abby's here?"

Abby sat silently on the futon while Erika took a large bite of rice from the bowl. A couple of grains tumbled off of Erika's fork, landing on her pant leg. She carefully picked them up off of her leg, placing them on the card table in a pile.

"I'm sorry," Abby said.

"Why now?" asked Erika between chews of her food.

"For complicating your life. Again."

"It's okay. I'm not mad at you this time."

"You stopped talking to me," said Abby. "You've been violently chewing the same two bites of rice for a while now."

"Just thinking and talking to myself," replied Erika.

"Anything you want to talk about?"

"Boundaries, Abby."

"Alright," replied Abby, "if you're not going back to Ohio, what are you going to do instead?"

"Drink," answered Erika. "Probably heavily."

"What if we did something? Just to kill the boredom."

"That's what the drinking is for."

"Erika, I'm serious."

"Like what?"

"What if I made you Thanksgiving dinner?" Abby asked.

"There's ramen and saltines in the cabinet if you want. The soy sauce and butter are good, but I wouldn't trust the ketchup. Might be some corn in the freezer too. Don't use the peas though – that's my ice pack. They might have been left out a few too many times overnight."

"I mean an actual Thanksgiving dinner."

Erika chuckled. "With what?"

"I could go to the store –"

"You can't. Stores are out of nearly everything by now, Abby. You'll be lucky if you can find cranberry sauce."

"I mean…" stammered Abby, "it…I was hoping I could have gotten some of it."

"It's the night before!" exclaimed Erika. "Shopping for Thanksgiving dinner is a weeks-long endeavor."

Erika watched as the hope faded from Abby's eyes, the corners of her mouth coiling into a defeated frown.

"There might be some stuffing left if you go now. But you'll be standing in a checkout line for 45 minutes to get it."

Abby looked away, thinking about what to do next. Erika carried her bowl to the kitchen. She opened the fridge and peered in, knowing full well there was nothing else to eat, but hoping all the same.

"How about we go somewhere for lunch or dinner tomorrow?"

Abby's head appeared just above the fridge door, causing Erika to jump.

"Warn me when you're going to sneak around like that," said Erika, clutching a hand to her chest.

"My treat," Abby said, her eyes brightening again.

"There's not a lot open," replied Erika, giving up on the fridge.

"I'm sure we could find something."

"Going out isn't cheap on holidays. There's not a lot open aside from expensive restaurants."

"I have plenty of money left. I promise, it's fine. Besides, when's the last time you went out for food that wasn't from a drive-thru?"

"Abby, I appreciate the thought –"

"It's the least I can do."

"Most places that are open will be booked or full."

"Leave it to me. Please?"

This won't work, Erika thought. But eating something other than rice and ramen did sound good. And Abby wasn't going to take no for an answer.

"Are you sure you want to?"

"I'm the reason you're not spending the day with family," said Abby. "That doesn't feel great."

Erika took a drink of her ginger ale, contemplating the offer.

She shrugged.

"If you can find somewhere that's open, okay," Erika replied. "But no Chinese food. That's for Christmas."

"But you're not Jewish?" Abby questioned with a confused look on her face.

"Nope, though I did play a prank on my mom in high school where I pretended to convert to Judaism for a week. Chinese is just delicious. That and they're the only places open Christmas day."

"I'll find somewhere. Just don't fill up too much before lunch."

"With what?" asked Erika.

"Good point."

*****

The next morning, Erika woke up early to call her parents before getting ready for "work". In reality, Erika put a dress shirt on and wandered around her bedroom acting like she was getting ready. On the other end of the video chat, Dwight and Kaytie Edens worked to start preparing Thanksgiving dinner – even without Erika, they were still expecting Kaytie's siblings and their children over for a large meal. After ten minutes on camera, Erika ended the call, tossed her button up shirt on the floor in front of her dresser, and curled back up in bed.

Erika woke up just after 9:30, feeling refreshed after her three-hour early morning nap. She walked out to the living room to find Abby curled up under a blanket on the futon, her head was propped up on one hand, and the other arm snuggling the pillow that typically sat on the far end of the couch. Abby stared blankly toward the TV, which flickered with the sights and sounds of a Thanksgiving Day parade. Without looking away from the screen, Abby acknowledged Erika's presence with a small wave.

"Thanksgiving isn't the biggest holiday of the year for Americans, is it?" asked Abby.

"Depends on who you ask," replied Erika. "It's big, though Christmas is probably bigger."

"Then why is there such a big parade? This just started and it's supposed to go on for another two and a half hours."

"People like parades."

"Why?" Abby questioned. "It's just a really long line being watched by other really long lines."

Erika raised a finger in the air and opened her mouth, nearly bringing herself to correct Abby. Before she could speak though, she put her finger down and cocked her head to the side. She couldn't find a fault in Abby's logic, even if she didn't agree with it.

"Want to watch it?" asked Abby.

"But you think it's weird," replied Erika.

"Yes. But it's also fascinating."

Erika walked over toward the futon to join Abby. Abby pulled her legs closer to her chest, giving Erika space to sit down. They watched the parade for the remainder of the morning, leading up to Abby's lunch plans. As they readied themselves for leaving, Erika bundled her coat tightly and put her keys in her coat pocket.

"So where are we going?" inquired Erika.

Abby shrugged and smiled. "It's a surprise," she said.

"It can't really be a surprise if I have to drive us there," Erika responded.

"I took care of that already. They should be here shortly."

"Who?"

"Tara offered to drive us to and from lunch."

"Doesn't she have plans?"

"Not sure. I didn't ask."

Erika and Abby exited the apartment where they found Tara sitting in her white sedan, bundled up tightly in a winter coat and a fluffy hat. The car's wipers flickered back and forth, swiping newly fallen snowflakes from the windshield.

"Happy Thanksgiving!" Tara exclaimed as Erika and Abby entered the car.

"Happy Thanksgiving!" Abby shouted back, equally excited.

"Thanks for driving us to lunch," said Erika. "Where are we going?"

"Well, I'm sneaking to the grocery store to pick up food for Jericho and Caroline while it's not busy," replied Tara. "You guys are getting some Italian food."

"There's an Italian restaurant open on Thanksgiving?" asked Erika.

Tara shrugged. "I know a guy who owes me a couple of favors. They're only open for dinner today, but he said he'd let you guys in before they open up."

"What's 'a favor'?" asked Abby.

"I did some bookkeeping for him. Tidied up the numbers and what not. I've been known to do a fair bit of magic."

"I don't follow."

Tara smiled. "I saved him from getting into trouble when some money came up missing. He owes me."

Abby tumbled the words over in her mind, slowly wrapping her head around what Tara had said. She didn't fully understand what Tara had meant, but appreciated her efforts all the same.

"Thank you so much," she said.

"Yeah," Erika said, her voice much quieter and unsure than before. "Thank you."

The rest of the fifteen-minute drive went by with Tara and Abby chatting in the front seats of the car about Abby's job search.

Erika spent her time searching for any restaurant – Italian or otherwise – that was open for business on Thanksgiving. Her search turned up nothing. Either Tara really did call in a favor or the place they were going to was still operating on a pre-social media business model.

"We're here," said Abby.

Erika looked up to a snow and vine-covered brick building in front of them. Boerio's Eatery. She'd heard about the restaurant from a few people, with everything she could remember being positive.

Tara led Erika and Abby to the front of the building and rapped her knuckles on the front door. After a short pause, an elderly olive-skinned man opened the door.

"Tara!" he shouted gleefully.

"Lino!" she exclaimed back, mimicking his intonation and happiness. Lino and Tara exchanged kisses on the cheeks, followed by a brief hug.

"How was Tuscany?" Tara asked.

"I assume it's beautiful," Lino replied. "But last I saw you, I was going to Tucson. Very different place."

"I can never keep up with you."

"Yet you'll always know how to find me."

Lino broke off his hug with Tara, finally noticing Abby and Erika standing behind her.

"Come in! Come in!" Lino beckoned as he motioned toward the door. "It's so cold outside."

They filed into the restaurant and out of the snowy Indiana afternoon. The main dining room of the building was only partially lit, in an effort to create some level of ambiance for any patrons of the establishment. Lino led them to a booth a little over halfway back the room, where he gestured for Abby and Erika to sit.

"Do you prefer red wine or white wine?" he asked.

"Oh, I really don't know," replied Abby.

"There's no need for wine," Erika interjected.

"Nonsense!" Lino responded. "Everything is better with wine! Tell you what. You read these. Take your time. I'll bring you a wine to go with your meal. On the house."

Abby gasped with excitement. "That's so kind of you!"

Lino handed Abby and Erika menus, then motioned for Tara to follow him as they walked back toward the kitchen and offices of the restaurant. Their shared enthusiasm for each other made Abby wonder how long they'd known each other. After they were out of sight, Erika quickly looked around to see if they were alone. Satisfied that no one else was in earshot, her demeanor turned serious as she addressed Abby.

"Are you out of your mind?" Erika inquired. "You'll be broke before the main course!"

"I promise I won't, Erika," replied Abby. "I told Tara about wanting to take you out to eat. Before I knew it, she was telling me about here, that they were open today, and to not worry about the cost. I swear this wasn't my first plan. Besides, it's not that expensive."

"The appetizers are $30! Do you realize how much that is?"

Abby reached her hands across the table and pulled Erika's wildly gesticulating hands down to the table cloth. Erika hurriedly pulled her hands away. Abby withdrew her own hands just as quickly, hiding them under the table.

"Erika," she stated, "it's fine. Just think of it as a gift. I won't eat much. You can have my leftovers. Okay?"

A door near the kitchen squeaked open, followed by the sounds of clicking shoes moving across the restaurant floor. Tara made her way from the back of the restaurant to the front, waving at Abby and Erika without stopping on her way out.

"Just call me when you girls need picking up," she shouted. "Ciao! Enjoy your date!"

"Wait. What?" Erika snipped.

Abby froze, staring at Erika with a cautious fear of what she was going to do next.

"Did you tell Tara this was a date?" Erika hissed.

"I said I wanted to take you out to dinner," Abby meekly responded, suddenly very interested in the tablecloth.

"Is this a date?"

"It's just a meal. I swear. It doesn't matter what Tara –"

"It does matter, Abby," stated Erika. "Is this a date?"

"No."

"I thought we had an understanding about boundaries."

"It's not a date," Abby mumbled, tears beginning to well up into her eyes.

"I thought I could trust you to do something nice for me without having any sort of romantic subtext to your actions. I should have known better though. You tried to hold my fucking hands just a minute ago."

"It's not a date," whispered Abby.

"Speak up!" yelled Erika, her voice echoing through the empty room.

"It's not a date!" Abby shouted back. "I'm just trying to say thank you! You saved my fucking life! You opened up your home to me! You've treated me as kind as you can despite the fact that I'm nothing but a constant source of frustration and anger for you!"

"Oh god, Abby," Erika said, taken back and now responding in a trembling voice. "You're not always frustrating."

"I clearly am!" continued Abby. "And I know I'm struggling with this. You are everything I wanted for so long. And now you're so goddamn close, but you're further away than ever. So yes, I *want* this to be a date. I want it so fucking bad. But you know what I want more than that? You to be my friend. Please let me try to be that, Erika. Please?"

Abby stood up from the table, leaving her coat in the booth behind her.

"I need a minute," said Abby, tears streaming down her face. "I can call Tara and have her come get us when I come back."

Abby swiftly walked to the far side of the restaurant and down a long hallway to the restrooms. Erika leaned her head back against the back of the booth, sighing heavily into the air. She put her hands over her face, wiping away the few tears that had begun to develop around the corners of her eyes.

Grace. Are you there?

"*Always am.*"

Why am I like this?

"*Like what specifically?*"

Why can't I trust her?

"*I think you can't trust you.*"

What do you mean?

"*Did you want this to be a date?*"

No.

"*But you did want this a long time ago. Romantic dinner. Candlelight. A beautiful woman – no, THE beautiful woman – across the table from you.*"

Erika sighed.

I did.

"*It's too perfect. Something was bound to go wrong. So you did it before anyone else could.*"

But she was just trying to be nice to me.

"*I'm not here to question your methods. But you did make her cry. And you're damn good at that.*"

"Do you ladies need more time?" she heard Lino say.

Erika removed her hands from her face and stared at the menu.

"No, but thank you," she replied. "Can I get your advice, Lino?"

"Of course."

"What wine pairs well with an apology?"

9
Precious

Cecil and Minerva scanned the restaurant again, trying to see Amy. It would be the first time they got to see Amy in person since meeting Erika and Abby. Minerva had planned to do plenty of venting to Amy about Erika's attitude, but a text from Amy a few hours before dinner put that desire in the back of her mind. Amy had some news she had to share first.

"She said she was here already, right?" Minerva asked as she scanned the dining room around her.

"I'm positive," replied Cecil. "I've checked and rechecked."

"I believe you. I just don't see her."

"We could go back to the lobby and wait. Maybe she ran to her car or something."

"Hey! Hey!" came a shout from behind them.

Minerva and Cecil turned around to see Amy flagging them down from a table in the corner near the front of the restaurant. Though the primary dining hall of the restaurant was expansive, Minerva shook her head, convinced they had checked that table shortly after entering. They walked over to Amy, with Cecil pulling Minerva's chair out for her once they arrived at the table.

"I hope you weren't waiting long," said Cecil as he took his own seat.

"Not at all," replied Amy, "maybe ten minutes at most. I would've ordered drinks, but I had no idea what you want."

"She'll have a glass of rosé and I'll have alcohol."

"Cecil, rosé is alcohol," retorted Minerva.

"Correct," he responded. "But I'm not picky about mine."

"The waiter should be back around shortly," replied Amy.

"If you're quick, we can probably send him back with both orders in one go."

"Are you in a hurry?" asked Cecil.

"To rush our dinner?" replied Amy. "Never. I just have a bit of packing to do before my flight tomorrow."

"Where are you going?" Minerva questioned.

"I've got some business in Toronto tomorrow. I'm hoping to be back before the end of the year."

"End of the year? You're missing Christmas?" asked Minerva.

"The plan is to have dinner atop the CN Tower on Christmas Eve," replied Amy. "Manny is staying to take care of the animals. I'll bring back a chew toy for Archer and some sort of trinket for Kalie to knock off of my shelves. They won't know the difference when they get their gifts."

The waiter arrived at the table, interrupting the conversation. He was a slender, young man with curly black hair.

"Looks like we have everyone here," he began. "What can I get everyone to dr – oh, hey Mr. Hughes!"

"Hello, Ronny!" Cecil replied excitedly. "How's your script coming along?"

"It's...going?" stammered Ronny.

"Was that a question or a statement?"

"I'm not sure at this point. It needs a lot of work."

"Come by my office during office hours this week and I'll help you. And don't save it for next week. It's due next Wednesday and there'll be a line out my door with the semester ending."

"Okay, okay, I will," replied Ronny. "Can I get you all drinks?"

"Food too, please," Cecil said, shooting a wink to Amy. "The lady has a schedule. I'll have the house ribeye, well done."

Ronny gave Cecil a judgmental look.

"Really?" he scolded.

"We all have our flaws, Ronny. It'd behoove you to remember that when working on your character development."

"Right, right," replied Ronny, taken back.

Minerva shook her head as Ronny took the rest of the orders. As Ronny left, she smacked Cecil's hand.

"You really had to turn your food order into a teaching moment?" she asked.

"You've been telling me that if I'm going to be a better instructor, I should try to make my teaching more relatable," replied Cecil.

"I meant in your classroom, not in a restaurant! Can you believe him?"

"Cecil does have a flair for the unexpected," answered Amy.

"Of course he does," Minerva mumbled.

"So, what's in Toronto, if you don't mind my asking?" Cecil pried.

Amy let out a long sigh and swirled her wine around in her glass.

"This stays between us," said Amy.

Cecil slapped at Minerva's leg, full of excitement and energy.

"It's finally happening!" he exclaimed. "Manny is going to become Mr. Nammu!"

Both Amy and Minerva laughed at Cecil's misplaced joy.

"No, no," answered Amy between laughs, "though I'd prefer to plan a massive party that I wouldn't get to enjoy the benefits of rather than what I'm going to deal with. There's a – let's go with growing resentment – towards conscientia and other android life in the halls of Washington. We're at the point where the legacy servers I've been using to house backups for anyone involved in our program are going to need to be relocated, as

Project Freyja isn't going to allow me to keep them on premises anymore."

"Isn't that why you were moving Abby and others like her?" asked Cecil.

"Yeah," replied Amy. "Thing is, it's accelerating."

"Fucking RPU money corruption again," Minerva said gruffly. "I heard that some of their members were considering forming a political party. Didn't we learn this lesson before?"

"Maybe the political climate will normalize once the midterms hit. Maybe it won't. Toronto is a precautionary move on my part."

"So why be out of the country so long?" asked Cecil.

"There's a surprising amount of red tape you have to go through when you're importing what amounts to trade secrets for a company into a country," replied Amy. "While I've taken care of most of the legal hubbub already, there are a few logistics I still need to work out. Once I get everything set up there, I'll either head back or bring Manny there. I'll be able to expand the program with some help, though there may be some intermittent outages in the meantime."

"Meaning what?" inquired Minerva.

"Meaning that it'd be best if none of the conscientia jump in the ocean for a few months once the moving starts," Amy quipped. "While I'll be able to restore them from backups, if their hardware were to be damaged to a point where I couldn't personally repair it, we'd have to purchase a new android that meets the needed specifications."

"Which isn't cheap," Cecil interjected.

"Not in the slightest," replied Amy, "though it would be easier than the alternative. Even so, a repaired android – particularly one that's significantly damaged – is never quite the same if they've required major repairs. It's just a drawback of the way current models of androids are built. We're still waiting on clearance to be able to do implant surgery in Canada. That's likely still a year or two away, but it's closer than the five or ten years we'd need for android technology to get where we need it to in order for there to be negligible data loss in the case of a massive repair. We could always fly someone to Finland or Japan if needed for that, but those programs are still very much in an alpha stage, and I'd prefer to limit costs wherever I can."

"I'd like to hope we won't need to use those backups," replied Minerva.

"Same," said Cecil. "I quite like who I've become since my last backup."

"And when did you last backup exactly?" Minerva stated.

"Ronny? Where is that waiter with our drinks?" Cecil said, doing his best to distract from the previous comment.

"I'll have to disable everyone's automatic backup while I'm traveling," continued Amy, "so if you're sitting on months upon months of not backing up, Cecil, I'd encourage you to do so tonight if you can."

"Thank you, Amy," he responded. "I'll try to be sure to do so."

"Do you really need to do this?" asked Minerva. "Or is this another one of your 'overabundance of caution' moments?"

"I'm hoping the latter," answered Amy, "though I have no idea. No matter how far we advance as a society, some groups always find someone to hate. I'm just worried that the tide has shifted hard against androids and conscientia – at least ones programmed to act like people – and that they are the next group we need to be allying for the protection of.

Ronny returned to the table, a tray of drinks in hand. He placed a glass of wine each down in front of Minerva and Amy, and a glass of bourbon in front of Cecil.

"Actually, Ronny," said Cecil, "bring us a second round too, would you? Put it on my bill."

10
A Puff of Dust

Three men and an older woman stood on stage in the back corner of the Side Pocket billiards hall. Two of the men grabbed bottles of beer off of stools beside them and took long drinks from them. One was an older man, with long, flaxen hair who held a crimson guitar. The other was much younger, baby blue bass in hand to go along with his baby blue glasses and shaved head. The drummer, Clyde, toweled himself. He was a portly man, wearing a bandana that held back his long black locks from his face. He waved at the bartender, pointing skyward to the vents blowing heat directly down on him. The woman – a petite, middle-aged lady with large purple-rimmed glasses – fiddled with the microphone stand in front of her, raising and lowering it repeatedly in an attempt to get the stand's height to her liking. After six or seven tries, she was finally satisfied, replacing the microphone atop the stand and turning back to the rest of the band.

"Are you good?" she asked.

"Can they do anything about the heat?" asked the drummer. "I'm dying back here."

"It's snowing out," the guitarist, Red, chided.

"Petra," the drummer pleaded again, "can you say something?"

"We break in ten, Clyde," the woman replied. "I'll chase down Millie then."

"Get another round for me and Brenden while you're at it," Red stated.

Petra shook her head and scooted a stool closer to the microphone. She picked up an acoustic guitar off of the stand beside the stool, slung the strap around her shoulders, and strummed it to check the tuning.

"This one's for anyone who just wants out of whatever they're stuck in," said Petra.

Petra began to strum on her guitar, beating out the opening riff to the song. She was soon joined by Brenden's bass playing and Clyde's drumming backing her softly. Petra then began to sing a song from the mid-2000s about feeling controlled by a life you're unhappy with. Songs like these were the only ones Petra actively suggested for sets, though none of the rest of her bandmates ever got the message.

On the opposite side of the bar Jericho lined up a shot with his pool cue.

"Far-left corner pocket," he said, squinting as he attempted to aim his cue so that the cue ball hit the 8-ball where he wanted.

"Your left or my left?" asked Abby.

"My left."

"You're not hitting that."

"For someone who had never played pool before two hours ago, that's a bold statement," replied Jericho.

"And I've beaten you twice," replied Abby. "You haven't intentionally made a ball in the opposite end of the table all night."

"That's because I wasn't warmed up yet!"

"Does drinking count as warming up?" Tara asked from a chair against the wall behind where Jericho was standing. Erika and Caroline chuckled.

"I'll make it," said Jericho.

Abby pointed to the rail at the far end of the table. "You've got a better chance if you hit it off of the wall here."

"The rail," murmured Jericho.

"Right," Abby replied. "Hit it off this rail and try to have it come back into the far-left corner pocket. Well. My far-left corner

113

pocket. Your far-left corner pocket is a bad choice."

Jericho turned around looked at Erika, pointing his cue toward Abby as he spoke.

"You're really going to let her talk to me like that?"

"Yes," Erika scolded mockingly, "because I want you to either win or lose so I can play again."

"Hun, just hit the ball," Caroline said.

Jericho sighed and lined up his shot again.

"Far-left corner pocket," he said. "*My* left."

Jericho pulled back his pool cue and struck the cue ball hard. The white ball missed its mark, striking the 8-ball on its side. While the 8-ball smacked into the side rail and spun harmlessly toward the center of the table, the cue ball caromed off and struck the far rail and opposite side rail before spinning its way back to the near side of the table, heading straight for the corner pocket opposite Jericho.

"Shit. Shit. Shit." Jericho grumbled.

The white ball tumbled into the corner pocket, clacking against the balls made earlier in the game. While Abby lifted her arms in the air triumphantly, Jericho slumped his head down, bringing chin to chest.

"Is there a game where one of us hasn't bought drinks at the end?" Caroline asked.

"Just the one where you and I played," said Tara.

"Jericho Desmond Fogg," stated Caroline. "I'm gonna need you to stop losing our mortgage payments to amateurs."

"She's got a computer in her mind!" pleaded Jericho. "Literally."

"Rack 'em up," said Erika. "Who am I against?"

"I think all that's left is you against me," answered Caroline, "Abby against Tara, and you against Abby."

"Are we actually round robining five of us?" asked Jericho.

"There's no one else in the bar playing pool," Caroline replied.

Despite Side Pocket's status as one of the few billiard and pool halls in the Indianapolis area, it was also by far the least frequented of them. Up until a few years prior, the bar had been owned by an angry man who refused to serve anyone he didn't like under the guise of religious freedom. It just so happened that his religious beliefs conveniently allowed him to choose not to serve anyone whose skin color didn't match his own. A hefty set of fines later and the man sold Side Pocket off to Millie St. Vincent, an entrepreneur who owned multiple bars in the area. Though the bar's reputation had improved slightly in the three years since the sale, most people still avoided it. Jericho and Caroline loved it because they could play pool for hours on end with minimal interruption, so long as they kept buying drinks. It also meant a shorter drive for Tara when she inevitably took an inebriated Jericho and Caroline home. It only seemed natural to bring Erika and Abby to the bar to try to get both of them out of their shells a little.

"Same drinks?" Jericho asked.

Erika and Caroline nodded in unison. Tara held up her glass to show Jericho she was still working on her drink.

"Do you want anything this time?" said Jericho as he pointed at Abby.

"I'm going to charge up in a bit," replied Abby. "Maybe after that."

Jericho walked off to get drinks while Abby arranged the pool balls in their rack.

"Are we playing?" Abby asked as she looked at Tara.

"Sure," Tara replied. "They'll drink now. You can charge while they play."

Tara walked up to the table and grabbed a cue from Abby. She picked up the blue cube of chalk off of the rail of the table and chalked the cue.

"I've never understood why you do this," said Tara. "I read

somewhere it keeps the cue from slipping when you hit the cue ball, but I'm not sure it matters when you're a garbage player."

"If you hit it just right, you can see a tiny puff of chalk dust when you make contact," replied Abby. "The lights above the table help me see it."

"No, *you* can see the tiny puff of chalk dust."

"You can't?"

"It's a difference in our class design," Tara explained. "Your programming lets you pay fine attention to quirks and nuances of people. Presumably, that extends to noticing small details when it's not related to humans – like the cue hitting a pool ball. My programming has an added emphasis on communication and calculation. You exist to form bonds with people. I was made to help people."

"But you've learned other skills over time," said Abby.

"Oh, of course. It's just easy for me to fall back on the skills I was programmed for. I do them subconsciously more than I realize. You're doing the same thing."

"Neat!"

Tara lined up her shot and struck the cue ball. The white ball broke the rack, spreading balls across the table, with the 5 and 13 balls dropping into pockets.

"Did you see the dust that time?" asked Tara as she stared at the balls coming to a stop on the felt.

After a few seconds of silence, she looked up to see Abby staring at their table, where Caroline was showing off something on her phone to Erika. Tara walked up to Abby, putting her hand on her shoulder to draw her attention. Abby snapped out of her trance, shifting her gaze to Tara.

"You alright?" Tara inquired.

"Yeah," said Abby.

Tara walked back to the cue ball, lining up a shot to try to sink the 11 ball and claim stripes as her target for the match.

"How do I look at her only as a friend?" Abby asked.

Tara struck the cue ball, causing it to careen into the 11 ball, sinking it into the side pocket. She lined up her next shot, this time taking aim at the 14 ball.

"Treat her like you treat me," answered Tara.

"But she's not you," Abby said, "There's a history. There are feelings. We live together."

"If you stick to the plan we drew up," interrupted Tara, "that last one won't be true three months from now."

"I'm still not sure if I want to leave, though" continued Abby. "I get that it's the right thing to do. And she's so kind for helping me. But…"

Abby trailed off as Tara hit her shot, sinking yet another ball.

"But what?" Tara implored.

"I like seeing her face every morning."

Tara sighed and walked around the table to Abby. She put her arms around Abby and drew her close, hugging her tightly.

"It'll get better," said Tara. "I've been there and it does get better. I promise."

Back at the table, Jericho arrived with drinks for Erika and Caroline, setting the drinks down in front of their respective owners.

"I'm just glad I'm done playing," Jericho joked. "You're going to bankrupt me."

Caroline smiled and grabbed Jericho's hands.

"Well, I appreciate you if nothing else," she said before pulling him over and kissing him on the cheek.

Jericho looked over at the pool table and saw Tara and Abby laughing as Abby lined up a shot. Abby struck the cue ball mid-laugh, causing her to miss.

"They seem to be having fun," Jericho stated.

"Good," replied Caroline. "Tara could always use more friends. Plus she's doing a great job helping Abby adjust. Don't you think, Erika?"

Erika took a long drink from her glass and nodded. As Jericho and Caroline began talking about upcoming Christmas plans, Erika watched Abby and Tara play pool. Tara began to struggle, giving Abby the chance to take control of the game, Erika couldn't help but smile to herself as she watched Abby's competitive streak come out. Abby held a steely focus with nearly every shot, calmly calculating before each time she pushed the cue towards the cue ball. To be able to make the calculations and decisions in her head that Abby was making befuddled Erika, even if she knew Abby found them to be simple. Against Tara, Abby's focus grew tighter, if only because she knew Tara was capable of similar abilities, though Tara herself never cared enough to try hard at pool.

Erika finished her drink, then leaned back in the booth as she watched Abby take the final shot to win yet another game. Tara made her way up to the bar to buy the next round of drinks -- following the band which had just finished the first half of its set. Abby found a plug in the corner at a table near the stage where she could begin charging.

"We're up," said Caroline to Erika.

Erika stayed leaned back in the booth for a few more moments, taking in the scene around her. Abby was finally fitting in with a group. For a brief moment, Erika smiled, excited that both she and Abby had found somewhere that they belonged.

11
Girl That Won't Talk Back

December 17, 2033

"Do you think she's awake?"

"Probably just drunk. Thots get a drink or two in them and they pass out like they're at home."

"You sure?"

"Give her a poke and see."

Abby woke herself out of sleep mode at the finger touching her shoulder. She looked up from her seat to see two members of the band that had been playing earlier standing over her.

"I told you she was asleep," said Brenden. "I'm sorry, miss, we just wanted to make sure you were alright."

Abby smiled at Brenden. "It's okay. I appreciate your concern. I was just resting my eyes."

Clyde nudged Brenden with a jab of his elbow to his ribs. Brenden pushed back shooting a glare to his larger counterpart. Clyde rolled his eyes and looked back at Abby.

"What my friend here wants to know is if you'd like to get a drink with him," said Clyde.

"But, only if you want to," Brenden quickly interjected.

Clyde pulled Brenden away from Abby by the arm, walking a few steps away and turning the two of them away before he spoke.

"What the fuck are you doing?" Clyde growled.

"Asking her to get a drink," Brenden snapped back.

"No, I was asking her to get a drink for you. Don't talk yourself out of it."

"I'm being polite."

"You trying to bed this girl or not, Brenden?"

"I'm only *trying* to see if she'd like a drink. Who cares if she wants to sleep with me?"

Clyde sighed, reached into his pocket, and produced a credit card. He handed it to Brenden.

"Go up to the bar and get three shots of whatever you want," said Clyde. "Drink one, then bring the other two back here. And for the love of god, stop being such a fucking pussy and follow my lead."

"But –"

"You don't want me telling your Uncle Red how ungrateful you are, do you?"

Brenden clutched the credit card tightly and walked to the bar as he was instructed. Clyde brushed dust and crumbs off of his shirt and walked back over to Abby.

"Sorry about him," said Clyde. "He's just nervous around beauty."

"It's fine," said Abby. "We've all been there."

"Listen. How's about getting a drink with my boy? I know he's nervous now, but he opens up once he's gotten a few drinks in him."

"I really shouldn't."

"Why not? Clyde asked. "He's a nice guy."

"I'm sure he is," replied Abby. "And I appreciate you trying to help your friend out. But I'm not interested in him."

"Ah, I get it. You need someone who's more of a man. Well darling," said Clyde as he patted his stomach, "there's plenty of me to go around."

"No. I'm saying I'm not interested in your friend. And I'm really not interested in you."

Red stumbled his way over from the bar, bottle of beer in hand. His graying hair trickled out from underneath a tattered baseball cap, both the hat and his hairline having seen better days. He walked past Clyde and leaned on the table in front of Abby, tipping his beer bottle forward. The liquid inside trickled out onto the table, creating a small pool on the edge that made its way onto the wooden floor below.

"You need help getting it up again, Clyde?" Red asked, his eyes looking over Abby repeatedly. "You'd think with one that looks like this you wouldn't have any problem at all."

"She's not for me, you old fuck," replied Clyde. "Brenden was eyeing her."

"Brenden doesn't eye anyone," said Red, "His aunt's been trying to give him these 'virtues' since he was a kid," Red made large, flailing air quotes over his head.

"You know she's a bot, right?"

"If Brenden wants to stick his dick in a toaster, that's his problem."

Red leaned in close and ran his fingers across Abby's chin.

"Though it is well put together," he said. "Someone really gave a shit what you looked like."

Abby slapped Red's hand away, knocking it into his beer bottle, causing the drink to crash to the floor and shatter.

"They made you feisty too!" Red exclaimed. "Maybe Brenden's right about this one. How much for a suck and fuck?"

"I'm not for sale," replied Abby.

Erika and Caroline had paused their game of pool momentarily with the sound of the bottle crashing to the floor. Erika walked up to the table, weaving her way between Clyde and Red, and sat down on Abby's lap. She wrapped her arms around Abby's neck and kissed her on the cheek. She then reached down and grabbed Abby's hand with hers and held it tightly.

"Hey babe," Erika said, beaming a smile toward Red and Clyde and she spoke. "Sorry my game was taking so long. Who are your new friends?"

"They were just leaving," replied Abby.

"Now why the hell would we leave?" Red jeered. "Things are just getting interesting."

"Yeah," Clyde chimed in, though in a much quieter voice than he had been using before Red joined them.

"Is this a two-for-one, or are you one of those freaks who actually has feelings for these machines?" Red inquired.

"What can I say?" Erika said. "I like the pretty ones. What about you? Tired of the cows back home on the farm? Or are sheep more your speed?"

"What did you say?"

"Of course, the pigs are too smart and an ostrich is a two-man job. Allegedly."

"Nice one."

"Fucking scicuck bitch!" he shouted. Red launched towards Erika, and grabbed her by the hair, pulling her violently off Abby's lap. Despite the double-vision, Erika couldn't fight the force with which he pulled her into him.

"Oh fuck."

"Smart mouth, huh?" With his free hand, he held Erika by the chin, prying her mouth open. His breath filled her lungs, the smell of whisky catching in her throat. "Shame to waste it on metal, needs something…warm."

"Alright, Red, come on –"

"Fuck off, Clyde."

Clyde raised his hands in surrender and left. Abby watched in horror as Clyde made his way to the bar.

"As I was saying," Red continued. He glanced at Abby, seeing her eyes beginning to well. "The fuck's your problem, got a leak?"

"What?"

Erika turned her face into Red's hand, and bit down hard. As

Red recoiled with a yell, she kicked him away and into the band's drum kit. Amid the clash of cymbal and snare, Erika grabbed Abby's shoulder and shoved her out of the way. Red quickly made up the gap and positioned himself between them. Erika watched Abby continue past the pool table and out of earshot.

"Smart mouth. Rough." Red grabbed her by the hair again. "My kind of night." He pulled her into him once more, his belly squeezing the air out of her.

A hand appeared on Red's shoulder. He turned around to see Jericho towering over him. Clyde glanced over, scanning the room for Brendan and Petra.

"You with the band?" Jericho asked.

"Yeah. What's it to ya?"

"You know 'Gimme Three Steps' by Lynyrd Skynyrd?"

"Song's real old for someone your age," replied Red.

"Do you know it?" Jericho asked again, this time more sternly.

"I can play the opening lick."

"Then why don't you? Or you can get a three-step head start on getting out of my friends' faces. Either way, you're going to stop harassing them."

Jericho squeezed his hand tighter on Red's shoulder. Red winced in pain. He let go of Erika as he strained to alter Jericho's unmovable grip. Erika walked out of his reach and towards Abby. Her hand had found its way into Erika's.

"Which is it?" Jericho inquired.

Red shrugged Jericho's hand away, heading toward the rest of the band at the bar. Petra walked briskly towards Red, slapping him across the face with a swing that echoed throughout the building as she made contact. As Red regained balance, he armed himself with a vague explanation, only for Petra to swing again. How many times, she screamed, how many more gigs did they have to lose? Tara and Caroline joined Jericho as they all watched Clyde and Brenden try, and fail, to contain Petra's rage.

"You alright?" asked Tara.

"I think so," replied Abby.

Erika squeezed Abby's hand, realizing that she still hadn't let go of the grip. "I think she meant me."

"Both, actually," Tara answered.

"He was just a creep," said Erika. "Not every day you've got Jericho around though."

"I really don't like playing the 'I'm a giant Black man who's ex-military card', but it has its uses," stated Jericho.

"And you didn't even have to play the full card!" joked Abby, giving everyone a laugh.

"Thanks, Jericho," said Erika.

"Don't mention it. Good job on the bite, people usually forget how dangerous these things are." He tapped his teeth together and smiled. Erika laughed.

The group cleaned up their drinks and left the bar, their excitement for a night out tempered by Abby's encounter with Red. Erika and Abby drove directly home. As Erika deviated from her normal path home to avoid red lights she'd have to stop at, Abby held her hand tightly, trying her hardest to hold back tears.

12
Nothing Good Happens After Midnight

December 17, 2033

Erika and Abby walked back into their apartment, both of them stomping the snow off of their shoes in the entryway. While Erika took off her coat and put it in the closet, Abby stood just inside the door, her eyes staring at the floor in front of her.

Erika walked into the kitchen. She grabbed a cold piece of pizza and stuffed one-third of the slice into her mouth in one bite. She looked up from her food and saw Abby standing in the doorway to the room, silent and with tears welling up in her eyes.

"You want anything while I'm up?" Erika asked, her mouth half-full of pizza.

"Vodka and something to mix it in," replied Abby. "I need a drink."

"Any food?"

"Did you buy anything?"

Erika opened the fridge door again, peeking inside. Abby's new job had allowed them to keep a bit more food around, though with grocery shopping being tomorrow, their stocks were still pretty bare.

"There's ham or peanut butter for a sandwich," Erika said.

Abby shook her head.

"Alright," continued Erika. "Well, there's ramen in the cabinet. Instant mashed potatoes and some corn too, I think."

Abby contorted her lips to the side, nothing Erika listed off appealing to her. Erika poked her head in the freezer, finding only bottles of alcohol and ice packs. She glanced down at her half-eaten slice of pizza before holding it out towards Abby. The gesture made Abby chuckle.

"Green peppers on pizza is disgusting," said Abby.

"You know, it's typically the pineapple that upsets people," replied Erika.

"And they're wrong. Especially if you're pairing it with ham."

"There's a full piece still in the fridge if you'd rather not have my germs on it."

"Is there anywhere delivering this late?" Abby asked.

Erika held up the half slice of pizza again.

"This is it," Erika answered. "Are you not okay with picking the peppers off?"

"I want a sub. Or at least something warm that I can dip in marinara sauce."

"They have cheesy breadsticks."

"Shit. That's the answer."

"Right? We'll have to get pop too if you want more than one drink."

"Yes please," said Abby. "I'll go order. Anything you want?"

"Make the cheesy breadsticks a double order," replied Erika.

Abby went to the living room and called the pizza shop. Erika found Abby's love of calling restaurants to order food befuddling, but endearing. The novelty of it to a conscientia was the exact opposite of how Erika felt about the act. Fortunately, most places had replaced the practice with electronic ordering in some fashion. Erika divided what little brown pop was in the refrigerator into two glasses, topping both off with ample doses of vodka. She took the drinks into the living room as she heard Abby end her call.

"Twenty-five minutes or so," said Abby. "They must be dead."

"I'd hope so. It's almost three in the morning," said Erika.

"It's 1:19," Abby corrected her.

"Seriously? My whole night is thrown off."

"Yeah."

Erika and Abby sat in silence, both occasionally sipping from their drinks. The pop had nearly gone flat, but Erika reasoned that with enough vodka in it, you could barely tell.

"I'm sorry," said Abby.

"Don't be," Erika replied.

They fell back into silence, Erika swirling the drink around her glass to watch what few bubbles of carbonation were still inside float to the top. Only three made it to the surface before the brown, syrupy liquid spun around in the glass with no additional excitement to catch Erika's attention.

"How long has it been?" Erika asked.

"Four minutes," replied Abby.

"You alright if I take a shower? I just want to kill some time before the food gets here."

"That's fine."

"You sure? If you need me I can –"

"Go. It's okay."

Erika grabbed her glass and threw her head back, downing the drink in one swift motion. She headed off to the shower, remembering as she entered the bathroom that she had taken one before they went out to the bar. Erika didn't want to take another shower, but felt committed to her plan, spending ten minutes standing under the hot water as it pelted her body. Most of her body still felt clean, though she did spend much of the shower scrubbing at her neck with a washcloth. Though they were no longer there, Erika could still feel Red's hands around her neck.

Erika toweled herself off and put on her favorite pair of pajamas. She walked back into the bathroom and stared into the mirror, which was still in the process of defogging from her shower. Her neck was lightly red, probably from the scrubbing, she reasoned. No fingerprints anywhere to be found – though that didn't stop Erika from staring and inspecting her neck for several minutes.

She walked back into the living room to the sound of a knock at the door. Erika opened the door and was greeted by a young woman with a pair of pizza boxes in her hand. Her long, brunette hair peeked out of the blue baseball cap that was part of her uniform.

"Erika?" the driver asked.

"Yeah."

"Cool. Here you go."

"Cute name," Erika said, reading the nametag on the delivery driver's shirt. Emilija.

"Thanks!" Emilija said. "My mom picked it out for me. Have a good night."

Erika twisted her body back into the apartment, kicking the door shut with her foot.

"What's the second box?" Erika inquired. "I know the big one is the breadsticks."

"Cinnamon sticks," replied Abby. "For dessert."

They sat on the futon, gorging on cheese and cinnamon sugar covered breadsticks and drinking boozy soda as they watched infomercials in the dark. Erika had forgotten how bad terrestrial television was after midnight, but the ridiculousness of the unitaskers being sold – along with the slapstick comedy used to demonstrate how hard life is when you don't have them – made her laugh heartily.

"Are humans actually like that?" asked Abby.

"Nah, we're much dumber," replied Erika.

"No, but…do people really not understand how to peel an orange?"

"It's hard when you don't have fingernails. Maybe?"

"The guy pushed the knife through his entire hand! How do

you even do that? And if you're that bad at understanding how knives work, how will that thing –"

"That thing," Erika interrupted, "is the Orange You Glad Fruit Peeling System and Coffee Grinder. Trademark."

Abby rolled her eyes at Erika's sarcastic tone.

"How would you use that thing without jamming it through your own hand?" Abby asked. "The coffee grinder attachment alone has five blades on it!"

"The five blades give you a closer shave," Erika said, smiling.

Abby gave Erika a playful push to the shoulder. Erika giggled, returning the light shove in kind. Abby grabbed the cushion next to her, and tried to land any hit against Erika's blockade. Erika grappled at the cushion before she found its edge, and pulled, drawing Abby into her. Abby's grip slipped; the cushion flew across the room as Abby landed on top of Erika. She laughed as Abby let out a cry of defeat, craning her neck to see where it had gone.

Giving up, Erika looked back and found Abby, their lips not even an inch apart. Before Erika could react, Abby kissed her. She pulled back, her eyes nervously scanning Erika for any signal, but Erika had barely moved.

"Sorry, I just –"

Abby's words were cut off by a hand weaving its way into her hair, and drawing her back down into Erika. Another hand moved down Abby's body, and slipped under her shirt. After a few moments, Erika twisted their bodies and pushed Abby down on the couch, pinning her down with her body weight as they made out.

"Stop it."

No.

"Stop it."

I've waited for this for years.

"You're going to hurt her."

Erika's kisses slowed.

I won't.

"You're going to break her heart. Again. She doesn't deserve that."

Erika stopped, sitting up on the couch by Abby's feet.

"Why did you stop?" asked Abby.

"I...I can't," replied Erika.

"Was that too fast? We can take this slow," said Abby.

Erika twiddled her thumbs and bit at her lip.

"We don't have to do this right now," continued Abby. "Another night."

Erika bit her lip harder, drawing the faintest amount of blood into her mouth.

"I just got caught up in the moment," Abby said, her voice accelerating the more she talked. "It just happened. And you were there. And, god. I couldn't help myself."

Say something.

"If this isn't what you want, I get it," said Abby frantically. "Or if it is what you want, but you're not ready, that's fine too."

Say something.

"It's just really hard for me," Abby continued, her voice on the verge of panic. "You're there and you're everything I ever wanted. And you kissed me tonight. And you saved me from those asshats."

Say something.

"And I appreciate it. And I appreciate you. So much. If you want this to be a thing now, great. If you need me to keep being patient, that's great too."

Fucking say something, Erika.

"I just need to know, Erika."

Abby stopped talking, looking up at Erika, her eyes begging

and pleading with Erika.

"Please?" Abby said timidly. "Just tell me."

Stop hurting her and say something. Time to be an adult.

Erika felt tears running down her face, but didn't know when she had started crying.

"I don't know," Erika mumbled. "I'm sorry."

She felt Abby scoot closer to her, leaving a small amount of space between them.

"What do you mean when you say you don't know?" Abby asked.

"I don't know."

"You must want something, right? You kissed me on the cheek earlier."

"I was just trying to help."

"You climbed on top of me and made out with me a few minutes ago."

"I know."

"Your hands were all over me."

"I know."

"Then how don't you know what you want?" Abby asked.

Erika couldn't answer. She couldn't explain why she was scared. Never mind Grace's voice inside her head constantly reminding her that she'd hurt Abby before.

"You know that not answering her is hurting her just as much as answering her would."

I know.

"Erika."

Erika snapped out of her thoughts, seeing that Abby was now standing in front of her instead of sitting beside her.

"Do you realize how confusing this is?" she asked.

Erika lowered her head, breaking her eye contact with Abby.

"I have never been able to get you out of my head," continued Abby. "You know this. You've always been my person. And if this is going to go somewhere, that's great. Even if that means I need to be patient."

Erika felt Abby's hands touch her shoulder.

"Look at me please," Abby said.

Erika did as Abby asked, her tear-stained face and bloodshot eyes finally facing Abby's.

"If I need to be patient, I will be," Abby repeated. "Do you understand?"

Erika nodded.

"I just need you to communicate with me," said Abby. "If you're not ready for this right now, that's okay. If you'll never want this, that's fine too. If you need time to figure out whatever the hell is going on in your head, I can respect that. The mixed messages are killing me."

"I'm sorry," Erika said, forcing out the words against her strangled voice.

"I know. Sleep on it?"

Erika got up from the couch, making her way to the kitchen with her nearly empty drink. She opened the freezer and topped her glass off with vodka, leaving the liquid inside tinted a pale brown from the remnants of the soda in the glass.

"Does it help?" Abby asked, watching Erika from the doorway.

"It helps quiet things down so I can sleep," replied Erika.

"You know if you need someone to talk to –"

"I know."

Erika grabbed the glass and started making her way to her room. She felt Abby's hand touch her shoulder, stopping her.

"Thank you for trying to help tonight," said Abby.

"Yeah. I'll do better next time."

Erika made her way to her bedroom and curled up under the covers. She closed her eyes, hoping her head would stop pounding. Within a few minutes, Erika was fast asleep.

"I'll love you until the day I don't exist! I'll love you until the day I don't exist! I'll love you! Please don't go!"

"Abby. I'm not going."

"But you just said you can't stay with me! You said you can't love me when you're going to get ridiculed and hated for loving who I am!"

"I'm wrong."

"What?"

"I'm wrong. And I'm so fucking sorry I ever said it."

Abby ran into Erika's arms, both of them holding each other as tightly as the possibly could.

"Don't ever scare me like that again," said Abby.

"I didn't mean it," Erika replied. "I didn't mean to fuck up your life."

"You didn–"

"I didn't mean to take away years of your life that you could have had to be happy with someone else."

"Erika, you di–"

"I'm so fucking sorry. I'm so so–"

Abby grabbed Erika by the back of her head and pulled her in for a long kiss. Erika smiled, returning the kiss back to Abby as she grabbed the back of Abby's shirt and crumpled it in her hand.

Erika bolted upright, her light golden-brown hair flying forward as she did so. She stared into the dark bedroom around her, taking a moment to recognize that the dream she was just having didn't actually happen. She carefully got out of bed, tiptoeing around her bedroom and out the door. Erika moved as quietly as she could through the kitchen, before arriving at the doorway separating the kitchen and living room. She peeked her head through the entrance, seeing Abby laying on the futon, reading one of the books from the bookshelf.

"Hey," said Abby. "Are you okay? I heard you screaming."

Erika shrugged.

"Just another part of being me," she said.

"Is there anything I can do to help you?"

Erika paused and thought. On one hand, this was the first time her recurring nightmare ever had a different ending. She felt like that had some level of importance and wanted to talk it through with someone. On the other hand, considering Abby's pleas from earlier in the evening, this also didn't feel like the right time to do so.

"Not tonight," answered Erika. "Maybe another time?"

"Whatever you want," Abby said. "I'm here if you need me."

Erika noticed a pile of books on the floor by the futon. She knelt beside them, picking through the stack. She recognized most of them as textbooks from the ill-conceived semester when she was a mythology and religion minor. But the book Abby was reading wasn't a textbook, rather, a very thin, worn book Erika vaguely remembered from her childhood.

"What are you reading?"

"A Dog of Flanders."

"I haven't read that in ages," said Erika. "Why are you reading such a sad story?"

"It's still a good story," replied Abby. "Not every story has to have a happy ending to be good."

Erika sighed, thinking about her recurring nightmare's different ending tonight. She walked back in her bedroom, grabbed her comforter and her pillow, and drug them out to the living room.

"What are you doing?" Abby questioned.

"I had a bad dream," replied Erika. "Well, kind of a bad dream. I don't want to talk about it, but I don't want to be alone either. So I'm going to sleep on the floor near you."

"Wouldn't me coming in your room be more comfortable for you?"

"I'm not doing that if I don't know what I want."

"Will you at least take the futon then?" asked Abby. "It doesn't hurt me to sleep on the floor."

"Fine," replied Erika. "Finish your book first though."

"I'm done already. I've read it four times tonight."

"Jesus. Why?"

"Not tonight," answered Abby. "Just get some rest."

13
Damselfly

Winter turned to spring, its cold snows melting away as grass and flowers began to peek through the mounds of fluffy, muddy decay lining lawns and curbs throughout the Midwest. Though the final day of March brought an unseasonably warm temperature of 72 degrees Fahrenheit to Indianapolis, many parts of the city still featured memories of winter in the form of piled, plowed, gray snow sitting in parking lot corners. Gone were the gargantuan peaks that stood ten to twelve feet high. Even those who enjoyed a few fluffy flakes recognized the remaining piles as eyesores, reminding the city's residents of the winter storm-filled few months that most would rather forget. Since Christmas, Erika had watched as the world around her suffered from the same slow, plodding change. In spite of the never-ending thaw, she felt the changes around her had arrived with the speed of a summertime lightning flash or the urgency of autumn leaves departing their trees.

After six long years as a customer service manager, Erika's repeated attempts at applying for a new job had finally paid off: she was now the manager of the call center's workforce management group. Instead of handling complaints, she'd handle staff and schedules – sure, it was a more background role, but it meant she'd be managing people she liked for a change. At least, that's what she'd thought. It wasn't long before Erika realized that most of her day consisted of having the four people who reported to her yell at the call center reps to get back on the phones. On the upside, it was less stress for more pay.

Meanwhile, Abby's job was progressing much quicker than Erika anticipated. Though she had only been working as a receptionist for a couple of months, Abby had managed to save most of her salary which, when combined with the stipend money that Amy had been providing her, had allowed her to get to the point where she could nearly afford Erika's apartment by herself. It had become routine for Abby to bring groceries home whenever she noticed Erika was running low on something. How Abby was so effective with money was impressive to Erika, and while she routinely reminded herself to ask Abby for tips, Erika never remembered to do so.

Part of why Erika could never remember to pick Abby's brain was because it seemed as though they had arrived at an unspoken agreement to continue being roommates. Abby could easily support herself and had met all the legal requirements to be able to be emancipated from Erika's custodianship. But anytime either of them was asked about this, both Erika and Abby brushed the question off, changing the subject to whatever else came to mind. Erika appreciated having the support, but she found comfort in the companionship even more.

The Friends of Al group had slowly morphed from Abby's support group to arguably Erika's closest friends. Tara, in particular, had become an invaluable resource to Erika, her financial prowess coming in handy when Erika needed advice as to how to handle her still recovering budget. Jericho and Caroline often invited Erika and Abby out to Side Pocket to play pool with them. And while Minerva and Cecil were around Erika infrequently, Erika even found herself growing to tolerate Minerva. Most of this last development was Cecil's fault, as Erika couldn't help but smile at Cecil's insistence on joking around at every opportunity. Erika found Minerva's strict straight-man persona paired with Cecil's jester mentality to be amusing, making Minerva ever-so-slightly less off-putting as a person.

But perhaps the most noticeable change for Erika was the new direction her recurring nightmare had taken. Following the encounter with Red at Side Pocket, the nightmare that had tormented her for years suddenly changed its ending. The screams of terror that had haunted Erika for nearly a decade where gone. Instead, as Abby's cries grew louder, Erika would reach into the screen, desperately trying to pull Abby towards her. She pulls, the screen flashing with brilliant, violent sparks that fill the air around her. Abby suddenly breaks free of her unseen shackles, the force ending both of them tumbling across the room. The computer's light now gone, Erika and Abby embrace and kiss, silencing any doubt it was the right thing to do. As time passed, the dream had become longer and decidedly more erotic, going from kiss and make up, to kiss and literally anything that Erika had ever fantasized about. It was as if instead of looking for an apartment of her own, Abby had taken up residence in Erika's subconscious, making herself at home in Erika's dreams and in her bed.

These dreams only served to add to Erika's increasingly conflicted mindset about Abby. Erika knew that the best thing for Abby – as well as for herself – was for them to maintain their friendship and nothing more. She had watched Abby become a more confident individual; more human even. Abby rarely had moments where she had to stop and think how a human would react in a situation. She was instinctual and natural (to the untrained eye, that is).

Even so, there was the occasional issue. How Abby reacted to the kiss at Side Pocket – as well as what happened later that night – was the first that came to mind. In the moment, Erika felt that she had done the right thing in trying to act like Abby's girlfriend. Subconsciously, Erika didn't think there was a way she could have been more convincing, even with a few months in the rearview mirror to think it over. There's only so much you can do to convince drunken, testosterone-fueled assholes to lay off before a fight breaks out.

Yet, in spite of it all, Erika had hurt Abby. Erika hadn't yet made good on her promise to come clean with Abby about how she felt about her. This frustrated Abby and though Erika had reluctantly accepted this fact, it didn't make the following weeks any easier. Any argument they had would inevitably end in Abby making a statement about Erika's inability to communicate with her.

Though Erika was typically proud to see Abby's growth as a more human-like conscientia, this particular development was exhausting. Abby had developed a pettiness in their fights, holding a grudge much stronger than Erika could have anticipated. This line usually led to one or both of them storming out of the room, only for Abby to later apologize for what she had said when they eventually did make up. Erika's past didn't help matters in these moments. Though their fights began as the trivial things roommates quarrel about – lights being left on, dishes not being done, schedules being forgotten – whenever that night would come into the equation, the bickering switched from a disagreement between friends and into a fight between estranged lovers.

Aside from their fights, their romantic past nearly never came up. Erika found Abby to be exceptionally patient in spite of the occasional snide remark during a fight. And though Erika knew Abby still had feelings for her, it was clear that she did her best to hide them most days. There was one exception, however.

Erika had subconsciously worried how Valentine's Day would go from the moment the calendar turned to February 2034. Though she didn't expect Abby to try to do anything on the day, the thought constantly lingered in the back of her mind. Much to Erika's relief, the day itself came and went without so much as a mention of the holiday itself. The next day – a Wednesday – Erika went to work and came home with a quiet evening planned: a microwave meal, a hot shower, and a good book in bed. Instead, she walked in to find six large heart-shaped boxes of chocolate stacked on her desk.

"What in the world?" asked Erika.

"They were on sale!" shouted Abby triumphantly.

"And?"

"And you like chocolate."

"Why?"

"Because chocolate tastes good?"

"Why six of them?"

"Why not?"

"This is so much chocolate," Erika said.

"I know," replied Abby, a grin widening across her face. "I'm quite proud of myself."

Erika didn't know where to begin. She didn't want another

fight, least of all today.

"Abby –"

"You should have seen the checkout guy's reaction when I walked up with six giant boxes of chocolate in my arms."

Abby paused, noticing Erika's concerned expression.

"You don't have to share them with me."

"Don't be ridiculous," replied Erika. "The chocolate covered cherries are mine."

"Would you like some wine with them?"

"Wine?" asked Erika.

Abby bounded off to the kitchen, where she produced four bottles of wine from the pantry, then skipped back into the living room.

"Red, white, rosé, or whatever's in this fourth bottle that I didn't bother to look at?" Abby asked.

"Why do you have four bottles of wine?"

"Well, five was right out."

"But, again, why?"

"Erika, just let me have the stupid chocolate and wine-fueled Valentine's Day I want," said Abby. "Please?"

Erika couldn't argue with that. And so, they ate chocolate and drank wine until the wee hours of the morning. Erika awoke the next morning with her head on Abby's lap.

"Hey," said Abby.

Erika groaned. "Why so loud?"

"It's my normal voice."

"I don't like it. It's too loud."

"Sorry," Abby said, her voice closer to a whisper now.

"What time is it?" Erika grumbled.

"Six thirty-five," replied Abby.

"How did I manage to wake up before my alarm?"

"Because you didn't sleep in your bed?"

"Yeah. Sorry about that."

"I mean, I know you didn't mean it," said Abby. "You just kind of passed out against me at one point."

"You could have helped me to bed," Erika replied.

"You looked comfortable."

Lights from a car pulling into the rear parking lot cut through the darkness of the kitchen, the brightness flooding into the living room and into Erika's eyes. She groaned again, squinting as hard as her dry eyes would allow.

"Can I stay home today?" asked Erika. "I don't wanna go."

"It's your job," said Abby. "You're an adult."

"Mmmmmk. I'm going to go lay in bed then."

Erika climbed off of the couch and started walking to the bedroom.

"You should go to work. You've still got shit for money."

I lost forty hours of PTO last year. I need to learn to use it sometimes.

"If you take a day off, people will think you're a slacker. You think you got that promotion because you take days off?"

Erika stopped, leaning against the kitchen wall to support her. She felt Abby's hand touch her back, helping to steady her.

"You okay?" Abby asked.

"I should go to work," replied Erika.

"You don't look okay," Abby retorted. "Rest."

"It's my own fault. I should go."

Erika entered her bedroom and turned on the overhead light. She screamed as the light met her eyes, covering them too late to block the brightness.

"Stay home," Abby said, pleading.

"She's not helping you."

"No," replied Erika.

"What if I stay home with you and take care of you?" asked Abby.

"It's just a hangover."

"And it's just my fault you had so much wine."

"She doesn't actually care. She just feels guilty."

"You didn't make me drink it."

"Why won't she listen?"

"Erika –"

"STOP!" Erika shouted.

Abby fell silent, backing a few steps away from Erika.

"I can take care of myself!" Erika continued. "I don't need you to play nurse or to feel sorry for me or whatever's going on."

"I didn't mean anything –"

"Then let me fix my own mistakes."

"But I want to help. I care about you."

"I care about you too."

Erika stopped. It just came out of her mouth. She couldn't stop it, but it was suddenly out. For the shock on her own face, Abby looked twice as stunned, her mouth ajar from surprise.

"You what now?" asked Abby.

"I care about you too," Erika restated. "And that's why I don't want you to help me."

Abby's gaze shifted from surprise to confusion.

"I don't follow."

"Me either. I still don't know how I feel."

"That doesn't mean you can't let me help you at all."

A jolt of pain went through Erika's head, causing her to wince.

"Look," Erika said. "I'll stay home today. But go to work. Please?"

Abby smiled slightly.

"Alright," she replied. "But go to bed."

"Way ahead of you."

After Erika's nap, she left the bedroom to find that Abby had gone to work as she'd promised. She had also filled the fridge with a stockpile of water and sports drinks, a box of microwave bacon, and a note.

Get hydrated. Eat some food. Rest. Please? – A.

14
Exit Strategy

"We must not only call for a return to a simpler time in American history, but we must also take action. Words do nothing if they are not acted on by people who know, in their hearts, in their minds, and in their God-given souls, that those words are right, just, and in the best interest of the improvement of society," said Congressman David Chuck of Indiana.

Congressman Chuck was positioned at the far left of a line of five podiums arranged in front of a slew of cameras broadcasting to any and all media outlets that would pick them up. He took a drink from a small bottle of water following his turn speaking. Next in line, a bespectacled Caucasian man with wispy dark grey hair shuffled his notes and began to speak.

"This is not just about taking action against a threat the five of us have tried to warn you against," said Congressman Michael Hayward of South Dakota. "It is about justice for families torn apart by the mechanical menace that the freaks and degenerates of society have chosen to let loose on America. While we were naive enough to let it happen, thinking there would be no negative consequences, we have seen the error of our ways."

The cameras shifted past the man in the middle of the line and focused on the fourth man in line. Like his peers, he wore a dark blue suit with an American flag lapel pin next to his microphone. He was nearly bald, the result of years of service to his country both in the military and in government.

"I can no longer stand idly by as my constituents leave me message after message with horror stories as to how this android menace has affected them personally," said Congressman Sherman Overton of South Carolina in his slow Southern drawl. "Just this morning, I received a message from a mother horrified that her son saw a young woman holding hands with a robot on the street. How was she supposed to explain this to her impressionable child?"

From behind the cameras, a young brunette woman in a business suit elbowed the man beside her.

"Did he actually get that call?" asked the woman.

"Probably not," said the man, who was Congressman Overton's personal assistant. "He's a racist chucklefuck who likes making up stories, but he's only here because he's trying to get extra funding for the state's infrastructure tacked on to this bill."

"If he's so bad, why work for him?"

"Pays the bills."

The fifth man in line took his turn to speak.

"If this were just about love and relationships – neither of which computers are capable of having – we could address this culturally over time," said Congressman Abner Junius of Idaho. "Two nights ago, an android killed Marienne Lakini and her three children, Talus, Meghan, and Katie right here in New Philadelphia. I, like all of the other Representatives here today, are not only here to support Congressman White and to co-sponsor his bill, but to make sure that Marienne, Talus, Meghan, and Katie get the justice they deserve."

The man in the middle of the line adjusted his tie and waited for the cameras to focus on him. He was the youngest of the five men standing at pulpits on this cloudy day, but he also drew the most focus of anyone in the room. His steely gray eyes and perfectly shaped black hair combined with his smiling, yet serious face to create this magnetic attraction that always seemed to draw cameras to it. He cleared his throat quietly and began to speak.

"Today," began Congressman Eugene White of Ohio, "Congressman Chuck, Congressman Hayward, Congressman Overton, Congressman Junius, and I, along with Congressman Cristina Abbott of Kansas who could not be here today, will be co-sponsoring and introducing the Protecting Americans from Digitized Destruction, Corruption, and Violence Act. This bill will not only aim to keep American families safe from conscientia and their horrid impacts on our moral fiber but also will impose harsh penalties on violent, miscreant conscientia and the individuals who choose to own them and associate with them.

"Though we recognize that a similar bill was defeated in committee last year, it is my hope that the unfortunate trend of android on human crimes – both violent and sexual – has caused more members of our legislative bodies to recognize the clear and present danger they present to us. America has overcorrected to the technologically-driven liberal agenda that we're on for far too long now. It is our responsibility, nay, our duty, as guardians of liberty and of the human race to ensure that the next Marienne Lakini will receive better justice than Marienne did.

"Make no mistake: there WILL be a next Marienne. I can personally assure you of that. I have watched as my hometown of Dover, Ohio, has descended into a hedonistic society where the youth of our country think it's acceptable to form relationships, partnerships, and even marriages with these subhumans.

"To my counterparts on the left who say this is nothing more than a ploy driven by hate, I assure you that nothing could be further from the truth. We are proposing this bill not because we hate people who are different. We are proposing this bill because we love America. We love the way this country has always been. And make no mistake, we are determined to ensure the country that we love does not spiral to the same depths that befell Sodom and Gomorrah."

*****

Abby ended her reception of the transmission of the press conference. She leaned back onto the couch, synthetic tears rolling down her face. From across the room, Erika sat in her chair and watched, afraid to get too close.

"Why did you watch it?" asked Erika.

Abby clenched her eyes tightly, doing anything she could to keep from looking at Erika's worried expression.

"Abby?"

Abby shook her head, her sobbing too hard to speak.

"Abby."

Erika got up from her chair and walked over to Abby, wrapping her arms around her. Abby shook her head again and half-heartedly tried to push away.

"Don't," Abby grumbled. "Just don't."

"It's just a bill, Abby," replied Erika. "We don't know if it's going to pass. We don't even know if it'll end up looking anything like what they're describing now."

"Why do they hate us? What did we do?"

"Not everyone –"

"Enough people do."

"Abby –"

"Humans made us for a reason, and what, it doesn't matter now?" Abby's breath was jagged, juggling crying with frustration. "No one needs us anymore, we're just taking up space? Oh right, because everyone misses heavy lifting, delivering mail, and caring for the dying elderly. And don't forget about picking fruit. I'm sure there's some blueberry farm owner tripping over their feet to pay a teenager a dollar an hour because farms are exempt from minimum wage laws."

Erika sighed. She pulled Abby in closer and hugged her more tightly. Abby didn't resist this time, returning her embrace as her crying slowed.

"We should run away," said Abby.

"Say what now?"

"No...no…" Abby stammered. "Not like that. Just to somewhere more…accepting. Or something."

"Where do you have in mind?" asked Erika.

"Canada's nice this time of year."

"It's April. Calgary is still buried under a metric fuckton of snow. And before you correct me, they do measure their fucktons in metric in Canada."

"I was thinking more of Nova Scotia than Alberta," replied Abby.

"We don't have the money to just move," continued Erika. "Plus, the Canadian citizenship requirements aren't as simple as 'oh hey, I want to move to Canada, I'm a citizen now, eh'."

"I know, I know!" Abby was becoming frenetic. "I just want to be safe. That isn't too much to ask for, is it? I used to feel safe. Now I don't want to leave the apartment."

"I know," replied Erika.

Abby nuzzled in closer to Erika's hug, prompting Erika to hold onto her tighter.

"Just a few more seconds?" asked Abby.

Erika nodded and kept her arms around Abby until Abby started to pull away.

"I need to get ready for work," said Abby.

"Do you want me to drive you?" Erika asked.

"No, I can get there fine. Take care of yourself for the day. The only way we can get through this is if we agree to take shifts."

Abby walked off to the now shared closet in Erika's room to get dressed for work – a suggestion Erika had made as Abby began to accumulate a wardrobe for her new job. Erika stared into space, perplexed at Abby's statement before leaving the room. Shifts for what?

After Abby left for work, Erika called Minerva. Even if she wasn't a huge fan of Minerva, Erika figured she'd be the right person to give her some advice as to how to help Abby.

"Why don't you come to dinner with us?" asked Minerva. "I could sit here and tell you how you should interact with Abby all day. But I think it'd be more beneficial for you and Abby both if you saw how Cecil and I are handling it in person."

"I guess that's fine," said Erika. "When?"

"Next Saturday? I assume tonight is too soon."

"Abby works late tonight, so next weekend would be better anyway. Listen, Minerva, I appreciate you doing this."

"I know you do," Minerva replied. "It's good to see you putting in the effort for Abby."

They said their goodbyes and ended the call. Despite her helpfulness, Minerva was still a dick in Erika's mind. Erika spent the rest of the day cleaning up the apartment – an activity that was sorely needed but that Erika routinely put off as long as she could – and trying to keep out of her own brain.

This last task was, as it always was, the hardest for Erika to accomplish. Her mind routinely flickered back to the press conference she had watched with Abby earlier in the day. It was one thing to hear stodgy old people talk about conscientia in the way they did. Erika figured that it was just part of a cycle. There were people who hated conscientia. Before that, they hated the LGBTQ+ community. Before that, they hated Blacks. Before that, they hated women. Before that, it was the Irish, or the news media, or immigrants, or Blacks and women again. It was hard to keep track of. Not that it wasn't all cyclical anyway. Not that any of the hate ever stopped.

Granted, this was an oversimplification of history, but it was, at its very core, accurate, even if the linear nature of things was not. Those who had power and felt like they were losing their power in some way were always looking for someone to place the blame on.

Seeing Congressman Eugene White as the ringleader of the group was more jarring. He wasn't young by any metric except in comparison to the others standing on stage with him – as he was nearly twelve years Erika's senior. Even so, he touted himself as the speaker for a new breed of youth. If someone that comparatively young and charismatic could spout hateful rhetoric so easily, all while being in a position of power, what did that actually mean for the next generation? Were Erika's peers more bigoted than she realized?

"This is why you broke things off with her in the first place."

We're just friends. And roommates.

"And no government has ever done anything bad to people who associated themselves with a persecuted class. Nope. Never."

That doesn't mean that's what'll happen here.

"Right. Of course not. It would only be a problem if someone found out about your past."

The past is the past.

"Or Abby's feelings about you now."

Stop it.

"Or whatever you're calling the mental gymnastics you call your feelings about her."

Nothing is going to happen.

"Until it does."

No one is coming after us.

"How do you know there's not a gunman in the courtyard right now waiting for her to come back?"

It was this part of Grace that Erika hated the most. Sure, the biting rhetoric and criticism hurt. Yes, Grace routinely made her rethink what she'd done and change her mood on a dime. But Erika knew no one was outside. It was irrational. There was no reason to indulge this paranoia.

"How do you know?"

Because it's irrational. And I know it is.

"It's irrational for a normal person to have a gunman waiting for them. It's not irrational for someone who's hated to have someone waiting for them. Or for the ones they care about. Go on. Look. It'll make you feel better."

Erika walked to the living room window and stared out into the courtyard in front of her building. There was no gunman – no angry mob with pitchforks and torches was here. Not yet, anyway. Erika went to check the parking lot behind the building.

No furious protestors there either. Just the old guy from apartment 1B, standing by the edge of the grass, shirtless, puffing on a cigarette in his pajama pants. At least that would never change.

With a deep breath, Erika finished her cleaning and made herself dinner. Though Abby did her best to make sure Erika ate reasonably healthy, Saturday nights were the one time that Erika could eat whatever garbage she wanted and not feel Abby's judgmental, though well-meaning, eyes staring at her. Erika had snuck two ham and cheddar Hot Pockets into the back of the freezer earlier in the week solely for this purpose. She microwaved her dinner, mixed herself a vodka cranberry, and took them into her bedroom. A few minutes after finishing off the last of the cocktail, Erika heard the front door unlock. Abby bounded into the room excitedly.

"Erika!" she shouted. "What are you doing?"

"What am I about to be doing?" Erika replied.

"Going out to dinner, dessert, or drinks, depending on if you've eaten and if you want to be sober."

"I had junk food."

"Hot Pockets again?"

"You know it."

"Was it at least any of the kinds with vegetables in them?" Abby asked as she sighed.

"Why would you ruin a perfectly good Hot Pocket with vegetables?" Erika said, disgusted.

"They're good for you!"

"It had cheese in it. Cheese comes from cows. They're second-hand vegetables."

Abby rolled her eyes.

"We're celebrating," she said, "or at least I am. I got promoted. I'm now an administrative assistant II. Or maybe it's pronounced administrative assistant eye-eye. Either way."

"Congratu-fucking-lations!" Erika shouted as she climbed out of bed. "You're right. Let's celebrate. How's dessert and drinks sound?"

"In that order?" asked Abby.

"Of course," replied Erika. "That's the best order."

They made their way out of the apartment. Erika had been doubly strategic with her suggestion of dessert and drinks. First, it allowed her to eat more junk food, which likely meant ice cream if Abby was picking. Second, and perhaps more importantly, the drinks would allow Erika to drown out that nagging feeling that some morning she'd wake up and the angry mob would be in her apartment's courtyard for real.

15
Catalyst

"The key to physical comedy is knowing when your audience won't see the humor in whatever it is you're doing," said Cecil as he gestured grandly to the restaurant patrons seated around him, unaware of their role as his audience. Abby, however, looked on in rapt attention as Cecil spoke.

"I learned this the hard way, of course," he continued. "Do you know what happens when you perform suddenly forgetting how to stand while in public?"

"I'm guessing it wasn't laughter," Abby said, chuckling a little.

"There was plenty of laughter," replied Cecil.

"Up until the police officer thought you'd had a heart attack," Minerva interrupted.

"Right. Well –"

"He started to call an ambulance, Cecil!"

"My point is," continued Cecil, "that knowing your environment is important. Take the same scene at a stage show, it would have produced uproarious laughter without a doubt, particularly given the right script. But if you're a street performer –"

"An unlicensed one," Minerva interrupted again.

"In a public place –"

"With no sign, no announcement –"

"You always run the risk of someone – even a well-meaning person – not knowing you're joking," Cecil pressed on. "That's when your comedy can backfire."

"We had a guy at the call center that liked to do that,"

interjected Erika.

"Be funny?" asked Cecil.

"Collapse. Or pretend to," replied Erika. "One of the other supervisors didn't know and started calling an ambulance because he thought the guy, you know, actually collapsed."

"Do people pass out often?" asked Minerva.

"You'd be surprised. There's a lot of medical emergencies when half of your staff is –"

Erika trailed off. The next words out of her mouth were going to be 'morbidly obese'. Which was true. Despite her company's best efforts to implement healthy living programs and other wellness-related items, most of the staff sat for eight hours a day – people would inherently gain weight. Back when Erika was a front-line employee, she had fallen into the same trap, gaining nearly thirty pounds in her first year, before spending the next four years working it back off. A person of Minerva's size and attitude, however, was not the ideal audience for this blunt honesty.

"–filled with people who have a history of medical problems," Erika said, finishing her sentence.

Minerva shot Erika a confused sneer, though her focus was quickly broken by Cecil's return to his dramatic lecture.

"Comedy isn't about getting people to like you," he said. "It's merely a way in the door. A misdirection, if you will. Being funny is just one way to get someone to pay attention to you. Once you have that attention, it's up to you to make them like you."

"What's the funniest thing you've ever seen someone do?" asked Abby.

"That's an interesting question," replied Cecil, leaning back in his chair, lost in thought as he searched his memories. "Something unprompted or as part of a performance?"

"Whatever was the funniest."

"Hm…" Cecil sipped at his glass before landing on a good story. "Ah, yes. A few years back, I was in this play – the name of it escapes me at the moment – with this gentleman named Brighton Mercy."

"Great name," interjected Erika.

"Very," replied Cecil. "If he hadn't gone into theater, I was hoping he'd develop a career as a hitman. Anyway. Brighton was playing this airheaded side character who was dating one of the incredibly serious lead female characters. They're supposed to have this dramatic fight where the woman realizes that Brighton's character is holding her back from everything she could be in life.

"So they're having this intense fight – screaming, crying, throwing things – the whole lot. It's supposed to leave the audience feeling incredibly awkward. Then at the end of it, Brighton's character becomes all serious, suggests they get ready for work, kicking off the events that lead to him eventually leaving her.

"We're having one of our final rehearsals before opening and they're running through their fight. They get to the moment where there's supposed to be this tense silence, followed by Brighton saying they should get ready. Instead, he says 'I'm going to go slip on a pair of black slacks'.

"Well, Brighton walks over to the bed where there are clothes scattered around it on the floor. Sure enough, he goes over to his black slacks…and slips on it like it's a banana peel! His legs fly into the air and he crashes to the floor. His poor partner was concerned he'd killed himself. To be fair, Brighton sold it like death. But when she gets over there, Brighton's laughing his ass off, saying how he's always wanted to make that joke."

Cecil wiped away tears of laughter from his eyes as his table struggled to maintain composure. Minerva rolled her eyes, though she couldn't help but smile at Cecil's story. Erika was barely keeping upright.

"So what happened?" Abby asked, suffering from an extreme case of the giggles.

"Our director told him to do exactly that every time going forward!" replied Cecil. "His character was always making jokes, even in the darkest moments, and it just fit with the real concern followed by constant disappointment of the character he was paired with. It was a thing of beauty."

Erika shuffled in her seat and smiled to herself while Abby did everything she could to refrain from literally being on the floor laughing. Minerva sighed and smiled at Cecil, before looking around for a waiter to flag down to refill their drinks.

"I'll be right back," said Erika as she got up from the table. "If I see a waiter on my way, I'll send them your way."

"That'd be great," replied Minerva.

Erika walked toward the bathroom, her small, yellow purse clutched in her hand as she walked. Once she was sufficiently out of earshot, Minerva nudged Cecil, who abruptly stopped his story.

"Are things still going well for you?" Minerva asked, a sense of urgency in her voice.

"Yeah, they are," replied Abby, giggles finally waning. "I really don't have anything to complain about."

"That's great to hear!" Cecil said excitedly. "See, Minerva, there's nothing to worry about."

Minerva ignored Cecil.

"You can financially support yourself now?" she asked.

"Yes," Abby replied, her voice tinted with a hint of confusion.

"Even if she gets scared off by being associated with you again?"

"I really wish Amy hadn't shared that with you."

"Well, she did. I'm only looking out for you."

"I'm not the one that needs it, it's Erika," replied Abby. "She's more fragile than she lets on. Don't get me wrong, she's a strong woman. But being human, she's fearful sometimes, even when she doesn't need to be."

"Is she okay?" asked Cecil.

"I think," replied Abby. "I wish she'd open up to me more so I could help her. Or at least so that I could get her talking to someone who could help her better than I can."

"You think she needs someone professional? Is she okay?" Cecil inquired.

Abby shrugged and sipped at her drink while Minerva stirred hers. The wheels were turning in Minerva's head – Abby could see that much. But she wasn't sure where she was going with her line of questioning.

"You know she was the one to suggest dinner with us, not me?" questioned Minerva.

"So?" replied Abby.

"She wanted advice for how to help you, yet couldn't just ask for it. She had to bring you along."

"Maybe Erika's just nervous?" Cecil interjected.

"She doesn't like asking for help," said Abby. "The fact that she did is great progress."

"I suppose," Minerva replied.

"I'm not worried," continued Abby. "I've got myself in a good position to take care of myself, if not more."

"And will you need to?" Minerva asked again.

Abby took a deep breath and stared toward the bathroom, mentally willing Erika to come back. Almost as if her will became reality, Erika emerged, pausing as a waiter carrying two trays full of food crossed in front of her.

"I trust Erika not to go anywhere," Abby said.

"Good!" Cecil said triumphantly.

Minerva sighed deeply, then gave a small, reluctant smile.

"It's a start," she said.

"Sorry about that," Erika said as she walked up to the table.

"I take it we're still waiting on food?"

"I've got plenty more stories," replied Cecil. "Besides. The tiramisu is worth the wait."

As dinner concluded, everyone said their goodbyes. Cecil and Minerva watched from the restaurant entryway as Abby and Erika entered their car. Abby clutched a carryout container holding a slice of tiramisu close to her. It had been her first time trying the dessert but Abby liked it enough to declare it her favorite thing that she had ever eaten – with the possible exception of hot cocoa, that is. Erika spent a good portion of the after-dinner conversation trying to explain to Abby that both items could, in fact, be her favorites, as hot cocoa was a drink while tiramisu was a food. Abby knew this, but continued her argument out of principle – it amused her to wind Erika up.

"Do you actually think they'll be alright?" Cecil asked. "Or were you just putting on an act to keep Abby calm?"

"A little bit of both," replied Minerva. "I think. I'm trying to be hopeful for her."

"She's adapting better than most of the conscientia we've worked with before."

"Is that because she's better programmed or because we didn't know what we were doing before?"

"A little bit of both," replied Cecil, smiling.

He held Minerva's hand and led her out of the entryway onto the sidewalk in front of the restaurant. He attempted to turn to the right while Minerva tried to go to the left.

"Where are you going?" she asked.

"Let's take the scenic route back," he replied.

"Cecil, it's chilly out."

"Then we'll walk quickly."

Minerva rolled her eyes, then clutched Cecil's hand tighter and strode with him along the sidewalk. They walked in silence for some time before continuing on with their conversation.

"Do you think we'll get another case before Abby's is done?" asked Minerva.

"Depends how quickly Amy can get everything set up," said Cecil. "My guess is that we will, but you never can tell."

"I was so hoping to get to ten successes before we had to call it quits."

"Why would we quit? There's nothing illegal about what we're doing. It's just easing integration. That's a good thing."

"Just because there's nothing illegal doesn't mean people want us doing it."

"*Some* people," Cecil stressed. "The vast majority of people we interact with accept us and see us as an integral part of modern society."

"The vast majority of people we interact with are in our social silo, Cecil," retorted Minerva. "They're going to agree with us."

"Are you suggesting that most people wouldn't if given the chance?"

"I'm saying that it's getting more dangerous to do what we're doing."

Cecil came to a stop, Minerva stopping shortly thereafter.

"I don't think we're doing this just to help others," replied Cecil.

"What do you mean?" Minerva asked.

"You want to help others. But you also want to see those like us have the same opportunities we do, yes?"

"Of course."

"But they won't, will they? The fact is, we both have a good bit of money and are fairly well-connected. And that provides us with opportunities that we would not otherwise be able to have. Especially me."

"True."

"So we help Abby. And others like her get jobs that suit them, get involved in groups that allow them to learn and socialize. That's what you did for me. So why stop? I've been able to go further than I otherwise would have in life – that's because of you."

Minerva blushed. "Cecil, you're sweet."

"But it's not just a matter of being a spearhead to help other conscientia," replied Cecil. "At least, not to me."

Cecil bent down to the ground, resting his weight on a single knee in front of Minerva. From his jacket pocket, he produced a simple green velvet box.

"I don't want our relationship to just be about what we do for others," continued Cecil. "I want it to be about how far we can take us."

Minerva knelt down on the ground beside Cecil, smiling and hugging him as she began to cry.

"I have this whole speech planned," said Cecil.

"You can tell it to me when we get home," replied Minerva. "The answer is yes. The answer will always be yes."

16
Il Gioco Siciliano

July 15, 2034

"Is this common?" asked Abby. "Having a party to celebrate someone's engagement?"

"If it is, it's news to me," replied Erika. "I always assumed you'd just text people. Or, if I absolutely had to, call them."

Cecil and Minerva's small home felt tighter than normal on this particular Saturday afternoon. It wasn't often that they had company over, let alone enough to necessitate bringing up chairs from the basement. Then again, it's not every day that you're celebrating your engagement. Minerva felt it was worth the time and effort, even if it meant people – including Minerva herself – couldn't maneuver through her living room quite as comfortably as normal.

Seated around the living room were a smattering of Cecil and Minerva – though mostly Minerva's – closest friends, as well as former members of the Friends of Al. Three of Minerva's work colleagues from the communications department sat closest to the door. Minerva had worked with Dr. Janice Cole, Professor Marian Lopez, and Dr. Micah Christensen-Alt for several years, though she rarely interacted with them outside of work. They were the quintessential work friends, in that the group was inseparable during the day, though they rarely spoke outside of the university's halls. The academics sipped margaritas as they looked at pictures on Professor Lopez's phone, laughing about something new every few minutes that would spiral them into an unrelated discussion.

On the couch, Cecil sat with Jericho and Caroline Fogg, patiently answering questions about their coming wedding as Caroline peppered them his way.

"Have you picked out colors yet?" Caroline asked.

"It's just something simple down at the courthouse," replied

161

Cecil.

"But you still have to have colors picked out. How do you know what you're going to wear if you haven't picked out colors?

"Minerva insists I need to wear pants. I figure I'm good so long as I do that."

"Good choice," interjected Jericho. "If you show up even before your wedding without pants, it's frowned upon. Or so I've been told."

"It was forty-five minutes before the wedding and you were still plastered from the bachelor party," replied Caroline.

"So were you."

"But I was in my dress!"

Against the far wall, Tara sat in front of an old wooden chessboard, contemplating her next move. Her opponent was Cerise Zurat, an Athena-class conscientia who was one of Minerva and Cecil's first integration projects. Cerise had long since moved out of Indianapolis, flying back to visit Ellie as she was able. Ellie's bubblegum hair made her stand out anywhere, especially against the intense chess match being played in front of her.

"Will you make a move?" Ellie shouted in a frustrated tone at Cerise.

"It's not her turn," said Tara, not bothered to look up from the board.

"It's not," replied Cerise, her expression focused on the pieces in front of her.

"I thought you just went," said Ellie.

"No," replied Tara. "I'm trying to determine how I want to handle Cerise's Sicilian Defense."

"It's a fair point," said Cerise. "If she botches this, her game could be in trouble."

"But this is taking forever! There's only been two moves!" Ellie exclaimed.

"The Sicilian Defense drastically changes the way both parties have to play their board," Cerise replied. "It puts me, as the black player, in an advantageous position nearly instantly."

"Cerise learned all about it from one of the masters of the tactic," Tara replied. "There's no one quite like Philidor to learn the Sicilian from."

"How long does this take?" asked Ellie.

"As long as it takes," said Tara.

"Is there supposed to be a clock? You know – to keep the game moving and what not?

"We don't play timed games," said Cerise.

"Indeed," added Tara. "We've been working on this same game for six years now."

"We only play when we see each other in person," said Cerise.

"Ahhh!" Ellie screamed, frustration rising in her voice. "I need a drink."

"Bring two," said Cerise, her focus unwavering. "We'll be here for a while, so you'll want more than one."

In the back corner of the room, nestled between the never-ending chess game and a plastic table filled with snacks, Abby and Erika sat, still unsure of the finer details of engagement party etiquette.

"Do you think Jericho and Caroline did this before their wedding?" asked Erika.

"From what I know, they had traditional bachelor and bachelorette parties," said Abby. "At least I presume going to strip clubs is traditional?"

"No clue. I've only gone to one."

"Strip club or bachelorette party?"

"Yes to both, but I meant bachelorette party," said Erika.

"Was it at a strip club?" Abby asked.

"No. We went to dinner at some Italian restaurant with overpriced wine, then spent hours on end at a casino. The bride was trying to win some extra money for the honeymoon, but ended up blowing it all on slots."

"Ouch."

"Yeah, it wasn't ideal."

"Was their partner mad?" asked Abby.

"I'm not sure he really cared," replied Erika. "Word is he was busy spending most of his free time with the bride's half-sister, so I don't think he really noticed."

"I can't imagine *that's* too common."

"Probably not. I didn't bother to ask questions. I was only there for the free drinks."

"Are you here for the free food?" Abby questioned as she motioned toward the snack table.

"I mean," replied Erika, "I'm not going to turn down pigs in a blanket."

Abby chuckled and grabbed Erika's plate off of her lap.

"Do you want anything else?" she asked.

"No. I'm going to grab another drink though. You want one?"

"So, I'm driving home?"

"This will be two," said Erika. "I can't even feel it yet."

"I'm going to make you blow me later to prove it."

Ellie, walking back in the room with two margaritas in hand, paused at Abby's statement before turning on her heels and heading back into the kitchen.

"That didn't come out like you meant it to, did it?" asked Erika.

"Not even a little," said Abby. "I really need to remember not everyone has a built-in breathalyzer."

Erika went into the kitchen where she noticed Ellie leaning over the sink, a drink still in each hand, laughing so hard she was crying. As Erika reached for the freezer to get a bottle of vodka, she noticed the soft sound of Minerva's voice coming from the far end of the hallway. She sounded like she was shouting, yet doing her best to keep whatever she was saying under her breath. Erika's curiosity got the best of her, leading her to follow the noises down the hall to a spare bedroom.

Erika peeked her head into the doorway, trying to keep her body out of sight from inside the room. Minerva was pacing back and forth, talking into a headset as her arms moved in animated motions.

"I'm not wanting you there for him!" Minerva hissed, trying her best to keep her voice calm and quiet as she did so. "I want you there for me."

Erika shuffled her weight towards her front foot, leaning harder against the door frame as she did so. In moving, she bumped the door further into the bedroom, its hinges squeaking as it moved a few inches further into the room. Erika froze, but Minerva was too intently focused on what the person on the other end of the headset was saying to notice.

"Because I'm your fucking daughter and it's my wedding!" she said.

Minerva paused, startled by whatever was said back to her.

"Sorry, I didn't mean...I know it wasn't very ladylike. I just want you...I'm not asking you to pay for the wedding. I...yes, I know that's off the table. I just want you there."

Minerva paused her pacing, staring at the wall in front of her. Erika could see Minerva's bloodshot eyes through the crack in the door.

"You went to all of the other kids' weddings. You even went to Christopher's wedding *after* finding out that she was an exotic dancer. You've spent most of my adult life begging me to get married, and now –"

Another pause. Minerva stepped forward a few paces, taking

her just out of Erika's line of sight.

"It shouldn't matter, mom. It's not like you and dad will be alone. Rebecca's doing her best to get a flight back from Dresden, so she'll be there."

Erika heard Minerva begin to tear up during the next pause.

"Yeah," Minerva said quietly. "I understand. If you change your mind, you know when everything is. Uh huh. I love you too."

Minerva took the headset off her ears, placing it down on the dresser near her. She strode a few steps across the room, sitting on the foot of the bed. Erika lightly knocked on the door, the soft rapping of her knuckles barely noticeable over the similarly quiet sounds of Minerva crying. Minerva took a few moments and gathered herself, then made her way to the door.

"Does someone need me?" Minerva asked, confused why Erika would be standing outside of her bedroom.

"No," Erika replied. "I went looking for the bathroom and got lost."

"It's the one behind you," said Minerva, pointing to the door across the hall.

"Right. Thanks."

Erika entered the room and closed the door behind her. She heard Minerva latch the bedroom door shut, though Erika was unsure if she had reentered the room or not.

"How was your 'we're not so different, you and I' moment?"

That just sucks. I can't imagine how she feels.

"Can't you? I feel like you at least have some idea."

Grace wasn't wrong. There was an outside chance Kaytie Edens wouldn't come to Erika's wedding regardless of who she was marrying, never mind if it were a conscientia.

Erika sighed. She finished using the restroom, washed her hands, and made her way back out to the party.

"Did you get lost?" asked Abby.

"Briefly," replied Erika. "I overheard something I wasn't supposed to."

"Oh? Want to talk about it?"

"Let's just try to enjoy the party."

17
Unmistakably Close

"Are weddings as exciting as people claim them to be?" asked Abby.

"No," replied Erika. "Weddings are a horribly boring waste of a weekend afternoon if you don't know the people getting married – and not much better if you do know the people."

"Even if you like them?"

"It helps. But that doesn't make the wedding itself better."

"I thought people liked weddings," Abby said, her voice wavering in confusion.

"What most people like is the reception, not the wedding," replied Erika. "That's where most of the fun happens. There's booze, dancing, food, booze, cake, drunken speeches from friends and family, booze, the occasional fistfight, music, booze –"

"Are you trying to hint at something?"

"We want booooze."

"I'm just saying that if weddings offered me a martini prior to the ceremony, I might find them more enjoyable," Erika answered.

"I can't imagine Minerva and Cecil's wedding will be too bad," said Abby. "They're starting at 2 pm and the reception starts at 2:45 pm. And the restaurant is in walking distance."

"It'll be boring, but fine," answered Erika as she fastened a bobby pin into her hair. "The fact that they chose to get married on a Friday afternoon helps. There aren't as many people out on Friday as there is on the weekend. Even if it is the summer."

Abby stepped through the door into Erika's bedroom, waiting patiently for Erika to turn around as she finished placing pins in her hair.

"As long as there's something greasy to eat somewhere along the way and a lot to drink, the wedding will...holy fuck."

Erika turned around to face Abby, dropping the bobby pin she held between the fingers of her left hand in the process. Abby twirled around in the doorway, the edges of her Egyptian blue dress spinning just above her knees as she did so.

Goddamn.

"Goddamn."

"Do I look alright?" asked Abby.

"You look...um...uh..." stammered Erika.

"Oh no. It's terrible. Is it the dress or the shoes?"

"No."

"Oh god. It's my hair isn't it?"

"If you don't compliment her right fucking now, I will never let you sleep again."

"No no. You...look amazing."

Abby stood and stared at Erika, her right hand tugging at the ring she wore on the middle finger of her left hand. Despite not typically wearing jewelry, Abby insisted on having something more than the gifted torii necklace from Amy on at the wedding. She bit down slightly on her lower lip, waiting to see if Erika would say anything else.

"Sorry," Erika finally continued. "I just had a moment. You look wonderful."

"Thanks," replied Abby. "Should I do something with my hair?"

"We're leaving in five minutes. I'll barely have time if I don't hurry up. You haven't even started."

"Erika? Android here, remember? It takes ten seconds to change my hair if I spend the first nine sleeping."

"Right. Then yeah, do whatever you want."

Abby walked into the bathroom and stood in front of the mirror. Her shoulder length black hair was typically kept in a ponytail, though from what she knew about weddings – context given to her largely by Erika, Tara, and Jericho – she figured a ponytail was too informal. After switching between a handful of hairstyles, she settled on a wavy, flowing cut that lengthened her hair by two inches as well as removing her typical bangs. Abby popped back into Erika's room where Erika was fastening a faux-pearl bracelet around her wrist.

"This work?" she asked.

"Is it over the line to say you look beautiful again?"

"No. I feel it."

"Good," replied Erika. "You ready to go?"

"Yeah. I just need to remember to take the gift to the car when we go."

"Go on down. I'll be there in two minutes."

Erika sat on the edge of her bed and pulled her black high heels onto her feet. She had packed a pair of flats in her purse for the reception but felt like she should probably show up dressed nicely to the wedding. After she heard the door close, Erika quickly selected her dad's number and called him.

Dwight Edens' raspy baritone voice wasn't as powerful as Erika remembered it being as a child. She couldn't figure out if it was because he was aging or if her younger memory was playing a trick on her. Yet every time she called, Erika would be caught off guard by how timid his voice sounded.

"Hey sweetie," said Dwight.

"Hi Dad," replied Erika.

"Been a while since I've heard your voice. You caught me driving back from the grocery store."

"So, Mom's not with you then?"

"You're funny."

"I try."

"No, she's at some art and wine class," Dwight said. "I find them boring, but she turns out good work."

"Sounds like her," replied Erika. "Look, I can't talk long. I'm about to go to a wedding."

"And you're not calling me to avoid going?"

"For once, no."

"Are you alright? If you need me to call the police, start talking about root vegetables."

"It's a work friend," said Erika. "Kind of. Actually, she's not a work friend at all."

"Are you sure you're going to a wedding?" Dwight asked sarcastically.

"Yes. I'm just nervous."

"Hot date?"

"Sort of. I don't know what it is anymore."

"Is it finally Abby?"

Erika stared at the screen of her phone, watching the seconds count up on the call timer. She couldn't bring herself to answer, yet she couldn't figure out why.

"I'm not going to tell your mom," Dwight said, his voice even more calm and quiet than it had been when he answered. "She good to you?"

"She's a saint," replied Erika.

"Don't put anyone on that high of a pedestal. Their image will break a lot more when they fall."

"Then she's kinder than I deserve. Better?"

"Much, though I think you still need to give yourself a bit more credit. Just have fun. Even if nothing comes of this –"

"Dad. Oh my god."

"Even if nothing comes of this," repeated Dwight, "just be the best person you can be."

"Okay. I need to go. I love you, Dad."

"I love you too. Good luck."

Erika ended the call and made her way to the car. Abby was already inside, singing along to a song Erika couldn't hear from outside the car. When she opened the door, the lyrics floated into the outside air, carried by a cool breeze from the air conditioner.

"Sorry about that," Erika said.

Abby held a finger her up in the air to silence her as she belted out the song's chorus in a haunting contralto voice. She finally acknowledged Erika standing by and paused the song.

"I don't know that one," said Erika.

"It's a song Amy used to listen to when she was working," replied Abby. "Every now and then, she'd want someone to talk to when working on a project – someone to bounce things off of as she tried to reason them out. I'd talk to her when she needed that. Mostly though, I'd stay quiet and just listen to music while she worked. Most of the songs faded into the background, but I fell in love with that one."

"Is it over?"

"There's more, but you came in mid-song."

"What's it called?"

"Hemorrhage. It's by a band named Fuel."

"You can start it over if you want. Sing to your heart's content."

"Good. It wasn't going to be a choice. Singing this song makes me happy."

Erika parked her car in a parking lot just down the road from the courthouse, giving her and Abby a short walk to the wedding. While the August air was hot, it wasn't nearly as humid as it had been earlier in the week, thanks to a strong line of thunderstorms that had blown through the city midweek. Erika tried to keep pace with Abby, excitement propelling her toward the venue at lightning speed.

Outside the courthouse, a homeless man wearing a fading gray hoodie sat on the sidewalk, a backpack at his feet and a nearly empty bottle of water in his hand. A pale gray cat – one that shared its fur color with the man's hoodie – nuzzled up against his leg, taking advantage of the shade the man's shadow provided. As Erika and Abby approached, the cat gave a big stretch and left its spot beside the man. It took a few steps forward, stopping directly in front of Abby and letting out a high-pitched meow. Abby chuckled at the cat, then turned to the man, digging her hands into the pockets of her dress.

"Is there anything I can do to help you?" she asked.

"Got a couple of bucks for more water?" he said, reaching out with his free hand to scratch the cat's head. The cat responded by nuzzling closer and purring softly.

Abby produced a five-dollar bill from her pocket, handing it to the man.

"May you be blessed, young lady," said the man, as he quickly pocketed the money. He gulped down the rest of his bottle of water, placing the empty bottle in his backpack after he had finished. He scooped the cat and the backpack up in one hand each before walking off toward the market around the corner.

"That was kind of you," said Erika.

Abby shrugged. "He needed water. It's hot out. You would have done the same."

Erika half smiled at Abby in an effort to try to give some level of confirmation to her. Flattering opinion, but still unlikely, she thought.

"It doesn't matter what I would have done," replied Erika, breaking away from her own train of thought. "It was still nice of you."

As they reached the county courthouse, they were met by a group of three men, all dressed in formal clothing, sitting on a bench and staring at their phones. At the feet of the tallest man was a pasteboard sign on a stick. She tilted her head to read the upside-down sign.

GO HOME 'ROBOT FUCKER', it read, complete with full capitalization and extraneous quotation marks.

"Do you think they'll do something?" asked Abby.

"Beyond yelling and being general assholes?" retorted Erika. "Probably not. It wouldn't be the first time some dipshit showed up to a wedding to yell about something."

"And you're not scared?"

"Oh no, I'm terrified. But there's only three of them and they're scrawny. Jericho could take them."

"Should I walk a bit ahead of you, just in case?" Abby asked.

"Please don't," said Erika. "There's safety in numbers, even if that number is two."

Erika and Abby entered the courthouse, cleared security, and made their way to the small room where the county processed small, quick marriage ceremonies. The watch on Erika's wrist read 1:56 pm, but they were still one of the last ones to arrive. Ellie Zurat came bounding down the hallway after them, her pink hair bouncing off her shoulders as she ran. As she entered the room, the officiant motioned at her to shut the door behind her.

"Is everyone finally here?" the officiant asked as she pushed her wire-rimmed glasses up the bridge of her nose.

"Yes ma'am," replied Cecil.

"Then let's begin."

The officiant motioned to a door off the side of the room where Tara was standing. On the officiant's signal, Tara opened the door, letting Minerva into the room. Minerva's simple white dress dangled fractions of an inch from the floor, though with each step she took, onlookers could make out a pair of sparkling navy shoes. She walked slowly across the room, her paces steady and short. Minerva did her best to contain her smile as she moved, though it broke through for good when she caught sight of Cecil crying, as well as Cerise holding up a video call of her

174

sister, Rebecca. Minerva arrived to the officiant and Cecil, handing off her bouquet to Professor Lopez before taking Cecil's hands in hers.

"Before we begin, I'd like us all to reflect on this very moment," said the officiant. "We do so many weddings here – sometimes with barely a few minutes between them to catch my breath. And they can often be hectic affairs. A spontaneous, heat of the moment decision, sometimes last minute, glad to be here but willing this part of things to be over and done with. And yet before me stand two people so clearly in love, and have taken the time to make this decision. Perhaps it's a little selfish of me to say, but I couldn't begin to tell you the last time I had a couple as happy to see me as the two of you are."

This elicited a chuckle from the crowd, punctuated by big smiles from Minerva and Cecil. Minerva wiped a tear away from her eye before grabbing Cecil's hand again.

"Alright then, ready?" the officiant asked.

Cecil and Minerva nodded.

"We're gathered here today in the sight of these witnesses," began the officiant, "to join together Cecil Hughes and Minerva Piccolo in matrimony. Cecil, do you take this woman to be your lawfully wedded wife, to have and to hold, to honor and to cherish, in sickness and in health, as long as you both should live?"

"I do," replied Cecil.

"And do you," continued the officiant, "Minerva, take this man to be your lawfully wedded husband, to have and to hold, to honor and cherish, in sickness and in health, as long as you both should live?"

"I do," replied Minerva.

"Do you two have a token, such as a ring, that you'd like to exchange to symbolize your vows at this time?"

Cecil produced a pair of rings from the pocket of his suit coat, placing one in Minerva's right hand and holding onto the other with his own. Minerva held out her left hand and Cecil attempted to slide the ring onto her finger. Minerva flinched at the motion, nearly causing Cecil to drop the ring.

"This is so awkward," said Minerva as she smiled at Cecil's attempts. The room around them chuckled along with the whole affair.

After a few tenuous seconds, Cecil finally got the ring on Minerva's finger. Minerva made much quicker work of getting the ring on Cecil's hand, slipping it on quickly in one fluid motion.

"And now that you've exchanged your vows and exchanged your rings, by the power vested in me by the state of Indiana, it is my pleasure I now pronounce you husband and wife. You may now kiss if you wish."

Cecil and Minerva embraced each other as a cheer broke out from the onlookers in the room. As the shouting died down, Cecil motioned to everyone gathered to quiet.

"Alright everyone," he began, "It's 2:18...wait...2:19 right now. We'll be meeting at Rio Brasilia at 2:45. Our reservation isn't until 3 pm, so please don't get there too far ahead of 2:45 if you can help it. And if you're not going to the reception, thank you for coming. We love you."

The party filed out of the small room, making their way to the lobby of the building. Erika stopped off at the bathroom on the way out, taking a moment to quickly get an eyelash out of her eye. As she turned the corner to the entry way, she saw the rest of the party was just exiting the building. Erika ran to catch up with them, only to come to an abrupt stop when she noticed that group of three men from before had grown. There was now a very large, very angry mob shouting at the wedding party.

18
Perfect Day

During their junior year of college together, Erika rushed to the hospital when she found out that Paulina had been involved in a violent car accident with a semi-truck. She arrived expecting to see Paulina fighting for her life or wearing a cartoonishly large body cast with various body parts up in traction. Instead, Erika entered Paulina's hospital room to find her roommate on crutches and wearing a splint on her hand, but not looking too worse for the wear.

Paulina had fallen asleep at the wheel of her undersized pickup on the drive home from work, rear-ending a semi-truck on the highway. According to the police, had she not been drifting left of center, death or paralysis would have been likely. Paulina figured this analysis was correct because the glovebox of her truck had been relocated into the truck's back seat. Instead, Paulina hobbled away from the wreck with a sprained knee, two broken fingers, and a mild case of whiplash.

In the days following the crash, Erika often asked Paulina to tell her about what had happened. The story fascinated Erika not just because she was stunned Paulina had survived her brush with death, but because of how fantastical the story of the crash itself sounded. It always played out exactly the same as Paulina explained it, almost as if she were reliving the moment a thousand times over. She woke up to the sound of screeching metal and the sight of her truck's hood raised nearly vertically in front of her windshield. In a split second, she took her foot off of the gas and placed both hands on the steering wheel.

"Well. That's not good," she said calmly – or at the very least, Paulina told Erika she said it calmly.

Paulina guided her truck to the shoulder of the highway, nursing it slowly to a stop behind the semi. For a few moments, she took deep breaths in and out, trying her best to slow her rapidly quickening pulse. Her heart wasn't supposed to be in her throat, but that's where Paulina felt it.

In an instant, time sped up. Cars on the highway began zooming by. The flames coming from the tires of the semi's trailer crackled ferociously. Sirens pierced through the night sky and stabbed into Paulina's ears. All she could do was cry a stream of tears that felt like it would never stop.

The way the story ended never shocked Erika. Panic and fear settled in and wouldn't go away until whatever terror mercifully ended. The sense of calm that Paulina had when the wreck began was so profoundly foreign to Erika that she repeatedly had to question whether or not Paulina was making that part of the story up just to sound like a badass.

In hindsight, when Erika exited the courthouse, she finally understood. The back of the wedding party stood in front of her. Abby was the closest to Erika, with the Zurats by her side. Erika stood in place, her legs frozen to the ground as she listened to the shouting coming from the crowd.

"You're an abomination!"

"Burn in Hell!"

"This ain't a wedding! It goes against God's word!"

Please don't say something stupid, Erika thought. Please, don't let anyone in our group say something stupid. They'll go away as long as we don't say something stupid.

"We're just trying to get to our wedding reception," said Minerva.

"Please," Cecil pleaded. "Let us through. We don't want any trouble."

"Metal don't mix with blood!" another man from the crowd said, his voice hoarse and deep.

"Where's the machine?" a second woman from the crowd shouted. The rest of the mob murmured in agreement.

Don't answer her. Don't answer her. Don't answer her. Don't answer her.

Erika tried her hardest to mentally will Cecil to keep his mouth shut. She noticed a police car come to a stop just down the street.

Just a little longer. Just wait it out. They'll notice us for –

"I love this woman and she loves me," said Cecil.

Oh goddammit.

"We're late, excuse us," said Cecil, beckoning the wedding party to follow. A few of the braver souls began to shuffle forward, Abby included, but Erika pulled her back, shaking her head. They stood with the rest, all still, wary of what may come.

No matter where he looked, Cecil's path was obstructed by person or prop. Despite the width of the courthouse's driveway, the mob had created too successful a blockade. Someone was going to have to move. He tried to pass between two of the protestors. They remained unwavering, staring him down. Cecil pushed again. Nothing. He laid a hand on one of their shoulders and tried to move through once more.

"Excuse me, sir," he said, waiting for the blockade to give way.

"Don't you touch me, toaster." The man threw Cecil's hand away from him.

"Get off of him!"

"I'm just trying to get through," said Cecil, still waiting for a break in the line.

"He just pushed him. We never touched you, who you think you are –"

"He did what?"

As those at the front of the blockade turned to address the crowd, Cecil pushed through. Minerva's hand lost his grip, leaving her stranded in a sea of rage and placards. Cecil looked back, terror filling Minerva's body with every second. Another man blocked his sight, grabbing Cecil's collar.

"Where you going? You're not gonna leave your blushin'

bride out here all alone?"

Cecil pushed the man away from him, with more force than he'd expected, sending him into the backs of other protestors. He scrambled to his feet, trying to see an exit from the compound.

"Men don't run from fights."

Cecil was thrown deeper into the crowd. A white-haired man loomed, a baseball bat in hand. He paused, savoring Cecil's wide-eyed fear, and struck him in the head. The wooden bat cracked and splintered, debris flying out from the barrel. The crowd descended on Cecil, stomping and kicking at him as he lay prone on the ground.

Minerva screamed, terror piercing through the clamor and echoing throughout the area. The crowd dispersed around her, trying to get a better angle on the fight. Caroline ran to Minerva as she fell to the ground sobbing. The policeman who had parked down the road heard the scream and began sprinting towards the courthouse. His partner bolted out of the car, slamming the door behind her as she followed suit. She shouted into her radio as she removed her weapon from its holster.

Jericho dove toward Cecil, his body greeted by kicks and knees as he did so. The man with the fractured baseball bat stopped mid-swing.

"Get out of the way!" he screamed.

Jericho tore bodies away from Cecil, moving between them as he attempted to cover Cecil's body with his own.

"Boy, I will end you if you don't move."

A hand shot out from the throng and wrapped its fingers around the white-haired man's neck. He dropped the bat, reaching for the crushing hold.

"Boy?" Jericho growled.

Erika grabbed Abby's hand.

"Come on!" Erika shouted. Abby didn't move.

"But he –"

"Abby, get inside."

Abby froze, staring at the escalating brawl. Erika twisted Abby's body with all her strength, shoving her back toward the courthouse.

"Abby Lin, get the fuck inside!"

Abby started to run to the doors, turning back to look at Erika.

"Go!"

Erika ran towards Jericho, who still had the white-haired man in his grip, Tara was pulling with all her might, to make him let go. Erika noticed that the crowd were focusing on Jericho and the old man, save for two younger men, golf irons in hand who were pounding at Cecil's head.

"Get away from him!" Erika shrieked, her voice raising nearly a full octave from its normal register. She dove at the men, startling them enough to send them running in the other direction.

Shots rang out in the air as the two officers both fired their pistols into the sky.

"Indianapolis police!" yelled the female officer. "Hands in the air."

All at once, time sped back up for Erika. The pounding steps of the officers racing towards them; Jericho and the white-haired man grunting and growling; Minerva's hysterical cries; the two men dropping their golf clubs as their hands went into the air. Everything instantly blurred together into a cacophony of shouts and thuds and clangs.

Erika sat up from Cecil's body, taking her first look at him. The illusion of him as human had been broken – the projection of his person had ceased, leaving a gray and black metallic body wearing a tuxedo behind. Pieces of metal were scattered all over the ground. His lower body was covered in dents, but nothing that looked like it couldn't be fixed. But his upper body had not been so lucky. His head was in several thousand tiny pieces, leading Erika to wonder if those pieces had appeared as blood before Cecil's projection stopped.

"Hands in the air, ma'am."

Erika wasn't listening.

"Ma'am."

Erika looked up to see the barrel of the officer's pistol as he stood over her. She raised her hands.

"Sorry."

"Are you okay?" The male officer held out his hand to help her up, eyes and gun refocused on the mob behind her.

"I…I guess," replied Erika. "Where's Minerva? The lady in the wedding dress? This was – is – *was* – her husband."

19
Doppler Shift

It took an hour and a half for the majority of the crowd to disperse, either away from the courthouse or into custody. Much to Caroline's relief, there were no charges against Jericho – there was always this underlying feeling that Caroline had that Jericho wouldn't be treated fairly by the police if he were to end up in questionable circumstances while Black. In a world where the massive police reforms of the early and mid-2020's didn't exist, things likely would have ended much worse.

Right now, however, Minerva was everyone's primary concern. Though the officers had managed to move her onto a bench, Minerva hadn't averted her gaze from Cecil's body as she softly cried. She sat with a blanket around her shoulders despite the warm August weather. Additional police personnel had set up a barrier around Cecil's body, marking evidence with yellow, numbered plastic stands.

On a bench near the entrance to the courthouse, Erika sat with her hands clasped around a bottle of water, surveying the scene around her. The policewoman who had responded initially had already taken her statement and though she had been released, Erika couldn't bring herself to go while Minerva was still there. She also couldn't, however, bring herself to talk to Minerva. Abby sat beside Erika, her hand occasionally running softly along Erika's back. After Erika had told her to go inside, Abby had watched through the glass doors of the courthouse amid the chaos.

"You did all you could," said Abby.

"I know," replied Erika dryly.

She took a sip of water. Beyond the barrier, one of the responding officers was instructing another policeman what they wanted pictures of.

"I didn't totally understand what you were afraid of," replied Abby. "Not until today."

"He's fucking dead! He died!"

"How could you have?" Erika replied. "Humans are shitheads, even at our best."

"Not all of them are. You're not a shithead."

"And you. You just ran in there. What were you thinking? You could have gotten killed! You weren't going to save him. You couldn't have!"

Abby watched Erika twirling the cap from the water bottle in her hands. She could tell Erika was listening to her, but her mind was clearly somewhere else.

"We have to get out of here."

Everything's calm now.

"Right. Now. These fucks will be back. And you were at ground zero of them killing a conscientia."

Where are we going to go?

"Literally anywhere that isn't here. Abby said she'd run away to Canada."

How am I getting money to go to Canada?

"You'll figure it out. You need to get somewhere safe. We do."

What about Abby?

"Clearly she's coming if she wants. You wouldn't have made her go inside before you dove on – and I cannot stress this enough – a dead fucking body if you didn't want her to come."

"Hey," Abby said, breaking Erika's train of thought with Grace. "What can I do?"

Erika shrugged.

Abby sighed and stared toward the people milling around near where Cecil's body was.

"This sucks," said Abby.

"We need to go! This is going to happen to us too. And you don't know it

won't. Cecil was better integrated into society than Abby. And this happened to him."

"He knows better – knew – fuck. Fuck!" Erika threw her bottle into the ground as she screamed. Abby pulled Erika onto her, hushing comfort as she held her.

"It's okay," Abby said.

"It's not though," replied Erika.

"I know it's not."

"Then why say it is?"

"Because I'm scared," Abby replied. "It could have been me. I know it wasn't. I know that I'm okay and therefore it's okay. But…fuck."

This time Erika put her hand on Abby's back, pulling her close for a single-armed hug.

"This is going to continue," Erika said.

"You don't know that."

Erika stood up from the bench. She gestured toward Cecil's body and the scene around them with both arms outstretched, spinning in an exaggerated circle to make her point.

"Are you seeing literally any of this?" asked Erika.

"It was one group of shitty people who did a terrible thing," replied Abby.

"They fucking killed him!" said Erika, trying, but failing to keep her voice from rising.

"I know!" Abby sniped back.

She grabbed Erika's hands and urged her to come back down to the bench. Erika relented, but not before kicking her water bottle, sending it spinning across the ground.

"I can't go talk to her," said Erika.

"Minerva?"

"Yeah."

"You don't have to right now," replied Abby. "Besides. She's got plenty of people with her right now."

Erika looked up to see Tara and Caroline flanking Minerva as she sat on a bench. Several other wedding attendees stood nearby, talking in small groups as they waited to give their respective witness statements to the police. Other than Jericho and Tara coming by to check on them, Erika and Abby had largely been left to themselves since Erika had given her statement.

"I should say something," continued Erika.

"Like what?"

"That you were too late?"

"I don't know."

"You could wait until tomorrow?" said Abby. "We could head back to the apartment? The police said we're free to go."

"I can't."

"They literally said we're both free to go."

"That's not what I mean," said Erika.

Abby clutched Erika's hand more tightly.

"Can we please go?"

"Why?"

"Erika."

Erika turned to look at Abby. Her eyes were leaking the synthetic tears much like Erika had seen before, but Erika noticed something different about Abby. The brilliant grey glimmer of her irises was dull and faded, much like they were when Abby was charging or sleeping.

"Are you alright?" asked Erika, concern suddenly filling her voice.

"Let's go home," said Abby. "Please?"

Abby wiped her tears with her wrist, failing at keeping up with wicking them away. Erika produced a tissue from her clutch, which she handed to Abby.

"I want to feel safe," she continued. "And that's not going to happen here. I want to go."

"Do you want Tara to take you back?" asked Erika. "I can ask –"

"You're so fucking dense some times." Abby replied angrily. "I need both things. I need to be away from here. And I need you there."

"Go. She needs you."

"Can we check on Minerva before we go?" Erika questioned.

Abby nodded and stood up, holding out her hand for Erika. Erika picked up her now empty water bottle and followed Abby over to Minerva. She was still sitting on her bench, with Caroline beside her, staring at Cecil's lifeless form on the ground. The two officers who had originally responded to the disturbance were trying to chat with her, though Caroline was doing most of the talking.

"When can she take him?" asked Caroline.

"For now, the body is considered to be evidence of the crime," said the male officer. "Until our investigation is finished, it's police property. With that said, there's a plethora of witnesses and cameras everywhere, so it should be pretty cut and dry."

"How long?" Caroline asked again.

"Maybe the end of next week," the policeman said. "If it'd help you, we know the name of a good recycling center that can help with your cleanup."

"What about getting him fixed?"

"We had an android at the station have something similar happen to it," said the policewoman. "It wasn't a beating like this, but it did take a gunshot to the head. Destroyed the head similar to what happened here. I don't want to say he can't be fixed."

"But you don't think he can be?" Caroline said, her tone steady and somber.

"It's not my place to say," the female cop said.

"Is this a hate crime?" asked Caroline.

"We can't comment on an ongoing investigation."

"Fine. Then comment in general. Is the murder of an android a hate crime?"

"It's definitely a crime," said the policeman. "And depending on how much the android was worth, the level of the misdemeanor that someone could be charged with varies. That said, androids are considered to be private property. Unless it's a state or federal employee, in which case, it could be a felony, depending on the nature of the android's responsibilities."

"This was murder," said Caroline.

"Unfortunately, that's not the way the law currently sees it," replied the policewoman. "I'm sorry for your loss. We'll be sure to get you the police report and any other documentation Ms. Piccolo."

Minerva broke down sobbing, burying her head into Caroline's shoulder.

"Thank you, officers," said Caroline.

The officers walked away, going over to the other police personnel who were busy taking pictures around Cecil's remains. Minerva continued to cry on Caroline's shoulder, pulling the blanket tighter around her shoulders in an effort to keep warm. From her pocket, Minerva's phone began to ring. She pulled it out of her pocket and looked at the screen. Caroline grabbed the phone from Minerva and tossed it to Tara.

"Go take care of that, please," she said. "Work whatever magic you need to."

Tara answered the phone and walked away.

"I'm sorry," Minerva muttered.

"Hun, you didn't do anything," replied Caroline.

"I'm sorry," Minerva repeated.

"It –"

"I'm sorry. I'm so sorry, Cecil. I'm sorry."

20
In My Veins

Eighteen days passed between Cecil's death and when the Indianapolis police department was finally able to turn his remains back over to Minerva. As soon as they arrived at her home, Minerva immediately called Amy. Though Amy couldn't get a good look at the damage herself over a video call, she had concerns about the practicality of attempting to repair such a damaged android.

"We can get a new model android body," said Amy. "The literal body it's in isn't going to impact anything."

"I'm aware of that," replied Minerva. "I'm already looking into the cost of repairing this one versus the cost of getting a new body. It seems like unless the repairs are under $10,000, it's more efficient to just buy a new one."

"I'd put your line at $5,000, but that's just me. What sort of condition are the memory box and personality processor in?"

Minerva looked around at the android parts strewn around the floor near her. She looked back at the camera helplessly.

"I've never seen the insides like this," said Minerva. "I have no idea what I'm looking for."

"The memory box should be about the size of a quarter. It's a cylinder that's either yellow or orange in your model. I can't remember which."

Minerva looked around the floor for a few minutes, but couldn't find what Amy was referencing. She then grabbed a small cardboard box off the table behind her.

"More parts?" asked Amy.

"There's a second one over on the couch too," replied Minerva. "This is the smaller one."

Minerva dove her hand down into the parts, producing a dented yellow cylinder.

"This?" asked Minerva.

"That should be it. How big is that dent?"

"It goes about a third of the way down."

Amy contorted her mouth at the news of the size of the dent in the cylinder.

"Can you look for the personality processor?" Amy asked. "It should be about the size of a playing card – maybe twice as thick. It'll have gold connectors on both ends of one side. There's usually a fourteen-digit model number written in the middle."

Minerva dug through the box again, this time having no luck in her search. She spent a few minutes searching the floor around her before going out of sight of the camera to check the box on the couch.

"I assume it's not a good thing if it's cracked to the point where it's about to split in two?" Minerva said.

"Not typically," replied Amy. "Can you show it to me?"

Minerva held the black processor in front of the camera, pointing out the crack that ran down it lengthways.

"I'll have Raymond visit you in the next couple of days to pick those parts up," Amy said. "Just keep them somewhere you won't lose them in the interim. Don't buy a new body until I've had a chance to look at them."

"Don't you have him backed up?" asked Minerva.

"He's backed up, in a very basic sense, but a lot of what he would have learned and developed over time is stored on those two pieces you have there. That and we still haven't been able to get our new backup system fully up…"

"It's been months, Amy!" Minerva shouted.

"When the government of jurisdiction in the place you're trying to help people is actively implementing legislation to hurt those same people, things move a hell of a lot slower," replied

Amy. "We're working as fast as we can, but getting all the programming from the remnants of the U.S.-based Project Freyja is taking much longer than we expected. We're to the point where raw data can be backed up here, but I can't do anything without having an android physically here to upload data to."

Minerva sighed. "Okay. When will Raymond be here?"

"Friday morning at the latest."

"Right. I think I'm going to plan a wake for Cecil. Just in case, you know?"

"Whatever helps you get through this."

Minerva ended the call with Amy. She walked to the dining room, digging out the bottle of wine Cecil had bought for their wedding night from the wine cooler. She popped the cork out, tossing it onto the table in front of her. Minerva took a long drink from the bottle before heading to the living room.

She stared at the broken android on the floor and table in front of her. It wasn't Cecil as she knew him. There wasn't a body to mourn. But her heart was crushed all the same as she stared at the metal fragments and stray electrical components around her. Minerva curled up on the couch and stared at the pieces of Cecil, taking long drinks from the wine bottle.

*****

"Have you heard from Minerva recently?" asked an Erika shaped mound in the middle of her bed.

"Not in a couple of days," replied Abby from the kitchen as she mixed a bowl of brownie batter. "I can ask Tara if you want?"

"Brownies first."

Abby poured the chocolatey batter into a glass pan, taking care to get as much of the mixture out of the bowl as she could. After tapping the pan on the counter in an effort to get bubbles out, she placed the brownies in the oven and set a timer. She returned to Erika's room, bowl and chocolate covered spatula in hand.

"You feeling any better?" asked Abby.

"It's just a cold," said Erika before sniffling. "That said, if brownie mix is what you're offering for medicine, I'm sick. So sick. Please. Give me medicine now."

"Brownie mix is not medicine."

"I'd like it to be administered orally and often."

"Phrasing?"

"What?"

"Nothing," said Abby as she handed the bowl to Erika. "Do you want to call Tara or should I?"

Erika looked up from the bowl, the handle of the spatula hanging out of her mouth.

"Never mind."

Abby left the room, leaving Erika alone with her brownie batter, a spatula, and a half-empty bottle of pop. Abby had been unusually giving the past few days. Perhaps it was because she was sick, but Erika couldn't help but notice that since Cecil's death, something had seemed different about Abby.

It wasn't anything overt, aside from Abby's sudden interest in attempting to make food for Erika. Her recent cooking spree wasn't that out of character, though Erika typically paid little attention to anything that wasn't prepared from a can or a box. Abby was, however, a lot more concerned about Erika's feelings than normal. Again, Abby's interest itself wasn't unusual, but the last few weeks had significantly amplified that behavior.

Despite those factors, they hadn't spoken once about the day Cecil had died. Daily discussions were had about how to help out Minerva, both between Erika and Abby, as well as part of their larger circle. There was a concerted effort to make sure someone in the group talked to Minerva every day, particularly after calls to a few local cemeteries unearthed the fact that Minerva wouldn't be able to bury Cecil's old body there due to environmental concerns.

But nothing about Cecil's death. Nothing about the terror Abby felt. Nothing about Erika diving on a dead body. Nothing about anything Abby or Erika had said that day. On the rare occasion Erika tried to bring it up, Abby dodged the question, quickly and unflinchingly changing the subject to something else.

Abby walked back into the room, holding the timer in her hand.

"Tara talked to her this morning," said Abby. "I guess she's going to call Amy at some point today to see what can be done about repairing Cecil's body."

"Do you think it can be done?" Erika asked.

"I don't know. I've never learned how android functionality works beyond what I need to know."

"Fair enough."

"But, if there is someone that can fix Cecil's current body, I'm sure Amy knows them. And if there's someone capable of restoring Cecil to what he was before, it's Amy."

"We can still have hope then, I guess."

"Exactly."

Abby watched Erika's unsteady expression, her mind flickering between thoughts. She took a deep breath and began to speak.

"Can we talk?" asked Abby.

"That's not good."

"About what?" Erika replied.

"There's a thought I can't shake. I said something the day Cecil died. I said it out of panic – out of trying to get you to listen to me. But the more I think about it, the more I realize I misspoke."

"What's that?" asked Erika.

"I said you were part of what makes me feel safe," answered

Abby. "But that's not true."

"Great. Now she doesn't feel safe around you either."

"You're the only thing that makes me feel safe," continued Abby.

"Oh."

Erika absentmindedly played with the spatula, unable to find words to reply to Abby.

"I don't know what it is about you," said Abby. "You've always made me happy. I loved talking to you from the first time we spoke. And you were this great friend and someone I saw as a huge part of my life. Even after we split up, I always hoped there'd be another chance for us."

"This is building to an ultimatum, isn't it?"

"When you agreed to come get me from Project Freyja, I was happy to have my friend back. But you became something else."

"Oh?" interjected Erika.

"You became my anchor," replied Abby. "You're the thing that keeps me from drifting off when I'm scared or when I don't understand why something's going wrong. I know it's been almost a year I've been living here. I'd like to think that aside from some early stumbles I've done a good job of keeping the boundaries you set for us."

"You have," Erika acknowledged.

"And I know you've said for a while now that you don't totally know what you want for us – if anything," continued Abby. "But I do know you care about me. And that if you're willing to throw yourself on a dead body for someone who you don't care about to the same extent that you care about me –"

"Hey, you don't know," interrupted Erika. "I might have secretly been enamored with Cecil."

"Barring that," Abby said, chuckling, "if you're willing to be that selfless for someone else, I can only imagine what you'd do for me. And even if nothing ever comes of this from a relationship standpoint, I need a friend like that."

Erika smiled. Abby leaned in and hugged her close.

"Maybe you won't break her heart after all."

Maybe.

"This isn't what you want though, is it?"

Yes. I mean no.

"Which is it, Erika?"

Erika broke off her hug and leaned back against the head of the bed.

"I had an epiphany a few days back," she said.

"What kind of epiphany?" asked Abby.

Erika sighed. She grabbed the bottle of pop and took a long drink from it, downing the rest of the soda.

"Vodka and brownies?" Erika said, waving the bottle at Abby.

"Erika," Abby said sternly. "You know I'm not doing that."

"Oh sure. Say you're going to be a friend, but then don't get me a drink."

Erika shrugged and scooped a bit more of the brownie mix out of the bowl with the spatula. She licked the spatula clean and continued talking, occasionally gesticulating with the spatula to emphasize her points.

"I look at people differently now," Erika said.

"How is that my fault?" Abby asked, taking offense.

"No, that's – do you know how long I've been single?"

"I don't."

"Four years. Not even a single date in the last three. It's crossed my mind. There's a girl at the grocery store who runs one of the checkouts – Michelle."

"Young-ish tall brunette with the nose ring and sleeve tattoos?" asked Abby.

"Yep," replied Erika. "I've seen her once or twice a week for about six years now. I even asked her out once a while back. She turned me down, but...there have been times where I've wondered what it'd be like to be with someone again. We flirt with each other, she's nice, pleasant to look at – when I think about it, she's typically been who's come to mind."

"Where's this going?"

"I was there last weekend like normal and she checked me out."

"I bet she did," Abby interrupted.

"Not how I meant it," replied Erika. "All I could think was how I wanted to know what her opinions on androids and conscientia are. Would she have been part of the crowd that attacked Cecil?"

"I highly doubt it."

"Me too. But that's the point. I don't know the answer. About her, about anyone. I can't assume she wouldn't hate you – wouldn't hate us if we were…you know –"

"I don't," said Abby flatly.

Erika sat there silently, spinning the spatula around in her hand. Her lips twisted and contorted as she struggled to come up with what she wanted to say.

"Have some fucking guts."

That's what the alcohol's for.

"Abby disagrees."

The timer went off in Abby's hand. Abby looked down, confirming it had, in fact, sounded before looking back at Erika for direction.

"Go," Erika said. "Don't let the brownies burn."

"We're not done, Miss Edens," Abby replied as she walked out of the room, tossing the timer onto the bed.

As soon as Abby had walked out of sight, Erika opened her

bedside table, the drawer squeaking in the process, and produced a flask. The vodka inside was always warm and burned as it went down. Desperate discussions call for desperate measures, Erika reasoned.

The flask, however, was empty.

Erika tipped the flask over again. She was sure she had filled it last week. Whatever, she thought, that's future Erika's problem. She walked over to her dresser, tugging open her sock drawer looking for the tiny bottles of rum she snuck into movies. Gone too.

"She did this."

With the hot pan of brownies safely placed atop the stove, Abby removed her oven mitts and set them down on the counter beside her. She heard the squeak of Erika's nightstand opening, followed by the thudding sound of both the nightstand and dresser closing. Abby stomped back toward the bedroom, her heavy steps alarming Erika as she entered the room.

"You don't have to rush," said Erika.

"What are you doing?" asked Abby.

"It doesn't matter."

"Erika."

"I told you."

Erika shoved her way past Abby, heading toward the freezer. Abby had a quicker first step though, getting her body between Erika and where the bulk of her alcohol was stored. Undeterred, Erika walked into the living room, retrieving her keyring from the entry table.

"This can't be how we coexist," said Abby.

"Why is it gone?" Erika mumbled.

"You can't drink just to talk to me."

Erika made her way back to her bedroom closet and turned on the light. Behind storage totes filled with old clothes Erika had promised herself she'd donate, Erika produced a deep black safe.

She fumbled with the key before finally placing it in the keyhole and unlocking the safe. Erika removed a bottle of aged scotch from the safe – a bottle her dad had bought for her as a college graduation present.

Finally.

"Just take a drink and say it."

Erika turned around to find herself face-to-face with Abby. She froze, gripping the neck of the bottle tight in her hands. Abby reached out and grabbed the bottle.

"Bitch."

"If you're not ready to talk, I understand," said Abby, her voice soft and calm. "But you can't do this to yourself."

"You poured out my flask, didn't you?" Erika growled.

"I'm worried about you."

"Where did you hide the rum?"

"When things get better –"

"Where is the fucking rum?" interrogated Erika.

"I know you're confused –"

"Give it back."

"This can't be how we talk. This isn't the real you."

"For fuck sake, Abby."

"Is the world so terrible? Or is it me you can't stand?"

"Don't patronize me."

"I'm not a monster, you don't need a drink just to talk to me."

"The world doesn't scare me as much as you do!"

Abby's hands slipped off the bottle of scotch, her mouth wide open from shock at Erika's statement.

"That's not how I meant it," Erika said, trying her best to backtrack.

Abby stormed to the living room, Erika following closely behind her, the scotch still in tow.

"I'm terrified of something happening to you. Not you specifically. Abby, please."

Abby opened a small storage container that held most of her belongings, she dug around for a few seconds, grabbing three small bottles of rum and threw them back at Erika with force. Erika caught one of the bottles with her free hand, but the other two smashed off the wall behind her and shattered.

Abby walked to the door, grabbing her keys and putting them in her pocket.

"Abby," Erika pleaded. "Wait."

"I need time to think," said Abby.

Abby slammed the door behind her, the sound echoing through the room. Erika stared at the closed door, stunned that Abby had actually left. She opened bottle of scotch, but the moment the liquid hit her lips, she stopped.

"Hey. Give me more of that. It's helping."

"No," Erika replied to Grace out loud. "No it's not."

"You don't fucking know. You can't do this yourself. She just left and it's your fault."

"It's your fucking fault!"

She threw the scotch into the wall, shards of glass fragmenting across the living room. The bottle of rum soon followed, alcohol pouring down a dented wall she had no idea how to fix. Erika collapsed to the ground, crying loudly into the carpet.

21
Great

September 5, 2034

"I better call Ms. Nammu," said Raymond as he held the cracked personality processor in his hand.

"That bad?" asked Minerva.

"It's been a while since I've personally done any repairs, so I could be missing something. I'd prefer not to say until I've talked with her."

"Do what you need to."

Raymond pulled a phone out of his pocket and placed a video call to Amy. After a few moments, she answered.

"Good afternoon, Raymond," she said as she put her glasses on.

"Good afternoon," he replied.

"I'm guessing you're done with your initial inspection?"

"Not exactly. I was looking at the personality processor and I think it might be beyond repair."

He carefully held the cracked apparatus up to the phone's camera.

"If the crack were running widthwise," he continued, "I think it could be salvageable with a limited repair. Since it's running long ways, I feel like we'd need to replace the entire thing."

"Right."

"I know it's hard to see, but can you take a look at it and see if I'm missing anything? I don't want to say the part is completely beyond repair if there's something I'm not aware of that we can do to fix it."

Raymond set the personality processor down on a nearby

table and hovered the phone's camera over it. He occasionally moved the camera around at Amy's instruction, tilting to odd angles to do his best to give Amy a better look at it. After a few minutes of inspecting the personality processor, Raymond repeated the process with the yellow memory box, complete with holding both the phone and the box at odd angles in an effort to give Amy a better look at things.

After twenty minutes of remote review, Amy ended the call with Raymond. He then took a few minutes to do some additional inspection of the memory box on his own before calling Minerva back into the room.

"Neither Amy nor I think there's anything we can do about the personality processor," he began. "She's going to call a guy she knows in Reno to see if he can repair it, but she wasn't optimistic. The memory box looks to be in a little better shape visually, but it's actually worse off. It's not responding to any tests I run on it."

"So what does that mean?" Minerva asked.

"For the personality processor, nothing at the moment," replied Raymond. "Until the repair engineer looks at it, there's nothing that can really be said one way or another."

"But it doesn't look good?"

"Not to me or Amy. We're not the experts here though. We know what we're doing and we can't fix it ourselves. If there's anyone who would know how to fix it, it'd be this guy."

"And what about the memory box?" Minerva questioned.

"It's not repairable," said Raymond. "I'm sorry."

Minerva rubbed her eyes and slid her hands down her face, frustration and sadness already beginning to set in on her eyes. She took a deep breath, let out a long sigh, and then continued her line of questioning.

"Let's say we can't repair one or both of them," Minerva stated. "What happens then?"

"Amy will take you through those options when and if we

have to get to that point."

"Let's call her now and talk through them."

"I think it would be prudent to wait and see what we can do to re…"

"I'm calling her now," said Minerva as she grabbed her phone and dialed Amy for a video call.

Amy's face popped up on the screen, the brown framed glasses from earlier now replaced with ones with thin, black wire frames.

"Good morning, Minerva," she said.

"What happens if we can't repair any or all of Cecil's parts?" Minerva asked impatiently.

"I assume Raymond has taken you through our repair plans?"

"I told him I needed to talk to you about what happens if we can't fix things before then."

Raymond poked his head into view of Minerva's phone camera, nodding in the background of Minerva's shot.

"There are really two possibilities left at this point," said Amy. "The memory box is beyond repair. Though there's still a chance the personality processor can be repaired, that will ultimately be a decision I'll leave to the specialist I've contacted."

"What if both pieces are done for?" asked Minerva.

"We could build a new android with Cecil's last backup."

"Which would have been before he proposed to me."

"Yes, though he wouldn't be exactly the Cecil you knew," replied Amy. "Functionally he would be, aside from whatever changes or upgrades you get in a new android body compared to his old one. And while he'd have the memories of whatever time you spent together before his last backup – as well as any memories of the rest of his life – without the locally stored data, the new personality processor might not process the emotions related to those memories the same as Cecil's old body did."

"And what if the personality processor can be repaired?" Minerva questioned.

"I wouldn't count on it being 100 percent being repaired. Even with the repairs, you run the risk of damage and corruption of the data it stores. The term personality processor is a bit of a misnomer. It doesn't just process emotions and other personality traits. It helps a conscientia to understand who they are. Conscientia don't just show up as full-fledged adult minds. They're like children in a way – they're always growing and learning. Eventually, with enough time, consistent backup, upgrades to new android bodies, and regular maintenance, conscientia will have a far greater knowledge and more complex emotional structure than we humans could ever hope to have.

"The problem, in this case, is that you're essentially going to be starting over. Cecil will have his memories thanks to the backup, so it's not like he's a brand-new program. But there's a ton he'll have to relearn. Even things that come as natural to you or me as social etiquette will be foreign to him. While I have no doubt that he'd still have strong feelings for you based off of his memories, the time it takes for him to reprocess them and relearn what those feelings mean could be significant."

"I don't want to do this," said Minerva.

"We don't have to have this discussion until we know one way or the other whether or not Cecil can be repaired," replied Amy.

"No. I mean I don't want to do this. I don't want him to have to go through all of that. *I* don't want to have to go through all of that."

The line went silent. Amy stared at something off screen, scribbling notes down out of sight of the camera. Raymond focused his eyes on the overflowing stack of dishes in the kitchen sink, his instincts telling him that even dealing with smelly, stuck on food would be an improvement over this suffocating quiet.

"I see," Amy said breaking the silence. "Raymond, could you take Minerva through what options she has for Cecil's remains so that they're properly handled."

"I can," Raymond said, peeking his head back into the view of the camera.

"Thanks," replied Amy. "I'm sorry for your loss, Minerva."

*****

"Welcome to a new America, they told us. Welcome to a world with a brighter future – a brave new world with endless opportunity where humans and robots can coexist peacefully, taking mankind into a stratosphere we could only dream of in our wildest fantasies and most ambitious science fiction novels."

Congressman Eugene White stood at a podium in front of a small crowd – around 1,500 people or so – in the town of Coeur d'Alene, Idaho. Over the past few months, White's public exposure had grown significantly with his selection as the Vice-Presidential candidate of the Humanist Party formed in late 2031. The Humanist Party was not receiving significant national traction, polling at less than five percent of the ballot in most states, though they were doing particularly well in states with heavy rural populations.

White's running mate, a megachurch pastor named Dan Friendly, had chosen a tactic of crisscrossing the United States in an effort to get the Humanist Party's message out to as many people as would listen to him. Friendly had been one of the earliest religious leaders to voice his support for the RPU, though he shied away from the group's more visible work as certain members grew more violent. Instead, he opened up his parish's coffers to help fund the RPU's offshoot political works – first the Humanist PAC then the Humanist Party – and gave financial backing to a cleaner, gentler, and better dressed form of hate.

The more people that saw the Humanist Party candidates in person, the better, Dan Friendly reasoned. Like Congressman White, Reverend Dan, as he preferred to be called, was a talented and charismatic public speaker. Their rally plan was simple: Congressman White would hold a small event in a small city where he'd speak about the coming fire and brimstone future conscientia would bring on humans. A few days later, Reverend Dan would visit the same city, making a follow-up speech wherein he'd share how the Humanist Party was a way to save humankind from its possible demise.

"I love a good science fiction novel or movie as much as anyone else," continued Congressman White. "There's nothing better getting lost in a work of speculative fiction set in a world similar to your own, knowing full well that the trials and tribulations the characters are facing will never happen to you.

"Part of what makes science fiction so great is that there's always a problem – a mortal danger – that humanity has to overcome. That enemy could be aliens, disease, even science itself. Yet one of the most prevalent tropes in early science fiction was the dangers of artificial intelligence and the android."

The crowd rabbled and clamored, with modest claps coming from some of the more enthusiastic members of the audience.

"In these works of fiction," said the Congressman, "non-human beings would live and work alongside humanity, to be part of the greater good – the greater good! – which come from their assimilation into our society. Humankind would be freed from the tyranny of being overworked and underpaid thanks to our robot companions. Earth would suddenly be a utopia where non-humans handle our menial jobs while humans get to live off of the well-earned fruits of our labors.

"But not every story has a happy ending. The robots would often turn on humans, usurping our authority, undermining our plans, and changing our society for their benefit, not our own. We become the tools used to make life better for the mechanical beings, otherwise we humans meet an untimely end."

A smattering of boos emanated from the crowd.

"If this were a reality just in the content produced by Hollywood and writers who live in their mother's basement, it would be disheartening, but it would be understandable. Fiction is meant to make us consider our own mistakes as humans, to learn from them, and ultimately to avoid them. My fellow humans: I am here today to tell you that we have not heeded the warnings of these stories and we have not learned the lessons we were meant to from these tales."

The boos turned into a chorus, deep and guttural in tone thanks to the predominantly older and male crowd.

"Settle down, settle down," stated Congressman White as he reinforced his words with arm motions in an attempt to continue on with his speech. "I know a lot of you are upset with the direction this country has taken. You likely wouldn't be here today if you weren't. And while I share the outrage and frustration that so many of you feel, I also see several faces in the crowd who are unsure about what you're hearing. You may interact with androids on a daily basis. You may find that they do, in fact, help you with your daily lives.

"I'm not here to tell you that all technology is bad. Far from it. Without technology, the message of the Humanist Party wouldn't be able to reach all of the open minds that we have to this point. I've said many times that we're intending to provide an alternative to the current American two-party system – one that focuses on the rights of humans, placing us all first. If it weren't for technology, the only people hearing today's speech would be those of you standing in front of me. The cameras videoing this speech and streaming it worldwide have made a huge, positive impact on our daily lives.

"Androids, even the dangerous conscientia versions that attempt to mimic human behavior and emotion, can also be a benefit to our society. I have conscientia in my life that I'm close to. There are even a few that I'd be tempted to call a friend if they were human. But we can only reap the benefits they'd contribute to society if we create laws, policies, and cultural restrictions that keep them in their place."

Congressman White took a drink of water from a glass on his podium. The crowd murmured in approval at his previous sentiments but patiently waited for him to continue on.

"I'm going to level with you," he said. "Not just because I'm an honest guy, but because I want to make sure you know the truth. The Humanist Party likely will not win the 2032 election. You know this. I know this. My running mate and the man I'd

207

love to see as our future president, the Reverend Daniel Friendly, knows this. While we are here to win, I will not consider us a failure if we are not taking the oath of office next January.

"We have started a dialogue in this country. We've opened the eyes of the average American to the dangers we face from those who try to portray themselves as being like us but are less than us. In turn, it has opened the door for legislation to help out the cause of the Humanist Party, even if we aren't in the White House this coming year.

"I have three days left on my current tour of this great nation, then I'll be heading back to Washington. Early this year, four other congressmen and I introduced the Protecting Americans from Digitized Destruction, Corruption, and Violence Act. While this bill failed to become a law, we found that there was significant support from the American public for some form – any form – of protection from violence towards humans by conscientia."

A man in the crowd shouted at the top of his lungs, "Fuck those robot scum!"

This elicited cheers from the audience around him.

"Over the past few months," continued Congressman White, ignoring the interrupting man, "brave Americans have fought back against conscientia and androids trying to decay our great American society from within. Many of these same Americans have been arrested from crimes like the destruction of property or, in more liberal states, assault, all while trying to protect what it means to be American."

The boos came again, louder and angrier than before.

"When I return to Washington," Congressman White said, "I will be partnering with a few other like-minded elected officials to introduce legislation to establish a dedicated national police force aimed at protecting humans from the technological danger that poses a danger to us all. The establishment of the Gold Tie Guard will not only be a way to keep Americans safe, but will also serve as a visual symbol that each and every American can look at, see the man or woman wearing that gold tie as part of their uniform, and know: I am human and I matter to my country."

Cheers erupted from the crowd, with a few in attendance shouting derogatory statements about androids and conscientia through the cheers.

*****

Minerva shut off the feed and collapsed back into her chair. For the first time in days, she felt something other than alone. It wasn't a better alternative.

22
Hemorrhage

"Congratulations. She's gone. Fine work, even for you."

Erika stared at the carpet beneath her face, now damp with her tears. There were thousands of little fibers spread across the living room floor. There'd been more than one time where she'd resorted to counting them in place of sheep. But she hadn't truly stared at them before this moment.

As she lay there, skin slightly scratchy against the synthetic surface, Erika noticed the disarray of the carpet in sharp focus before her. When standing, the material clearly had fibers, but was one uniform entity. At this distance, she could see individual strands of carpet trying to break away from others. One specific strand had succeeded, sure to be picked up by the vacuum whenever Erika or Abby next decided to clean.

If she comes back.

Tears began rolling down Erika's face again. They took no effort to cry, appearing without Erika's input, then trickling away as they pleased. Gone was the energy to scream the guttural cries and the pained wails from hours before. But the pain remained.

"And whose fault is that?"

Her gaze shifted to the far wall. The dent was larger than Erika initially thought it was. At least it looked that way from the floor. She couldn't really tell. Maybe the light was playing tricks on her. Maybe she'd just made an existing hole a little bigger.

"It can never be simple, can it? To find someone, anyone, that can tolerate your bullshit. You're too damaged, too broken, not interested, it's raining, it's snowing, it's too hot, it's too cold, it's a Tuesday – there's always something, some little reason you convince yourself to be true. But you know better than anyone that it's all a lie.

"You aren't damaged goods, Erika. You aren't unlovable. Your palate is

bland, and your desires are no more twisted than a teenager discovering porn. You aren't looking for something exotic or exciting in any way. Truth is Erika, the saddest part of your pitiful existence, is that there's nothing wrong with you at all."

Erika squeezed her eyes closed, trying to shut Grace out, but it only made her louder.

"People like you die alone. Unnoticed. Only when the rent stops coming will someone look for you, that's how little an impact you've made. Think about it: when's the last time someone called to say 'hi'? You've got mom and dad right now, but most parents don't outlive their kids. Not that your mom would miss you anyway."

Erika opened her eyes. Maybe she could crawl to her escape. She tried to move, but it was as if her bones had turned to metal.

"The lies you tell yourself. No one's too busy for you, no one has other places to be. They just don't care. But the one person who did? Look around, Erika. She couldn't run fast enough. Who did that? Who took something so simple, so pure, and ruined it? How this should have played out is pretty simple. You – moderately attractive girl, protagonist of your own story – feels lonely and unloved. You're longing for the love you once had. Pining for the woman who you wronged, who you threw away.

"And yet, by divine providence or some other bullshit, you're given a second chance. Not only that, but she's real now. She's not someone you have to keep at a distance. She's there. She's living in your fucking apartment. And she's still into you. It's everything you could have wanted! All you had to do was be normal, and you couldn't even do that right. Second chances like that are like a drug to losers like you, and you blew it."

"Stop," Erika sobbed aloud.

"You're a liar. A manipulator. A coward."

"No – "

"A machine built to love, and you denied it from her. A machine that fell for you – that loved you and you alone – and you took that from her. She calls on you, and only you, for rescue, and this is the best you could do? An alcohol-stained safe haven and TV dinners? Abby gave you everything you asked for, did everything you told her to. God forbid you hold up your end of the bargain.

"She isn't the girl who got into your head, you clawed your way into hers. This isn't love or heartbreak. This is fear of reprimand, of being alone as a consequence. But let's face it, it's the least you deserve."

"Please," Erika begged. "No more."

Her words blubbered out as she curls on the floor, tearing at the carpet with her fingernails. Her feet kick helplessly, toenails catching the carpet, running a race from which there's no escape.

"You can stab and scream all you want. You can drown yourself in the 'healing power of alcohol', or whatever whimsical wording you've given it now. But you can't kill the thought of her fixing you. Of this dream that she'll complete you. You're addicted to it – like everything else you love.

"And now that opportunity has vanished, leaving you far behind. Which is what you wanted, right? To be left alone, free from her clutches. So why waste your time with all of this inane crying?

"Is it because...that isn't true? Was that another lie? Is it, perhaps, that you have truly ruined something beyond repair? Thing is, it's not like you wanted rid of her. You didn't before. You tore yourself apart before deciding to break things with her. You cried for days before and after. If she was even a little human when you first knew her, she would have known what was coming. Your tear-stained face and bloodshot eyes would have given you away. But she didn't. She was innocent. You took that from her.

"It's why we got to know each other so well. I've always been there. I just bought more stock in your mind when you abandoned her. And you couldn't abandon her. Not again. That wouldn't happen. So you push her away. Sure, you didn't know Cecil would get killed right in front of the two of you. How could you? But you always knew that SOMETHING could happen.

"It didn't happen to you. It didn't happen to Abby. It doesn't matter. It's not safe to have Abby in your life. It's not safe for you."

Erika's movements slowed, her body tiring from the frantic crying and pained movements. She stared at the wall, her vision blurred with tears, helpless.

"You can't – you won't – abandon her. But she won't be safe with you either. What to do? Do you let the big bad world out there have its way with her and destroy her? No. You're selfish. You want to break her down bit by bit yourself. You've driven everyone who has ever loved you away. Who knows

where Abby is right now? Your little therapy group never really liked you anyway. What's left for you? Who is left for you?"

Erika held her breath, unsure of where Grace would go next.

"Surprise, sweetheart. It's me. That little voice in your head, reminding you of your limitations, your flaws, your fuckups. You tried to stop me with that therapist. It's like you don't understand how valuable I am to you. You gave me a silly name. Grace. It doesn't fit me well. I deserved a better name."

Erika let her breath go, trying to control her breathing with Grace's pause. Erika tried to focus on a long-unused tactic her therapist had taught her.

"I can see the wall," she said between sobs. "And the TV stand. And the fibers in the carpet. And my hand. And –"

"Do you remember the first time? The first time the booze shut me up?"

Two nights after she broke up with Abby, Erika sobbed uncontrollably in her room. Paulina showed up with a bottle of tequila from their RA. They drank until who knows when in the night. Erika woke up with a massive hangover the following afternoon, having passed out on the floor.

"The silence was wonderful, wasn't it? To be able to think about nothing at all. To not hear my voice. To not hear whatever song is stuck in your head. To not be bouncing back and forth from thought to thought so fast you repeatedly struggle to keep track of whatever you were trying to think of. Just beautiful, serene silence. God, that was good. Wasn't it?

"It's not coming back. It only works for so long. We drive people away. Your drinking. My existence. It's why Paulina hasn't talked to you in years. It's a shame. For you, not for me. She was good at taking your mind off me. She tried to put up with you. But having a drunk for a best friend drains the soul.

"Abby's no different. She's gone. She's tired of you. Just when it felt like there might be some hope. Just when everything felt like it might be coming together for you for once. It all comes crashing down. You lose your friend. Your desire. Your hope. Again."

"Why?" Erika mumbled, her words pained as they leave her lips, drool and tears pooling on the carpet beneath her. But Grace was silent.

213

"Why?"

Erika felt herself begin to shake. She was growing cold, as if the room had lost its ceiling and let in the chilling autumn winds. Erika couldn't hear Grace, but she could feel her judgment bearing down on her.

"Why?"

She felt a gripping tightness around her body. Everything was blurring. The sound of wind echoed through her ears. What was once a whisper turned into a whistling, howling gale all around her. Her head was spinning, ready to explode from the deafening roar. Erika tried to make herself louder than the furor; she could feel sound escape her body. But nothing could silence it.

Her larynx burned with every sound she made, crying out for rest. Erika writhed in anguish, thrashing until her head hit off of the wall behind her. She hit it again. And again. And again. Anything to make the noise stop. A sharp pain flashed across her forehead. Erika shrieked.

She began to choke, something running down into her throat and stopping her from breathing. Erika felt herself shoot up, though not under any power of her own. She tried to reach out and grasp something – anything – but her arms were clamped tightly to her torso.

The wind was changing, morphing into another sound. Rhythmic. Almost soothing. Erika slowly realized it wasn't the wind at all, but the sound of Abby's voice, trying to shush her screams.

For a moment, as Erika collapsed into Abby's arms, the world stood still. The calm after the storm. As quickly as serenity came, Erika's mind gave up the fight. She could save the apology for when she woke up.

23
U-Turn

October 19, 2034

Jericho Fogg carefully pulled a deep roast pan out of the oven, the small ham inside glistening with the combined juices from the meat itself and the rings of pineapple atop it. He cautiously set the pan on the burners on the left side of the stove, taking care to avoid the pan full of green beans cooking on the opposite side.

"Does it look done?" Caroline shouted as she mixed and mashed a bowl full of boiled potatoes with an electric mixer, slowly adding whipping cream in an attempt to turn the mashed potatoes smooth.

"The thermometer says it is," he replied. "Though the skin didn't brown up quite the way I wanted to with this new glaze."

"I'm sure it's fine."

Caroline shut off the mixer, grabbing a spatula and scraping down the sides of the bowl.

"Is Tara on her way?" she asked.

"She's usually here around 6:30," Jericho answered. "It's still only 6:16."

"Sorry. I'm just on edge."

"I think we all are."

Caroline finished with the potatoes and began setting the table while Jericho finished up with the ham and the beans. With platters and serving bowls full of steaming hot food on the kitchen table, Jericho and Caroline had just sat down to eat when Tara walked in.

"Hey," Caroline said as she poured Jericho a glass of water.

"Hey Caroline," replied Tara. "Hey, Jericho. Can I live here?"

"That's an unexpected question," said Caroline.

"You alright?" Jericho asked.

"It's going to get worse," replied Tara. "It's going to get much, much worse before there's any hope of it getting better."

"What happened?" Jericho inquired.

"Same old shit," Tara answered. "Same new shit? Either way. Between politicians going on TV and putting bills through Congress trying to make my life matter *less*, now I hear it in the streets. Not in hushed whispers anymore either. It used to be you'd get a smile one minute then some asshole would say snide shit behind your back. They're not even hiding it anymore. I don't want to deal with it."

"You're emancipated though," stated Caroline.

"Why does that matter?"

"Legally you have less to worry about than a typical conscientia."

"Legality doesn't matter to some jagoff with a five iron or a shotgun."

"Come eat at least," interjected Jericho. "We can talk it through when we're not all on empty stomachs."

Dinner passed relatively uneventfully, save for Jericho dropping a piece of ham on his white polo shirt. The stained shirt was added to an overflowing hamper situated by the top of the basement stairs – a chore both Caroline and Jericho regularly put off for as long as they could. After dinner, Jericho took the hit and made his way down to the washer with a hamper of clothes, while Caroline plated slices of Dutch apple pie for dessert.

"The accounting firm must be some kind of security for you?" Caroline asked.

Tara, rinsing off the large plates from dinner, sprayed the dishes frantically as she thought over her response. She cleaned off all of the plates and placed them in the dishwasher before she finally gave an answer.

"The money makes things more secure," she said, "though it's not like I couldn't make good money as an independent CPA. I have enough clients that'd follow me if I left. Even people who hate conscientia seem to be fine with one of us handling their money."

Caroline nodded.

"I feel like I've heard that somewhere before," replied Caroline.

Tara looked at her, thinking of how to best phrase the thoughts whirring through her head.

"Can I run something by you?" Tara asked.

"Sure?" Caroline replied, confused by Tara's hesitation.

"I'm already your accountant for your business."

"And a very good one at that."

"I have plenty of clients I could bring over if I started freelancing. There's selling my house and the money I have in investments. I could live off of that."

"Is this a question or are you bragging?"

Tara closed her eyes and sighed; Caroline was never good at nuance.

"I'm saying while I get my business up and running – which won't take long, I might add – I can still pay rent."

Caroline tossed a dish towel at Tara, her face feigning disgust.

"How dare you?" she tutted.

"I can do other things. I'm more help than you realize. Pick your poison."

"Can you do the laundry?" Jericho asked as he climbed up the last few stairs.

"If that's what you want."

"Sold! When can you start?"

Jericho walked over and feigned shaking Tara's hand, only for Caroline to smack it down. Jericho turned toward Caroline and stuck his tongue out at her before offering his hand to Tara a second time.

"Is this really what you want?" asked Caroline. "I know you like having your time and space to yourself."

"I do," said Tara. "I've been thinking about it for a while. There's safety in numbers, and I don't just mean with money."

Caroline looked at Jericho, still waiting to shake Tara's hand.

"We do need some help around here," she said.

"We'll need more soon," he replied.

"When are you wanting to move in?" Caroline asked.

"Whenever," replied Tara. "I'd prefer to sell the house sooner rather than later, but I can hold off as long as you need."

"Give us a week to clean up some space somewhere in the house for you to live. Maybe the basement? You can work on selling the house after you move in here."

"As long as there's wifi."

"You can shake her hand now," said Caroline to Jericho.

24
Fragile Dreams

November 17, 2034

Erika woke up to the sound of Abby screaming, her voice piercing through the darkened apartment. Erika bolted out of bed and ran to the living room, where she found Abby staring at the ceiling, her eyes wide open as she screamed. She wrapped her arms so tightly around Abby that her shoulders began to burn from the tension.

"It's okay! It's okay!" Erika said over and over again, gently rocking them both as she tried to soothe Abby. The screams soon calmed, giving way to panicked breathing. When that finally subsided, Erika released the embrace.

"Are you alright?" asked Erika.

"I think so," replied Abby. "Just a bad dream."

"I didn't realize you dreamed."

"Conscientia have the capability, most just choose not to. It's more power efficient to completely go into total sleep for a half hour or so. If I'm dreaming, it takes me five to seven hours to recharge, depending on how vivid the dreams are."

"Then why have them at all?" Erika questioned.

"To understand you better," replied Abby. "I've just never stopped."

"I'm guessing this means you can have nightmares too?"

"Apparently."

"Do you want to talk about it?" asked Erika.

"Not really?" replied Abby.

"Was that a question or a statement?"

"I really don't know."

Erika rose up from the couch and stood in front of Abby, nearly tripping over the stack of mythology books still sitting on the floor.

"If you need me, come get me," replied Erika. "I'm going to go back to bed until then because it's fuck early o'clock."

"It's 12:08 am," said Abby.

"Shit, really? I'm getting old."

Erika left the living room and crawled back into bed, burying her head in the pillow repeatedly in an attempt to get comfy. She laid there for a few minutes, growing increasingly annoyed at her inability to get comfortable. Erika poked her phone's screen, temporarily blinding herself just to see that Abby had been right about the time.

As the screen shut back off, Erika heard her bedroom door open.

"Can we talk now?" Abby asked.

"Yeah," Erika said, giving up on her attempts at a comfortable slumber.

Erika sat up and motioned Abby to come join her in bed. Abby did so, pulling the covers over her legs and leaning against Erika.

"There's this myth around human dreams…about how the last thing you think about before you sleep is what you're going to dream about," said Abby.

"God, I hope that's not true."

"It's only half-true," replied Abby. "Or at least that's my understanding of it – wait. Why would that be a bad thing?"

"My last thought is usually how I don't want to wake up in six hours."

"Sounds boring."

"It is."

"Well, there is some evidence that it can somewhat control

the subject matter of your dream. But it's not a hard and fast science like it is with conscientia."

"So what were you thinking about before you went to sleep?"

"They just...beat him. He looked human and they killed him. He was more human than anyone who attacked him."

Erika looked down at Abby. Though she expected Abby to be crying, even in the dark it was clear she wasn't. Instead, Abby stared off into the distance, her eyes blankly gazing at some point past the far wall of the room.

"How can so many people do that?" Abby continued. "One person I sort of get. You could have a serial killer with their blue-orange morality. They kill someone, maybe even torture them, because it makes sense to do so. In their mind anyway.

"But a group. I...I just...They didn't care if they hit each other. As long as they hurt him."

"I don't understand us either," Erika interjected.

"It's not a 'you' thing," Abby replied. "It's a human thing. A species that commits genocide and lynchings with one hand, only to cure disease and create us with the other. I can upgrade myself whenever I want with information released seconds ago. Human change takes generations. Even then, only if enough people care. Or if the right people care at the right time. It makes it feel like change will never come."

Abby went silent for a few minutes, still staring across the room. Erika started to grow tired, her body comfortable leaning against the wall behind her. She willed herself to stay awake, though she did find her eyelids starting to droop. Luckily, Abby started talking again, causing Erika to snap back awake.

"It must be hard," said Abby.

"Yeah?" Erika said in an inquiring tone.

"Our fight when everything ended. I get it now. It sticks with you. It haunts your dreams. No wonder you had nightmares."

Erika chuckled. If only. The more she thought about it, the

harder it was to stop.

"What?" asked Abby.

"Those aren't the scary dreams," replied Erika. "I mean, yeah, you'll wake up in a cold sweat from them. But you realize they're just a dream. The fears are real, sure. But the dream is just that – a dream. Nightmares aren't always about what's been done to you."

"What do you mean?"

"My nightmares after you moved in weren't new."

Abby leaned her head up a little bit, breaking her stare to look at Erika.

"I'd had them for eight years," Erika said. "They were always about you."

Abby frowned a little, struggling to follow Erika's line of thought.

"When I broke up with you," Erika said, "I just spoke as fast as I could. I knew that if I didn't, I wouldn't be able to go through with it. For eight years, I replayed that night. I was a wreck. I didn't sleep. I couldn't. I was terrified that, one day, I might see you in person. You'd see me and just…hate me. And that's the last thing I ever wanted. But even that I could have lived with. Eventually. So you shouldn't be scared."

Abby nodded, and then stopped, mentally replaying what Erika has just said.

"I don't follow your logic."

Erika rubbed her eyes and stared into the dark room, trying to think of another way to explain the confusing nature of humanity, even if she didn't fully understand it herself.

"Love and hate are opposite ends of the same scale. They both consume you, right? Well, there are all these people that feel like the existence of conscientia alone threatens them. And that's probably a valid feeling for them to have.

"But they don't know what it's like to have a conscientia as part of their lives. To see one as a friend, as a colleague, as an equal. Never mind romantically. They see you as something lesser. I don't totally know why, but we always fear the outsider as our default reaction. But that'll change with time. Not necessarily from one individual person, but from society as a whole. It might get worse before it gets better. But there are enough people out there on your side."

"Do you really believe that?" Abby asked.

"I have to try," replied Erika. "It's what lets me have hope in humanity."

Abby laid her head back down on Erika's shoulder, leaning in close. She pulled the blanket tight around her waist.

"I'm not perfect, you know," said Erika.

"I know," replied Abby.

"No. I mean…I don't mean little shit. Not my crappy taste in food. I mean –"

"What?"

Erika closed her eyes and took a deep breath in. If what she had to say was going to come out, it had to be now. She felt Abby nuzzle in closer, as if she were encouraging Erika to go on.

"I think. I…think I drink too much," Erika began.

"Why do you think that?" asked Abby.

"I… I keep finding bottles."

"So?"

"I find them in places I don't remember putting them. Or I think there'll be two or three somewhere and there's nine. They're always the empty ones."

"People forget things all the time, Erika."

"I found a bag of empties in the closet yesterday. Abby, I don't know where they came from. I can account for my full ones. There's always three to five around. The empties just reproduce faster than I remember."

Abby leaned up and put her arm around Erika's shoulders.

"I can't think of the last time I went to bed and just…dreamt. All I have are nightmares."

"Erika –"

"There are days I don't even know how I got to work. Well I do know, but I don't remember the journey."

Abby let go of Erika, and faced her. A stream of light leaking through the side of the window's blind shone across Abby's face. Erika could see Abby didn't fully understand her, but she had to continue.

"I shouldn't be missing bits of days. Why aren't they staying in my head?"

"I – I don't know –"

"I don't even like what's in there most of the time, but you'd think I'd remember getting behind the wheel of a fucking car."

"Ok, but it has been a rough few months, so maybe –"

"I stay up late so I don't dream. I wake up early to stop any dreams from turning bad. I hate silence, I can't stand being alone with my thoughts. And she has a point, I'll probably never get blinds that fit my windows because I'm pretty sure I'm kinda scared of the dark. At my age? Who's scared of the dark at my age? Who the fuck am I?"

Erika looked away, trying to mask the newly formed tears from Abby's gaze.

"She's right. I… I really feel like I'm losing my mind."

"…who?"

Erika looked back.

"What?"

"You keep saying 'she'. Who's 'she'?"

Erika blinked. How did that happen?

"She's…Grace."

"Who's Grace?"

"Horrible."

Abby held Erika's hand and squeezed.

"I said who, not what."

"I had a therapist. When I was younger. Said I had this inner monologue, a critic. Or whatever she technically said it was. We called her Grace to make it – make me -- seem less...crazy."

"What does she say?"

"Nothing much, she's usually just an asshole," said Erika.

"Hey."

Erika gritted her teeth, willing herself to stop crying. "I can't get rid of her. I've tried so many times, but nothing ever works."

Abby heard Erika start crying as she leaned her head into Abby's arm.

"We'll think of something," said Abby, holding Erika close.

They sat in the darkness as Erika calmed. She felt Abby reach out for her hand, and grasped it, their fingers intertwining together.

"I'm worried what people will think of us," said Abby.

Erika squeezed Abby's hand tighter.

"Can...would you mind if I stay?"

"Sure."

"I'll be right back."

Abby walked out of the bedroom, quickly returning from the living room with her pillow from the couch. She tossed her pillow at the left side of the bed, climbing back into bed beside Erika. When Erika scooted back down from her seated position, she felt Abby wrap her arms around her.

"Thank you," said Abby.

"For?"

"A second chance."

"That seems backwards. Shouldn't I be thanking you?" Erika asked.

"I'm listening," said Abby.

Erika returned Abby's embrace the best she could, though giving a hug to someone who was laying behind you was more of a challenge than Erika realized.

"Thank you. Can we sleep now?"

"Yeah."

Erika released Abby and rolled over to go to sleep. Within a few minutes, Abby could hear Erika softly snoring by her side. Abby laid there, trying her best to capture this moment in her mind. It'd give her something to fight off the nightmares when they made her want to scream the loudest.

25
Gatekeeper's Lullaby

The lights in Minerva's house were all turned off. They always were now.

Minerva lounged in the bathtub, a half-full bottle of wine on a card table beside her, with a smaller, empty one on the floor beneath the table. She took a long drag on a thin cigarette – a habit which she had mostly managed to bury while Cecil was alive, but that had resurfaced in the days since his death. Throughout her teen and young adult years, Minerva alternated between smoking and vaping, whatever happened to be cheap and readily available at the time. By the time she was 27, Minerva went through two packs of cigarettes every day, leading some of her co-workers and friends to intervene. After some persistent nagging, worried co-workers and friends had led her to largely kick the habit, albeit in the form of a social smoker on the weekends.

None of that mattered now. Nothing did.

The speakers in the bathroom typically brought Minerva joy. Cecil had installed them shortly after moving in as a surprise for Minerva's birthday. Minerva would spend her long, luxurious baths listening to Brahms, Mendelssohn, Bach, and Wagner, and so on. On sleepy weekend mornings, Cecil would play music throughout the entire house as he made breakfast, *Don Giovanni* or *Tosca* echoing through every room. After breakfast and cleanup, the music would transition to the bathroom and to Minerva's preferred classical work of the day while she bathed, while Cecil would retire to the living room and read.

On this evening, the speakers did not play the classical orchestral fare that Minerva so loved. Instead, they played a song from an old movie she watched earlier in her relationship with Cecil. Though Minerva could never remember the name of the movie, the song never failed to make her think of him. While Cecil was convinced not everyone wanted to rule the world, he was the one person Minerva was convinced didn't actually have that desire.

The song had been on loop for nearly two hours now. Though Minerva's body was pruny and cold, she couldn't bring herself to get out of the tub. Partly because she knew she was too drunk to stand steadily. But also because she knew what was to come. She had crafted the plan meticulously, running it through her head several times over the past few days. Minerva knew she'd have to get up eventually. But even making it to this point in the plan, getting out of the tub meant it was coming to its end. There'd be no turning back.

Minerva made her favorite dinner tonight – steak, cooked medium, with sautéed mushrooms and onions, garlic mashed potatoes, and steamed asparagus. She paired the dinner with a bottle of red wine a colleague had given her following Cecil's death, then paired that bottle with a second bottle she had laying around the house. Literally. Minerva found it on the floor and figured she couldn't let it go to waste.

After dinner, she took a long bath, complete with a bath bomb Cecil had bought her a few months back. She'd enjoy the bath, along with the remains of her wine, then spend some time in her robe in bed. After all that was done, she'd go out to the living room, and sit in Cecil's chair. Then, once she was ready, she would end her life with the .38 caliber revolver her brother, Patrick, had gifted her upon moving into her first apartment alone.

The plan had gone off without a hitch to this point. The food, the music, the bath – it was all meant to bring some sort of mental calm to Minerva. It was working in a way. She did feel closure, though not in the way she expected. Instead of providing the peace of mind she'd hoped for, Minerva felt overwhelmingly like a door was being slammed in her face – and that she couldn't do anything about it. A part of her life that she desperately craved to continue. But it was ending. No amount of trying to hold on to memories of Cecil would change that.

Outside the bathroom window, an otherwise starry and

cloudless night saw the wind pick up, its low, guttural howl increasing in pitch and turning into a shrieking wail. On nights like these, Minerva would curl up under the covers with Cecil, holding him close while the wind droned on and on. There was no one to snuggle with anymore. At least, not the person she wanted. Even if Amy could have given her Cecil back in some form, anything less than the Cecil she knew wouldn't be the same.

The wind blew harder, catching the screen door on the back patio and slamming it open and shut. Minerva began to pull herself out of the tub, reaching for a towel she had set on the lid of the toilet. She dried herself off, grabbed her robe off of the hook on the bathroom door, and started making her way to the living room.

With each step she took, Minerva became less and less sure this was what she wanted to do. For years now, her life seemed so certain. It had a purpose. It had meaning. It had a goal of marrying the man she loved and growing old with him. At the same time, there was so much in life she still valued that hadn't gone away. Her work was still there, patiently waiting while she was on leave. Her friends and even her family regularly checked in on her as best they could.

By the time Minerva got to the living room, she had talked herself out of the end of the plan, if only for tonight. She was drunk and sad for sure. But she needed another night to think about it. Maybe sleep would bring clarity to her life, even if only partly.

Minerva reached for the gun from the table where she had left it, intent on unloading the ammunition from its cylinder and placing the bullets back in the box where she stored them. The gun, however, was not where she had left it. From behind her, Minerva heard the sound of the hammer of the gun cocking. She slowly placed her hands in the air, her towel falling to the ground beneath her robe as she did so.

"Whoever you are, you can have whatever you want," she said, her knees rattling together with fear.

A slow, monotonous voice grumbled out from behind her.

"I'm here to help cleanse this world of those who seek to bring chaos to this realm," it said. "Order must be maintained for humanity to survive. All who seek to oppose it must perish."

The sound of the gunshot roared through the house, rattling the chinaware that Minerva kept in a cabinet on the far side of the living room. Her body collapsed forward, her bloody head crashing onto the ground below.

"Janus thanks you for your sacrifice," the voice said.

The shadowy figure then left the house through the patio, letting the wind slam the screen door behind them. As suddenly as the wind had blown to life, it dissipated, leaving an eerie calm in its wake.

26
The Clockmaker

December 1, 2034

Abby and Erika waited at a booth at Side Pocket, Abby sipping on a glass of iced tea while Erika was working on her second Pepsi. They had agreed to meet Tara, Jericho, and Caroline here at 6:30 pm so that they could call Amy and hear whatever Amy's grand plan was for them following Cecil's death. Minerva was originally supposed to join them too but texted Abby earlier in the afternoon saying she'd chat with Amy separately; what she needed now was a long bath and a night in.

The clock on the wall read 7:22 pm, its big hand resting just past the Roman numeral four on the face. Erika had struggled to keep her eye off of the clock all night, growing frustrated both at the lateness of the rest of their group, as well as the clockmaker's choice of how to notate four on the clock.

"Why do they do that?" asked Erika.

"Who?" replied Abby.

"The people who think you can make a four like that."

"But four I's is technically correct."

"It's IV."

"But both are technically correct," continued Abby. "Ancient Romans are believed to have used the IIII notation before the language progressed to be the IV notation."

"Abby."

Abby turned and looked at her. Erika placed her finger on Abby's lips.

"That four," said Erika, "is wrong."

The clock ticked past 7:30 pm before Tara, Caroline, and Jericho walked in.

"Sorry we're late," said Caroline. "Something came up."

"It's fine," replied Abby. "I'll let Amy know and see when she wants us to call."

"Cool," replied Caroline.

"I'll get drinks in," said Tara. "You two need another round?"

"Sure," Abby responded.

"Iced tea and…?" asked Tara.

"Pepsi," said Erika.

"Pepsi and…?" Tara prodded.

"Just Pepsi."

"Cutting back?"

"Something like that."

Tara walked off to the bar while Abby dialed Amy for a video call. Amy joined the call quickly, waving excitedly at everyone as she picked up.

"Good to see everyone!" Amy said excitedly. "Are Tara and Minerva there?"

"Tara's grabbing drinks," replied Jericho.

"And Minerva's having a date with a bubble bath," said Abby.

"I'll give her a call later then," stated Amy. "While we're waiting on Tara to get back, congratulations Jericho and Caroline!"

Abby and Erika stared at Jericho and Caroline, perplexed looks on their faces.

"We hadn't gotten to that quite yet," said Jericho.

"Oh!" Amy exclaimed. "Shit. My bad."

"It's okay, we can do it now," replied Caroline. She turned to Abby and Erika. "We're going to have a baby."

Abby let out a squee and bolted out of her seat in the booth to hug Caroline and Jericho. Erika's reaction was more subdued, substituting sprinting for a more casual walk. Tara came back to the table with drinks, nearly getting clotheslined by an overly excited Abby in the process.

Once everyone settled down from the excitement, Amy continued on.

"My news isn't quite that exciting," she said, "but it is still good news. First off, we should have backups back online by Easter. The hope is sooner, but that's the more conservative timeline I've been given."

"That's welcome news," said Tara.

"Ideally you all won't need it aside from routine maintenance. Especially with the second part of my good news. I've been working with a company up here to get you all – as well as the rest of the conscientia that I've helped out over time – to relocate to somewhere else."

"What do you mean relocate?" asked Caroline.

"I just want to ensure after what happened with Cecil that you're all somewhere…" Amy's voice trailed off.

"Safer?" Erika asked.

"Somewhere that isn't as risky to live in," Amy corrected her.

"And where would that be?" Jericho inquired.

"I've done my best to spread a relatively wide net in an effort to increase the safety that you all are provided," continued Amy. "I can get into the details more with each of you separately if you'd like, however, for you, Caroline, and Tara, I'm looking to have you all relocate to Calgary."

"That's not a possibility," Caroline said firmly.

"I'm not saying that's finalized," Amy replied. "There are several options I've been looking into. With you having a kid on the way, I want to be sure you're provided with everything you need for your own health and the wellbeing of your child."

"It's not that," said Caroline. "I'm not running from this."

"None of us are," added Jericho.

Abby shuffled awkwardly in her seat.

"Tara, what about you?" Amy asked.

"I'm going to stay with Jericho and Caroline," she replied. "I don't know what lies ahead for me, but I want to help the people who helped me out."

Amy made notes on something off-screen for a moment before looking back up.

"Okay," she replied. "If you change your mind, just let me know."

"We will," answered Jericho.

"Abby and Erika," continued Amy, "what about you?"

Abby shot a look at Erika, unsure of what to say.

"Can we talk about this with you later tonight?" asked Erika. "I think we'd like to talk it over before we make any sort of decision."

"Sure," replied Amy. "Do you want to know your choices first?"

"Just send them to us, if you could. We'll look them over and then call you back when we're ready."

*****

Erika stared at the map on the tablet screen in front of her, with the six options Amy had sent to them plotted out on a map. Yet doing so only made the choice seem more daunting in her mind.

Each location on the map was denoted with a red pin: Tallinn, Estonia; Vigo, Spain; Midori, Japan; Adelaide, Australia; Gaborone, Botswana; and Halifax, Canada. Erika couldn't see the connection. All that she knew was that each of the locations were places where Amy had lined up workers' visas for both Erika and Abby and would be able to quickly start the citizenship process for both of them.

"Are we sure we want to do this?" Erika asked.

"What are you concerned about?" replied Abby, who was busy looking up information on the various locations herself.

"Everyone we know is here. At least most of them."

"It's not like we're going away to a parallel universe and not speaking to them for five years. Email exists. Video calls exist."

"I know," said Erika.

"Knowing Amy, she probably has a plan to make sure you can get back here if you need to," Abby replied.

"Does she have unlimited funds or something?"

"She's better connected than people realize. Safe houses on five continents that we know of? Think about it."

"We don't know what her whole plan is," said Erika.

"You know there's a way to fix that," answered Abby smugly.

"I just want to know what our answer will be before we call."

"I already know my answer."

"I know," Erika sighed.

"And it would be easier if you had an opinion too," replied Abby.

Erika held up the tablet to Abby, the map and its red pins facing towards her.

"Pick," she said.

"I want to go *somewhere*," Abby stated. "I just don't know where."

"That's not an answer."

"More than you've given."

"Then can I pick?"

"If we still have no strong preference after the call, sure."

Abby called Amy, waiting patiently for the video call to pop up on the screen. It was nearly 10 pm, but Amy still looked wide awake, no doubt fueled by the half-full pot of coffee in the background.

"Good evening, ladies," she said, quickly shoving a forkful of food into her mouth.

"We can call you back if we're interrupting," Erika said as she moved closer to Abby to get in the camera's shot.

Amy shook her head and wiped her mouth with a napkin.

"Cake can wait," Amy said. "Have you two talked?"

"We'd like to know more about your plan," replied Abby. "Just to be sure."

"You've reviewed the map and the documents I sent you?"

"We have," said Abby.

"Are you really getting us both jobs as part of this?" asked Erika.

"I am," replied Amy. "Depending on where you go dictates how quickly you can start them, but there will be jobs lined up for both of you. I've tried to line up job choices with your skill sets, even if it's not an exact industry match. It'll make integration into your new home nations easier, I would think."

"And the pay will be enough to cover our expenses?" Erika asked.

"Housing and any related costs will be taken care of by my local associates. Your salaries will cover the rest. They'll be modest, but since you won't have a ton of bills you'll need to pay, it'll be like having a good paying job in the States."

"What if we need to come back to the U.S. for any reason?" questioned Abby.

"In the unlikely event you need to return," said Amy, "I'll make sure travel is arranged for you. That said, I'd hope you'd agree to keep costs somewhat low, as there are quite a few conscientia being relocated."

"How many?" Erika asked.

"Forty-five in the first wave," replied Amy, "along with fifty-five humans. The second wave will be a little larger – probably in the one to two hundred range. The goal with this wave is to get those that are the most valuable projects, and therefore the ones I have the most stake in, out of the country first."

"Aww," said Abby. "You really love me."

"Of course I do," answered Amy. "I love all my projects."

"…less than me." Abby whispered, chuckling to herself.

"Yes, you know you're special."

"Where is the safest place for us to go?" Erika asked.

"Any of them," replied Amy. "It's just a matter of what's going to be the best fit for you."

"Where would you recommend then?"

"If I were the one moving, I'd suggest Estonia or Japan. That said, I feel like there's the most need for you in either Canada or Botswana. We need help getting other safehouses set up in Botswana, while Canada will be an ongoing project because of how many of the future moves will likely end up here."

"Do you care?" Erika asked Abby.

"If I pick my preference, will you come with me?" she replied.

"Of course."

"We'd like to go to Halifax," stated Abby. "It keeps us close enough that Erika could come back if we need to visit her family, plus it gives us the best opportunity to help you if you need it."

"You two can help me from anywhere, you know," said Amy.

"I know," Abby replied. "But I think we want Halifax." Abby looked at Erika for confirmation. Erika shrugged and nodded.

"Lovely," Amy said. "Can you two be on a plane at 6 am tomorrow?"

"That's a quick turnaround," replied Abby.

"I know. I'd rather be safe than sorry. If you two need more time to pack and say goodbyes, I can find another flight."

"We'll be there," interjected Erika.

"Good," Amy stated. "You'll be flying to Toronto first, spending a day or so here with me, then heading to your new home in Halifax."

"Business dinner?" asked Erika.

"Something like that," replied Amy. "It gives me a chance to get to know you better."

"Oh," said Erika. "Well, now I'm terrified."

Amy finished covering the logistics of the trip and ended the call. The night was getting late, but with an early morning flight – even on the private plane bringing Abby, Erika, and Raymond all back to Toronto – there was a ton of packing that needed to be done. Both Abby and Erika packed light, Abby with one suitcase and a carry-on, Erika with two small suitcases and a duffel bag.

Erika sent a message to Caroline and Jericho, offering them all of the food left in her apartment, as well as promising to send them money for any cleaning they could do. Amy had promised that she'd take care of any loose ends about her apartment, but Erika still felt bad that someone other than her would have to clean it. Her car would get sold and Erika would get the money, though she couldn't imagine who'd want to buy it.

Shortly before 4 am, Raymond arrived in a white SUV that he had rented at the airport. Abby and Erika tossed their stuff into the back hatch of the vehicle, and left, vanishing from their previous life like an early winter snowflake on a heated car's hood. The trip to the airport was silent, as Raymond focused his weary mind on driving. As Abby rested in the front seat, Erika leaned her head against the rear passenger window and tried to get a little sleep before their flight.

27
With Our Eyes Turned Skyward

December 26, 2034

"Happy Boxing Day!" shouted Erika, bouncing around the living room of their apartment.

Amy had done surprisingly well in finding her and Abby somewhere to live. Their new apartment was nearly double the size of the old one, not including the second bedroom, which served as a makeshift office.

"What's so happy about it?" moaned Abby as she pulled the covers over her head.

"I don't have to work today! Neither do you."

"Neither one of us have to work anyway, not unless Amy needs us."

"Like I said, happy Boxing Day!"

"For a seasonal grouch, you're strangely festive."

"I'm doing my best to make an unexpected situation better," replied Erika. "Besides. This is basically just second Christmas. Or at least Canadian Christmas. Which I assume is just Christmas, but more polite."

"Where's Erika and what have you done with her?"

"Do you need to go back to sleep, little killjoy?" Erika said mockingly.

"I'm seven inches taller than you. Why are you calling me little?"

"Because I'm standing and you're not."

Abby sighed and shuffled out of bed. She grabbed a red and white checked long sleeve shirt from the closet and put it on over the black tank top she was already wearing. Erika continued her excited bounding, darting out of the living room and down the hallway.

"Good morning," she said.

Abby stared blankly at the clock on the wall. "You do realize it's a quarter till seven?"

"And if we hurry up, we can see the sunrise over the beach."

"You hate nature. What's wrong with you?"

"I've had coffee!" Erika replied triumphantly.

"Clearly. How much?"

"Two cups."

"How long have you been up without me hearing you?"

"4:45," said Erika. "I couldn't sleep."

Abby rubbed her eyes. "Trying to eat food to recharge is fucking with me."

"Because you need sleep?"

"Because I consistently need more than thirty minutes of it."

Erika walked over to Abby and put her hands on Abby's right arm, unbuttoning the sleeve.

"What are you doing?" asked Abby.

"Fixing your sleeve."

"Why? It was already buttoned."

"Just trust me," replied Erika. "They'll look better rolled."

"That's not how long-sleeved shirts work. They're long for a reason."

"Exactly. And I'm showing you that reason."

Erika meticulously rolled the sleeves up to just below Abby's elbows, first the right one, then the left one. After she finished, Erika took a step back and proudly admired her handiwork.

"How long do I have to keep them like this?" asked Abby.

"Just through sunrise," said Erika.

"You're lucky I don't get cold as easily as you."

Erika led Abby out to the kitchen, grabbing a pair of insulated mugs off of the counter.

"*More* coffee?" asked Abby.

"One's coffee and one's hot cocoa," replied Erika. "You can have whichever one you want."

Abby grabbed the mug closest to her and took a small sip. She smacked her lips together and handed it back to Erika.

"Switch," she said.

'You need coffee?"

"No. But you don't."

"But hot cocoa's your favorite," Erika said, smiling at Abby.

Abby sighed and smiled back.

"Fine," she said, before switching mugs back with Erika and planting a kiss on her cheek.

Their new apartment was a short walk from an inlet cove surrounded by a park. In the summer, the park would be filled with families enjoying the sun and the water. In the middle of December, however, few people found Nova Scotian beaches to be hospitable, let alone before the sun came up.

Abby brushed a coating of light snowfall that had come down the night before from a bench while Erika unbundled a pair of blankets from the backpack she had brought with her. Erika laid the first blanket down on the bench, splitting it equally between the metal seat and wooden backing. She wrapped the second around herself, before putting it around Abby's shoulders as well.

Erika and Abby sat on the bench as the winter sun slowly began to peak over the horizon. Waves from the nearby ocean came crashing against the rocks in the distance. Erika reached over and took Abby's hand, locking their fingers tightly.

"I think," said Erika, "well, when I was younger, I thought, at least, that I'd always find a way to end up on a bench watching the sunrise with you. Now that we're here, it's not exactly what I was expecting."

"No?" asked Abby.

"No. It's better."

Erika rested her head against Abby's shoulder and watched the waves in silence as she clutched Abby's hand. Abby leaned her head against Erika's, her tears unnoticed. How can such a perfect moment exist? Just a few months ago, she felt like her life was in imminent danger – could it have happened without that threat?

She thought about Jericho, Caroline, and Tara, and having to raise a child in a community that legally classified Tara, a family friend, as its threat. She thought about how neither Minerva nor Cecil will ever get to experience moments like this. She thought about Amy, hoping she'd stay safe as she worked to get other conscientia out of the country.

A small nudge to Abby's forearm broke her concentration.

"Are you still there, Abby?" asked Erika.

"Yeah, sorry," replied Abby. "My mind drifted for a moment."

Erika squeezed Abby's hand.

"This was a good choice," said Erika.

"Keep it in your pants," replied Abby.

Erika raised her head off of Abby's shoulder. She stared into Abby's dark grey eyes and smiled.

"What?" asked Abby.

"Can I kiss you?" asked Erika.

"That'd be nice."

Their lips inched closer together for what seemed like an eternity. As their lips touched, both Abby and Erika felt so happy that they could have sworn time had stopped and the world around them had gone silent.

After a few moments, Abby and Erika broke the kiss apart to the sudden realization that the world around them actually had gone silent – save for a howling wind that had just kicked up. A pale blue light appeared in the sky in front of them, quickly growing both in size and brightness. An explosive sound sent a shockwave around them.

The blue light advanced towards the bench, coming to a stop around thirty feet or so in the distance. Upon closer inspection, the light was much more than just its glow. It was an illuminated circular door, covered in a series of cryptic symbols and images. The symbols pulsed in color between the pale blue of the door itself to a much darker blue. The slow flashing light towered over Erika and Abby despite its distance from them.

"If we kiss again, will it go away?" Abby asked.

"What the actual fuck."

Acknowledgements

Good lord. This book is a long time coming. I originally came up with the idea for this book just after the 2016 US Presidential election. I started writing it in December 2016 and dedicated the better part of three and a half years of my life to making it suck less than anything else I've ever written. I am going to forget someone who has helped me along the way when writing these acknowledgements. Please know that it's not intentional. The support and guidance I've received when writing *Kotov Syndrome* has been nothing short of extraordinary.

I intend to write more thorough, gushing thank yous to people on my blog, complete with tangents and digressions that people who know me well have become used to hearing. That said, there are some people without whom this work would not have happened. I want to call them out here.

A ton of thanks is due to my beta readers for this book, as well as other folks who gave feedback on scenes or chapters as one-off occurrences. The feedback provided by Eve, Katie, Stetson, Tabitha, and Tina helped clean up some of the book's rough edges, including a pair of very different endings that were ultimately better relegated to the drafts pile.

Additionally, a huge thank you is due to various folks who have supported my writing over the past couple of years. Their input didn't (typically) come directly on this book, but it did give me the confidence to publish this book in one way or another. So thank you is due to Amanda, Ann, Bella, Casey, Cherie, Courteney, Darci, Dr. Gbur, Erin, Jeremy, Joan, Jon, Kaytie, Krista, Lola, Mike, Rebecca, Stephanie, and Steve.

I want to give a special thank you to Eve and Charlotte for their intentional guidance on how certain characters and scenes in the book developed. Additionally, a big thank you is owed to Stephanie for being able to provide me with similar feedback, all without knowing exactly what I was talking about, as she had asked not to be spoiled. A thank you is also due to my wife for making sure my occasionally poor grammar didn't come through in the final product.

I would also like to thank Lauren Restivo for the amazing work she did creating the cover for this book. This was my first time being involved in the cover art process from start to finish and I'm blown away by how Lauren took my simple idea and ran with it, truly transforming it into a work of art I could never imagine.

Finally, a significant amount of praise is due to my editor, Charlotte Laidig, who helped me to turn a good idea into a great book and eventually into a powerful story. I've learned in working with Charlotte that she gets annoyed when I dump praise on her. But the truth is that this book would not be anywhere near as polished as it is without her guidance, her critical mind, and her willingness to challenge me to improve as a writer.

CPSIA information can be obtained
at www.ICGtesting.com
Printed in the USA
BVHW030430040921
616049BV00003B/150